AMBUSH!

A clatter of AK fire from the rear caused a simultaneous chorus of "Medic, medic!" from the infantry. Franklin's turret was already swinging when the first hostile face came aboard the tank. Franklin reached for his .45 when three more pajama-clad figures appeared in his peripheral vision.

"Five, button up, yer buried," Alveretti said over the radio, and Franklin dropped, pulling the hatch down with him. He heard a high-pitched scream as a grenade went off on top of his hatch. A quick drumroll of tinking sounds pattered over the side of the turret while Alveretti "scratched" Franklin's back with machine-gun fire.

Alveretti's tank was also covered with enemy, but Alveretti was an old hand at this. He had his driver peel the uninvited passengers off by driving through a burning hut . . .

JUNGLETRACKS

RALPH ZUMBRO
and
JAMES WALKER

POCKET BOOKS

New York   London   Toronto   Sydney   Tokyo

An *Original* Publication of POCKET BOOKS

POCKET BOOKS, a division of Simon & Schuster Inc.
1230 Avenue of the Americas, New York, NY 10020

ISBN: 0-671-66418-2

First Pocket Books printing July 1989

10 9 8 7 6 5 4 3 2 1

POCKET and colophon are trademarks of
Simon & Schuster Inc.

Printed in the U.S.A.

JUNGLETRACKS

Chapter One

"SHUT THE DOOR!" A METALLIC VOICE BLASTED FROM one end of a long, unpainted, plywood and screen tropical building. "You people born in a frigging barn? Don't you shut the door when you come into someone's house? This is my house, so shut the goddamned door!"

"Not exactly your warm, motherly type," Lieutenant Jeremy Hawke said to his friend, Lieutenant James "Jimbo" Franklin, as they set their duffel bags down, slamming the offending door.

"Whatever Old Uncle has planned for us," Franklin replied, "I don't like already. That soup out there would slow Erwin Rommel down to a crawl."

Their arrival at Camp Enari, just south of Pleiku City, had coincided with the onset of the winter monsoon, and the two armor officers were beginning to have grave doubts about the wisdom of their choice of stations.

The lieutenants had met in the basic tank course at Fort Knox, Kentucky, and had formed an immediate friendship, finding that their differing personalities were a perfect complement. Hawke, tall, black-haired, and of a hard athletic build, looked at the world through gunmetal eyes and automatically took charge of any situation. Franklin, slightly shorter and considerably leaner, wearing G.I. issue glasses, was a bookish, studious individual with a talent for detail and organization.

Holding court over the line of incoming officers was a diminutive, baldheaded master sergeant, whose bellowing voice was totally out of proportion to his size. Glittering black eyes sunk deep in hollow sockets, and a pinned left sleeve attested to his past association with combat.

"Lieutenants Hawke and Franklin," the master sergeant suddenly erupted. "Take your forms from the specialist, fill each one out in triplicate. . . ." His instructions were voluminous, complete and tedious. And the two officers soon found themselves excreted from the rear of the Paper Machine, sitting on their bags, as a tall, sunburned staff sergeant approached them.

"Excuse me, gentlemen. Are you waiting for transportation to the Orientation Center?"

"That's right, Sarge," Jeremy said. "I take it you're from the 'Charm School'?"

"Yessir, I'm Sergeant Strickland. I'll be your platoon guide during your two weeks of in-country training here at Camp Enari.

"I'll take you over to HQ, get you signed in and issued some equipment, first off. Then you'll have to attend the Division CO's orientation for new officers. You can put your gear in the three-quarter-ton truck out front, while I round up any others who might be ready to move out."

"Thanks, Sarge," the two officers replied, heading out the door. It had begun to rain heavily again, and rather than sit in the cramped cab of a vehicle no larger than a civilian pickup, they opted for the canvas-covered rear bed of the truck. Neither of them said anything while they awaited the return of the driver. Only the uninterrupted patter of the rain against the bowed canvas intruded on their thoughts.

"Think quick!" came a boisterous shout, as a duffel bag hurtled through the opening over the tailgate.

"Hey, watch where you throw that thing, man," Hawke yelled, the bag nearly burying him.

Close on the heels of a sputtering, overly dignified, young black captain, followed the grinning, hook-prowed visage of an intelligence officer they'd met during their transit through Oakland, California. They'd initiated a fleeting friendship with Lieutenant Salomon "Sal" Epstein, although neither of the tankers expected to see the chunky information specialist again.

"Epstein, what got you up here into God's country?" Franklin asked. "We figured you for some nice cushy job in an officers' club down around LBJ Base."

"Fuck you, and the mule you rode in on, Jimbo," shot back the profane Brooklynite. "I heard you two were coming up here. . . . Somebody had to see to it that you didn't lose the war all by yourselves."

Dropping into a seat next to Hawke, Epstein wrung a flood of water out of his boonie hat, scrunching his plumpish form into a more comfortable position. "Nuthin' like this in the travel brochures, was there, Jer? I think I'll ask for a refund at the next stop and transfer to the Gobi-fucking-desert.

"You two look like Charlie's already got you by the balls. Why so happy?"

"Hell, Sal, we don't even know where we're going yet," Franklin said. "All the scuttlebutt says we're fresh meat for the Legs. Piss on that noise. I ain't no damned gravel cruncher."

"My sentiments, exactly," Epstein said. "Look, I know a guy in the G-1 personnel shop up at Division whom I'm going to work on. Maybe we can get us some duty where we can use our training. They've got three full armored cavalry squadrons assigned to the division, plus a tank battalion. With all the combat I've been hearing about lately, there sure as hell should be some openings."

Jimbo Franklin managed to look hopeful and doubtful at the same time. "Who's your buddy up at the head shed—your brother?" he asked somewhat sarcastically.

"Not exactly. He's my brother-in-law, and we get along real good. In fact, he owes me a few favors."

Hawke and Franklin glanced at each other with a measure of relief. Maybe there was a light at the end of the tunnel. The slam of the cab door signaled the arrival of the driver, and conversation ceased.

"Grab hold of something, gents. The road to the school ain't too swift," the driver shouted over the roar of the engine. The ride, bone-jarring even in the soft mud, lasted only a few minutes before the tailgate slammed down, and Strickland announced their arrival at the Charm School, formally known as Division Orientation Center.

Shortly, the officers had run through another paper gauntlet, and been delivered to the division commander's briefing room. They'd been met by a spit-

and-polish headquarters captain who'd led them through a maze of corridors in an H-shaped building and parked them in the map-walled room, telling them, "Relax, have a cup of coffee. The general is busy, but he never misses new officers. He'll be here in a few minutes."

Instead of sitting, each of them drew a cup of steaming brew from an electric urn and walked to the large, map-covered dais at one end of the room. Surprised at the huge size of the AO (Area of Operations) shown, and at the incredible number of sweeps, probes and small battles indicated, the three lieutenants engaged in spirited speculation until Hawke sensed a "presence" entering the room, as a door from the general's office swung open.

"Gentlemen, we have something over twenty-one thousand troops assigned to us. We are the largest division in II Corps, and in USARV. We have an area of operations stretching from the South China Sea on the east, to the Cambodian border in the west—from Ban Me Thuot in the south, to north of Dak To. It's the largest, toughest AO in the country."

The young officers had all snapped to attention at the first sound of the general's deep, commanding voice. The man's carriage, walk and almost overpowering manner, all spoke of power. The tall general ambled to the front of the room, put the men at ease, and straddled a chair opposite them, resting his arms on its back.

"Take a seat, gentlemen, I won't keep you long. I believe that it's important for all of my officers to get at least some knowledge of the man who controls their destinies, and those of their men, while they are in this command. It is my responsibility to acquaint you with the policies and activities of this division, so that you know from where they came . . . to avoid as much scuttlebutt as possible.

"You people are all armor officers, and we have the finest armor and armored cavalry in the U.S. Army in this command. Their exploits are the stuff of legend. I've found that no other branch has produced junior officers more immediately fit for field command than yours."

After a pep talk and tactical situation briefing, the general introduced them to the key members of his staff, closing by wishing them good luck and advising them to "Keep your butts down."

The young men shuffled from the briefing room silently. Saddled with impossible goals and awesome responsibilities, the general had spoken simply and without histrionics or platitudes. Few men, even in the rarified strata of general officers, have the innate ability to generate trust in their peers, let alone their subordinates. But this man did. He laid it on the line with no apology, and he made a man proud of the opportunity to serve his country.

Back in the prosaic world of young armor lieutenants, they'd just finished stowing their gear in one of the wood-framed tents, when Sergeant Strickland rapped on the screen door. "Gentlemen, chow isn't till 1730 around here. Since that's an hour from now, would any of you care to take a little ride around the camp? I'll be happy to give you a running narrative about all the sights."

"Sure, Sarge, sounds like a good way to kill an hour," said Hawke.

The other two lieutenants agreed, and they all headed for the waiting jeep.

In just forty-five minutes, Strickland had shown them the key unit and facility locations within the vast base. Despite the late hour and inclement weather, the major route through camp remained congested, and the covered jeep was inching along.

"Sergeant, where do the enlisted men go for off-hour entertainment?" Hawke asked.

"Well, sir, usually each battalion has its own NCO and EM club. There's also brigade club, and a division club. That's coming up. It's the long building, painted gree . . . Uh-oh!" he exclaimed, punching the brakes. "Looks like we got a little extracurricular activity about to happen."

Strickland pointed to a group of G.I.s gathered at the end of the walkway leading to the club building. The group encircled three men, two obviously facing off against a lone individual in a rather unique uniform.

The entire jungle fatigue uniform had been spray painted in a brown and gray camouflage pattern of sorts. He wore an olive green bandanna around his head, and a black and white feather sprouted from a knot in the rear. Instead of G.I. boots, he wore canvas Foreign Legion boots.

The two he faced were not exactly regulation in their garb, either. The larger, standing something over six-four, was wearing black cowboy boots with silver-capped, pointed toes. The other wore a longshoreman's cap and carried a swagger stick made from a pool cue.

"Sarge, don't you think we'd better break this up before it really gets started?" Hawke asked. "The two big guys are about to pound the little dude into the ground."

"Well, sir, I suggest we sit tight until the small guy

teaches those two REMF's (Rear Echelon Mother Fuckers) a lesson in etiquette. They're new in-country, and don't know the rules yet.

"You see that uniform? The little fellow's a Lurp, slang for LRRP, or Long Range Reconnaissance Patrol. They're ranger types who live in the bush for weeks at a time. Crazy muthers! They don't take shit from nobody they don't respect. This oughta be interesting, gents," Strickland said with a chuckle.

"But, Sarge," Franklin said. "The one guy has a weapon."

"Well, that's his problem," Strickland said, laughing. "It won't do him any good, and he might wind up wearing it for a hemorrhoid compressor."

The larger of the two belligerents circled his opponent, looking for an opening. As the stocky troop with the swagger stick closed on the Lurp's rear, the cowboy moved in on his side. Like the strike of a jungle snake, the canvas boot lashed out, striking the cowboy just above the inside of his knee. Face contorting in pain, the man dropped like a poleaxed steer.

In a fluid follow-through, the Lurp shoulder-rolled and came up in a standing crouch, facing the man who'd been to his rear. A barroom lunge was easily sidestepped by the Lurp, and the man's momentum was converted to a wrenching judo throw that bounced him into the mud. In the process, the weapon found its way into the hands of the ranger. When the action ceased, the swagger stick was pressed against the owner's windpipe, held in place by the Lurp's knees. As Strickland had predicted, the weapon was proving to be a liability.

"Now is when we break it up, sirs. They've had their lesson," the sergeant said. But Epstein was already gone. He'd seen what no one else had—the flash of metal.

Now a new threat menaced the young ranger. The taller assailant had recovered partially from the kick and was approaching from the Lurp's rear, holding a wicked-looking switchblade in a high, stabbing position.

As the cowboy reached the kneeling Lurp, who'd pinned his buddy, the knife suddenly slipped from his hands, his vision beginning to gray out. He became aware of bone-crushing pressure on his carotid artery and Epstein's Brooklyn snarl in his ear.

"On your knees, asshole, or I'll put your fucking lights out."

Just as the man went down, Hawke's heavy, parade-ground voice, inherited from a cavalry sergeant grandfather, boomed.

"Get gone, soldiers, NOW! It's all over. I say again, the entertainment is OVER! Anyone still here in three zero seconds is going to be up in front of the provost in the morning, and behind wire before noon!"

Franklin had already grabbed a pair and shoved them in the direction of the clubhouse door, starting a general exodus. And Hawke's threat caused the assembled troopers to vanish like smoke in a breeze. . . .

Soon the officers and Strickland were alone with the assailants. Epstein dropped his man with a contemptuous sidekick, picking up the knife almost as an afterthought. "Beat it, scum," he growled. And the man, along with his buddy, slunk from view.

"Jesus Christ! Epstein, where'd you learn that?" exclaimed Franklin. "You dropped that creep like a sack of potatoes."

"The numbers were gettin' real crappy, Jimbo. The

odds of survival are bad enough over here without some pricks like those two making 'em worse."

"Sal, you're just full of surprises," Jeremy said. "Where the hell did you collect that little bag of tricks?"

"I grew up in Brooklyn, Jer. Do you know what it's like for an undersized, four-eyed Jewish boy in a racially mixed neighborhood?

"I got sick and tired of getting my ass stomped, so I did something about it. I took the money my folks gave me for dancing lessons and bought judo lessons instead. I've been studying various styles of martial arts for fifteen years now. NO-body is ever gonna kick my ass again, without making a payment in his own blood."

The officers hadn't noticed the approach of the Lurp and as Epstein concluded his comments, the man came forward with his hand extended.

"Thank you, sir, for taking out the ape with the knife. He coulda parted my hair real good with that thing."

"What's your name, soldier?" Hawke asked.

"Elias Benteen, sir. Sergeant E-5, 75th Rangers, attached to the LRRP Platoon of this Division."

"What was the problem with those two?" Franklin asked.

The hooded gray eyes darkened as the trooper seemed to crawl back inside himself.

"Come on, man, we won't put you up on charges," Jimbo said. "Something must have started that fracas."

"Well, sir, I'm half Indian; Ponca, from Ponca City, Oklahoma. Those two jerks decided to entertain themselves at my expense. You know the type, especially them goddamn drugstore cowboys from Texas

—all mouth and no guts. I've put up with their 'half-breed' comments and threats all my life. They're always trying to impress their buddies, and of course they're always in a group. Never saw one of them damn Texicans worth a shit by himself. Nobody screws with my heritage, sir."

"I know where you're coming from, man," Epstein said. "I've been there, too." Experimentally popping the switchblade, he added, "I always wanted one of these things . . ."

"Sergeant Benteen, can we buy you a drink?" Franklin asked, as the group moved back to the idling jeep.

"No, sir, I think I'll just mosey on back to the team hootch and stack some Z's. Besides, it's against regs for an enlisted man to drink with officers—in base anyway."

"Okay, Benteen, the invitation's good anytime, but I hope we get a chance to see you again, under different circumstances."

"By the looks of your uniforms, you all are new in-country. Right?" Benteen asked.

"Yeah, Sarge, we're over at the Charm School, fresh in today. Would you believe?" Hawke answered, almost sheepishly. "We're about as green as you can get."

"I won't forget the good turn," Benteen said, as they climbed into the jeep. "If you ever need help out in the hills, just ask for The Chief. I'll find you."

"That's one man I'd like to have at my back out in the bush," Hawke said as the jeep rattled its way back to the compound. "In fact, it wouldn't surprise me one bit if we ran into him again."

Chapter Two

War is a series of unpleasant surprises. Not only are the intentions of enemy commanders unguessable, but the machinations of one's own command are unpredictable.

The division training command—Charm School— was supposed to be a boring two-week course of orientation, culminating in a sample patrol in a "safe area." However, Lieutenants Hawke, Franklin and Epstein were dealt a wild card on the day of the graduation patrol.

Epstein, upon his arrival at Camp Enari, had contacted his brother-in-law, resulting in his assignment to the Division G-2, or intelligence shop. He'd received some information too, which he passed along as they all relaxed, one afternoon, in the school day room.

"I got some semi-good poop for you guys. Word has

it that there's going to be a large number of line unit vacancies this month. I've got a private *ear* at work, trying to find out just when and where. I should know something when you two get back from your hike."

The reference to "you two" wasn't lost on Hawke. "What do you mean, Sal? What will you be doing?"

"Hey, guys, sorry. I forgot to mention that my assignment is effective 0001 hours tomorrow. The Boy Scout hike has been waived for me, thank you. I'll keep an eye out for you, though. Victor Charlie's been known to hit those school patrols from time to time. Kind of runs his own graduation exercise.

"But just in case you should need some . . . er . . . 'specialized' assistance out there, here are some of the key radio frequencies from the Division SOI (Signals Operation Instructions)." Epstein handed Hawke a tightly rolled slip of paper.

"Don't let that off your body, man. That's the freqs of DivArty, TacAir, Spooky and the Special Forces MIKE team, just for starters. It'll be my ass if someone finds out where you got those."

"Damn, Sal," Jimbo said. "You've been at it already, before you've officially started. You're un-fucking-believable, man. By the way, how're you going to be able to keep an eye on us while we're out there?"

"Jimbo, the G-2 shed has radios tuned to virtually every active unit in the field, including LRRP teams and the closer Special Forces camps. If the shit hits the fan, I'll know about it pronto, and we'll get the troops to you ASAP."

The school patrol consisted of three thirty-man platoons, divided into three squads of ten men each.

Every trainee unit would be accompanied by a member of the school cadre and would be equipped as a normal line infantry platoon.

The three platoons, conforming to normal U.S. Army training doctrine, were designated as Red, White and Blue elements. All the members of this group were either NCOs or junior officers. The patrol leader was a Signal Corps captain, named Hensch, who held the position because of his rank. He had no combat or advanced infantry training.

The school patrol's departure was logged in at the Division Operations Center at 1315 hours. Their arrival at intermediate CPs (Check Points) would be similarly logged in. The plan of operations was to exit the camp's south gate on a southwesterly course, turning more to the west at each CP.

They had a small stream to cross, which also curved around to the west. The stream ran in a deep, jungled ravine, and the point where they would enter the defile was designated CP1. Upon leaving the far, or north, side of the cut, each platoon in turn was to call in and then strike out due west for their objective, a relatively clear knoll where they would set up for the night.

Blue Platoon led out, followed at half-hour intervals by Red and White platoons. All operational combat units in the area had been notified of the existence of yet another group of "newbys" and would keep an eye out for the greenhorns. The base patrol choppers reported sightings of the patrols right on schedule. Division Artillery had plotted concentrations all along the proposed route of march, just in case they were needed. All eventualities had been covered.

Lieutenants Hawke and Franklin were squad leaders in Blue Platoon, the forward element of the patrol. Hawke was in the lead, while Franklin bossed the trail squad of the long file, as the platoon wound its way through the jungle. Blue reported arrival at CP1 without incident at 1526 hours. Communication between platoons, and with base, was loud and clear. Red and White platoons, however, were falling behind schedule, and would need to make up time in order to reach bivouac before dark.

At Check Point Two, Hawke radioed to base once again, and then led Blue down into the ravine, which crossed their path at an angle, seeming to come from their right rear. As they sloped down into the streambed, its course curved around to the west, nearly paralleling their route. Nothing out of the ordinary was sighted, and at 1615 Blue reported that it was approximately ten minutes from its final objective. So far, the day was proving to be an uneventful training exercise, except for the tardiness of the trail units.

Red Platoon, commanded by Captain Hensch, had picked up their rate of march since departing CP2 and begun to curve down into the defile. Due to their haste, they'd gotten slightly off course and entered the defile a bit downstream of the point used by Hawke and Franklin.

The creek was nearly two meters wide, and the point man crossed it by leaping to a rock in the middle and then to the north bank. As his feet touched dirt, he froze in his tracks, eyes raking the thick undergrowth.

Seeing this, the school NCO, SSG Jensen, a short, wiry individual, who was the second man in the column, signaled the rest of the unit to halt and watch their flanks. Crossing the stream himself, he saw that the point man had found a line of commo wire paralleling the bank. Charlie, apparently alerted by the passage of Blue Platoon, and knowing the school's pattern, had set up shop.

Due to the fact that military tactical radios are FM, or line of sight only, Jensen could not reach base or any other unit from the defile. The outfit would have to get up to high ground in order to transmit.

After a fast conference with Captain Hensch, who was technically in command, Red Platoon began to cautiously but quickly ascend the north slope. Gaining the top, they set up a hasty defensive perimeter, and Jensen and Hensch scanned the brush carefully from this new vantage point. Observing nothing out of the ordinary, they signaled the men to move out, and began to search for Blue Platoon's trail, some two hundred yards north of them.

No sooner had they found the trace left by Hawke and Franklin, and regained radio contact with White, which was hurrying to catch up, than a sustained burst of M-16 fire echoed up from the rear of the column.

One member of the trailing squad had spotted an NVA soldier squatting behind a bush near the edge of the ravine. The man had been facing away from the American column, covering the route that Blue Platoon had used almost an hour earlier. Their navigational error had kept them out of an ambush.

The last man in the trailing squad, an unnerved rookie trooper, dumped an entire magazine into one NVA. He, in turn, was fired on by five or six enemy soldiers who'd been hidden farther from him. The G.I. was hit in the legs and side, falling instantly. The remainder of the squad had gone to ground, and by the grace of the Gods of Battle did not panic, but didn't lay down suppressing fire, either. The squad leader called the platoon leader, reporting heavy fire and a man down. He'd no sooner reported in, than he took a round in the head, his radio antenna obviously zeroed in on by a sniper.

With their radio out, and no effective leadership, the squad's situation turned sour. Lacking the training to return controlled fire, and concerned only with burrowing deeper into the mud, they became a pinned unit. Upon hearing the commotion to their rear, First and Second squads had immediately dropped to a crouch and anxiously begun searching the surrounding brush.

The ambush had misfired—a situation which the NVA commander set out to rectify. He called in his troops from farther upstream, and started a circling movement meant to bring flanking fire on the Americans. At the same time, after figuring out what'd happened, and knowing that the school platoons would rally to the pinned unit, he sent groups to set ambuscades ahead of Blue which was west of him— and White which had yet to enter the area.

Captain Hensch, rather than informing Blue and White of his predicament, or calling base, kept on trying to reach his Third Squad. No one in that element was going to show his butt to answer the frantic calls emanating from the radio. Every time someone made a move toward it, a flurry of shots would drive him back to cover. Red Platoon was now three separate groups, strung out in a line. Two squads were stationary, and the First, under Hensch and Jensen, was moving warily back toward them.

Third Squad, which had made the initial contact,

now had one more casualty, an M-79 gunner who'd been hit in the head—but not killed. Their other grenadier was pinned in the open and could not fire effectively. The squad was slowly being shot to pieces, when a heroic effort by a pair of buck sergeants got their machine gun into action, firing from behind a small mound of earth. Rather than set up the weapon, they'd rested it directly on the mound, keeping low.

Just as that weapon opened up, Second Squad, only one hundred meters west of it, came under intense fire from one of the returning NVA groups. There were over forty of them, heavily armed with grenade launchers, machine guns and AK-47s.

Fortunately, Hensch's group heard the fire in time to avoid stumbling into the same trap. They formed an assault line and moved swiftly toward the sound of NVA weaponry. Jensen nearly tripped over a prone NVA grenadier, but quickly put a burst in the man's back.

One gung-ho infantry sergeant, spotting a pair of RPD (Russian light machine gun) gunners who didn't see him, leveled his M-16 and pulled the trigger, only to find that he'd forgotten to change magazines in the heat of his first battle. Pulling a grenade from his webbing, he popped the spoon, gave it a two-count, and lobbed it, underhanded, as he grabbed dirt. The missile arced up, exploding one foot over the two NVA. Both communists should've been killed, but one tried feebly to crawl away. The buck sergeant, seeing this, exploded out of concealment like a great jungle cat, and drawing a huge hunting knife, repeatedly stabbed the NVA until the man quit moving.

The enemy commander, under fire from both sides, and not knowing the size of his opponents' unit, withdrew to the edge of the defile to reassess the odds. This eased the pressure on Second Squad, and Hensch rapidly joined them and began setting up a rough defensive circle.

The status now: One American squad pinned but gradually regaining fire superiority. One detached NVA unit and one American unit in nervous positions about a hundred meters from each other. Neither outfit could move without exposing itself to the other. Stalemate.

Blue Platoon had nearly closed on their night position when the firing broke out behind them.

"Red 6, this is Blue 3-1," Franklin hollered into his mike. "What's the firing in your area, over?" No response. So he changed frequencies.

"Blue 1-1, this is 3-1, do you hear the fire to our rear, Jer?"

"Roger 3-1, we're heading back your way at a gallop. Saddle up your troops and we'll fall in behind you. Wait until we get there. We don't know how many gooks are out there, but it sounds like a real shit-throw; 1-1 out."

White Platoon had also heard the firing and was heading at full steam right into the blocking ambush that the NVA honcho'd set up for insurance.

Jeremy's school NCO, Sergeant Strickland, had contacted Division G-3/operations, providing what scattered details he'd obtained while they trotted back toward the firing. Within two minutes, every major command in the area was aware that the Charm School patrol had been hit, and the ADC (Assistant Division Commander) was on the way in a command chopper. Artillery had been alerted, and a section of tanks diverted from road patrol.

Sal Epstein at G-2 also knew that his friends were in the soup, and was pacing with anxiety and helpless frustration. Help was on the way. But could it arrive in time?

Back at the ambush site, the young captain's innards had settled down to some degree—just under his tonsils—and he was beginning to sort things out. The two squads in his immediate vicinity weren't under direct fire, but they weren't going any place anytime soon. He'd still had no contact with his Third Squad, but gunfire from that direction told him that someone was still alive—including what sounded like one very good machine gunner.

Captain Hensch got into contact with the trailing platoon. "White 6, this is Red 6."

"Red 6, this is White. We hear and we're on our way to give you a hand, over."

"Negative! Negative!" Hensch screamed into the mike. "Stay in place until we can sort this out. There's probably another ambush waiting for you behind us. Don't come any further. Set up a defensive perimeter now."

Hensch was dead right. White Platoon'd been trotting up from the streambed when the call came in, and nearly blundered into a classic L-shaped ambush. At a curve in the trail, the NVA had set up a pair of Russian-made RPD machine guns, aimed straight down the narrow track. Along the trail, parallel to the segment that would be swept by the guns, ten men lay quietly in the thick brush—waiting.

The White Platoon leader, immediately after receiving the captain's warning, set up his unit at one side of a little clearing through which any attack would have to come. Once they were in place, he quickly flung out small patrols to his rear and flanks—just in case.

Then a new factor was added to the action. "Red 6, this is Mongoose Lift, over."

"This is Red 6, over," responded the captain to the unknown voice that had intruded itself in his firefight.

"Red 6, be advised that we have a Spike team in the air about zero five from your location. We can put them down to the rear of the bad guys and mess up some of their day."

"Break, break," intruded a stronger signal. "Red 6, Mongoose, this is Bronco 5. I'm en route to your position; break, Mongoose, good idea! Drop your Spike team on my command. We'll provide grid coordinates when we're over the contact area."

"Holy shit! That's the ADC," exclaimed Jensen, who was monitoring the captain's radio.

Overall command of the engagement had just been transferred about six hundred feet—straight up.

Hensch delivered a fast situation report and was informed that Blue Platoon was coming to his rescue —and that heavy armor was on the way.

The Northerners, apparently made somewhat nervous by the sound of choppers, increased their fire, probably starting to think about breaking contact.

"Bronco, this is Red 6. We're beginning to pick up heavier activity. Can we get some Redleg in here?"

"Affirmative, Red 6. Give me your exact coordinates, and we'll relay to the 155s."

"Break, Blue 1-1, this is Bronco. Did you monitor my last?"

"Roger, Bronco, this is Blue 1-1," Hawke answered. "We copy and will hold in place till the Redleg stops."

Radio traffic flickered back and forth between command and ground elements, setting the stage. Hawke, whose position allowed him an overview of part of the battle, drew the task of adjusting artillery rounds.

A white phosphorous marker round came screaming down from the distant 155 millimeter guns. The thick white smoke curled from a spot just within the ravine to Hawke's front. "That's in there. It's in there," shouted the excited lieutenant. "Add one hundred, shift right and left two hundred—for effect —over."

"Roger, Blue 1-1, understand. Add one hundred and walk it sideways," came a voice—presumably the artillery FDC (Fire Direction Control).

"Roger, Redleg," Hawke shouted. "Give 'em hell!"

Twenty seconds later, a deep, throaty whistle signaled the approach of ninety pounds of destruction. The shell slammed into the brow of the gorge just below its crest, lifting a fountain of gooey dirt and vegetation. It was closely followed by four more, and then the concussions became continuous as the distant gunners found their stride, ramming powder and shell into their gaping weapons. The cannonade continued for almost ten minutes, with the guns walking their fire up and down the draw, and to the rear, to cut off the escape of any NVA who attempted to exfiltrate (bug out).

As the last of the rolling barrage echoed into an eerie silence, White Platoon's radio punched through the dirty, gray smoke that filled the hollow. Their patrols had finally found the ambuscade that'd been laid for them.

"Bronco 5, this is White 1-1. I've got a blocking element to my immediate front—too close for arty. What do you recommend?"

Rather than answer directly, the ADC surprisingly got in contact with the commander of the mysterious Spike team. "Mongoose, what is your ETA at the drop point, over?"

"This is Mongoose. We're there, over," came the instant response from the LRRP team shepherd.

"Affirmative, Mongoose. Execute," Bronco 5 ordered. "White, did you monitor? . . . Mongoose will deal with your problem, over."

"Roger, Bronco. We'll keep our ears open."

While the tactical maneuvering continued between air and ground, Hawke and Franklin were on the move again. Following the barrage, they'd altered course, plunging back into the draw. Slipping and sliding, they tore down the steep, green, heavily vined slope, leaped over the stream and scrambled up the opposite side, heedless of thorns and thick brush.

They were now on the south bank, somewhere opposite the NVA who were, at last report, somewhere on the north bank or actually in the draw itself, either trying to finish off Red Platoon's trapped Third Squad —or beatin' feet before the situation blew up in their faces.

After an unsuccessful attempt at getting the enemy's location from one of the swirling command choppers, Jeremy divided the platoon into two reinforced squads under himself and Franklin. Probing toward the presumed position of the enemy, they kept the men in a loose column formation.

By moving rapidly while the area was still obscured by the pall of gunsmoke, the two squads had gotten a chance to circle to the enemy's rear—provided, of course, that there were no NVA on the south bank. Suddenly, the point man of the righthand column froze, attention riveted on the nearby bank. Every man dropped to the ground, searching the foliage directly in front of him. Hawke and Franklin moved cautiously forward to check out the situation.

What had become visible to the point man, were two wide paths ending at the defile some thirty meters ahead. The paths opened wider as they neared the edge, and enemy troops were plainly visible, dug into the north rim of the defile.

The NVA were invisible to Red Platoon and Hensch, but they'd neglected to cover their own rear. After a speedy conference with Sergeant Strickland, Jeremy sent a pair of experienced infantry sergeants out on solo probes to find the ends of the hostile line.

"Jer, the guys in the birds don't know our position," hissed Franklin. "We'd better let 'em know as soon as we open up on that bunch over there. Also, we don't know how many slopes are in that ambush in front of White, and that NVA honcho is bound to have a tactical reserve hid out somewhere. We're not facing any dummy!"

"I know, Jimbo. I hope the LRRP bunch can take some of them out of the picture—or at least keep them occupied until we can take care of business here. Hell, we don't even know if there are any bad guys on *this* side of the creek."

Their worried speculations were interrupted by a flurry of automatic gunfire and a series of sharp explosions from White Platoon's assumed location.

"Must be Mongoose dippin' in that ambush squad's shit," Franklin said. "Hey, wait a minute. Feel the ground. There're tanks movin' around here."

Franklin had detected a subtle vibration through the soles of his jungle boots, and now Hawke doffed his helmet and pressed his ear to the ground. "Right," he said. "Those tanks Bronco mentioned are around. I hear the rumble."

With his head tilted to the west, Franklin said, "I just picked up engine sounds, off that way." He was pointing in the direction where Hawke figured that Red Platoon's pinned squad would be.

Jeremy Hawke could keep track of an astonishing number of small units. And now he was beginning to worry about just where the tanks would enter, when a howling sound like a thousand angry hornets moaned through the underbrush, and several men yelped in alarm.

"CANNISTER! Hit the deck," Hawke ordered. The swarm of pellets was followed by a series of authoritative thumps as the muzzle blasts of tank cannons reached through the trees.

"I didn't know guns could be fed that fast," Franklin said, as the concussions became a stuttering roar, rapidly increasing in volume.

"Look, Lieutenant," Strickland said, pointing bug-eyed at a section of the northern bank. A half-dozen NVA exploded from the brush, running in blind panic. A tree, easily sixty feet in height, slammed to earth, followed by the muzzle and bow of an incredibly battered M-48 tank. Its ninety millimeter gun crashed again, and two NVA were turned into a red mist that blew away on a fitful breeze while tattered rags of cloth drifted to earth.

On either side of the emerging tank, two more thundering, olive drab giants smashed through thick underbrush, and the three plunged headlong down the bank. Scarcely halting at the bottom, they pivoted hard left, charging after the remaining hostiles.

Jeremy saw one NVA knocked down by a piece of rubber thrown from a worn track, and the man's face instantly turned blood red and exploded as the churning right track caught his feet, forcing his body fluids out.

Briefly, Hawke caught sight of the name painted on the tank's gun tube—"Ballbuster." *They got that right,* he thought, as he ordered, "Keep yer butts down. A buttoned-up tank can't tell one side from . . ." His words trailed off in wonder when he noticed that the tank commanders were exposed head and shoulders, eyeballing their shots, actually firing from the hip.

While the trio swept by below him, Hawke had a chance to observe the battered machines. Not one of them had a whole set of fenders. The treads were worn almost smooth, some of the upper rollers were missing, and the turrets and hulls were sprinkled with lead spalls and bullet dings. Here and there, were actual gouges in the armor where some heavier weapon had struck. One turret had a massive bolthead protruding where someone had simply run a steel bar through— to close a wound.

Baggage, ammo crates and ration cartons were wired down all over these machines, and water cans and track sections were festooned from the turret sides. Looking down into a built-up box on the rear of one turret, Hawke was somewhat shocked to see a stack of beer cases—packed in ice.

"Looks like those suckers were made out of spare parts in the Creation and told to fight till Judgment Day," Jimbo observed.

As the last of the NVA in the streambed vanished under the tracks or were cut down by machine gun fire, the three tanks pivoted half-left up the north bank, tearing into the thunderstruck invaders. The approach of the heavy armor had been obscured by trees, and their engines drowned by the small arms fire. One NVA, obviously an officer, stood yammering at his men and pointing—just as he turned to vapor. Again, Hawke was amazed by the rate of fire of the hand-loaded cannons.

At least half of the exposed Northerners turned and charged the tanks which by now were halfway up the bank, engines straining and pouring out clouds of oily, black smoke.

"Damn fools," Franklin said, "charging a tank barehanded."

Then they all saw what the enemy was really up to. Being used to this kind of battle, they knew that each tank would have at least one hatch open. So they were trying to get grenades or bullets inside. In addition, there were at least four of them bringing RPG (anti-tank) launchers to bear. The situation could still turn to shit, because many of the experienced jungle fighters were already under the guns of the tanks, and swinging aboard.

"Shoot the buggers off the tanks," Jeremy ordered. And his hill instantly exploded with twenty M-16s, four grenade guns, and three machine guns sweeping the opposite hill and hammering among the tanks.

Hawke was worried lest the TCs (tank commanders) take this for another assault, and swing those awful tubes in his direction, but they seemed to recognize the sound of American weapons, and went calmly about their business. All but one—a tall, lantern-jawed individual who had a hostile directly behind his TC hatch, rapidly bringing a carbine to bear on him.

The tank commander was clawing for a shoulder-holstered .45, and the loader's hatch was opening—but no one was moving fast enough. The tank honcho was looking death in the face when his opponent dropped off the hull, pierced by a burst from Franklin's M-16. Startled, the tank sergeant's eyes followed the line of fire back up the hill, his eyes meeting Franklin's for an instant. The two exchanged the warriors' half-salute, and each went about his business.

The tanks were now roaring up over the crest of the north slope. With the impromptu boarding parties cleared from their decks, all the turret hatches popped open and a perfect rain of grenades preceded the tanks as they dropped back level and growled from sight. The coaxial machine guns were probing ahead like vipers' tongues searching for prey, as empty shell casings, mixed with a few beer cans, arced out of the hatches.

"Cease fire, cease fire!" Jeremy shouted, as he ran down the line of his frantically firing troops. "They've had it; save yer ammo."

Franklin, doing the same thing with his men, moved rapidly to the far right, or upstream end, of the line—nearly freaking out at the sight that met him. Moving quietly down from the east was yet another group of combatants. They must be the reserve from the original ambush, he figured, and they were in the right place to roll up the flank.

He ran back to Hawke's position to report his sighting . . . "We is in some deep shit, Jer. The NVA CO must've pulled in his reaction force. There's a bunch of Charlies comin' down the draw from the east."

"Reckon we better get the hell out of here," Hawke said. "We can't defend this area against a determined assault, and they seem to be damn determined . . ." His eyes ran down the list of frequencies that Epstein had given him. "I can't even call those tanks back—they were a wild card."

There was a sudden flurry of fire, and a rippling series of closely spaced explosions. Something new had been added. They could see thick, white smoke engulf the troops in the bottom of the defile. The sound of automatic weapons continued for another few minutes, gradually dying off to isolated bursts. Then the metallic clacking of the AK-47s ceased—and one final shot from an M-16 terminated the episode.

The NVA column, a unit of over twenty men, was now a shredded mass of limbs and bloody heaps. Nothing moved, except the rapidly dissipating smoke. Only the stink of cordite and death remained. The stream was now running red in places. And in the distance, the rumble of idling tank engines could be heard.

"Lieutenant, look, there's somebody coming through the bushes over there," yelled one of the "thump gunners," as he reloaded his M-79. Hawke's eyes followed the line of the man's arm, and he saw three, maybe four shapes materializing out of the smoke-filled gloom.

"Don't shoot till I give the command," Hawke barked to his men, unsure of just who or what was coming.

"Looks like Lurps, sir," Strickland said, nodding toward the approaching shadows. Slowly the forms began to take recognizable shape. The stubby CAR-15s, spray-painted fatigues and cammo sweatbands, all identified the men as members of the elite unit.

"Hey, Jer, that's our old brawling buddy, Benteen," Franklin said.

"Guess that kinda makes us even, don't it, pard?"

drawled the grease-painted warrior to the two grinning lieutenants. "Heard you was havin' a little git-down, so the boys an' me thought we'd just stop by and say hello."

"How the hell did just four of you do so much damage?" Franklin asked. "We thought there was a whole company down there."

"Naw, man, these guys were easy to spot and follow—they left signs like a herd of blind cattle. Remember, I learned to track on open plains—this's like a book to me. We spotted them from the sling, moving this way about two klicks back. The pilot got a bead on 'em, then we cut over to see about that ambush that White Platoon spotted.

"Damn fool bunch of gooks didn't even have any security out. There was only about a dozen of 'em anyhow. We slid in behind 'em and set up a claymore barrage. That was the first big bang y'all heard, just before the tanks hit."

Sergeant Benteen went on to explain. "Our 'eyes' brought us back past this group here, to see what they were up to, and we set up a little hasty ambush of our own. We set out a 'U' of ten claymores, and got ourselves up high, out of the blast patterns—and just waited for the suckers to walk into it. Nothin' but a turkey shoot." He sighed, shaking his head.

"You're welcome to join us anytime," Hawke said. "You guys fit very nicely into a firefight. . . . Talk about the cavalry coming to the rescue. First tanks, and then you guys to roll up the edges."

Benteen had been anxiously scanning the western sky as they talked. "I'd say that you fellers oughta be thinkin' about gettin' back to the cantonement area before you lose your light. Chuck might have a few surprises planned for you this evening. This ain't no place to be taking rocket or mortar fire—too open."

Franklin butted in at this point. "Jer, Bronco 5 just came back on the horn. Says he'll have two hooks on the way out to pick us up—wants us to set up an LZ on top of the south lip. He said we're to police up all weapons and paperwork that might have been left in the area and check for any wounded gooks."

"Let's get to it, troops, you heard the man," Hawke ordered, rising from a semi-kneeling position to survey the carnage below.

"Jimbo, call Red and White back; have them marry up with us over here ASAP. Have Red keep a close lookout for any dinks that might have bugged out and slipped between us and the Lurps. And Jimbo, have—or should I say, remind the captain to get a dustoff out here right away. It sounded like he had at least one seriously wounded."

"Heard him doing that a few minutes ago, Jer. Sounded like he took four WIA, and at least one KIA. Man, if that don't give you the shits. Less than two weeks in-country, and you go home in a rubber bag." With a shudder, he remembered that the entire West Point Class of 1950 had been killed in Korea.

"Sergeant Benteen, do you people need a lift back?" Hawke asked.

"Much obliged, Lieutenant, but our mother hen is waiting for us to give him a call. He's circling up there with the brass and other birdshit."

"Okay, Sarge, but thanks again for the rescue. We owe you one," Hawke said. "Come see us again, Chief; I hope we'll be in one of the armor units by this time next week."

The oncoming whup-whupping of the choppers

could now be heard in the predusk quiet of the jungled hillside. A smoky haze still lingered over the now silent jungle, with nothing but torn earth, mangled bodies and shattered trees to attest to the violence which had so recently visited.

Chapter Three

HAWKE AND FRANKLIN WERE DRAPED WEARILY OVER THEIR bunks in the barracks tent when Sal Epstein found them the next evening. "Hey, turkeys, don't get too comfortable," he said. "Just because you're big combat jocks now doesn't mean you can take a vacation."

No one even twitched at his words, so he lowered his voice to a near whisper. "Hey guys, your orders are in."

Both of the lieutenants suddenly jumped from their bunks, almost bowling Epstein over in a rush toward the bulletin board. Anxiously they searched the roster, to no avail.

Frantically, Franklin turned to Sal. "I don't see our . . . Epstein, you prick!" The prankster was standing behind them, grinning and dangling two freshly cut sets of orders between thumb and forefinger.

The two men leaped on the unprepared Epstein.

"Okay, spill it, man," Hawke threatened, and the three collapsed in a tangled heap on a bunk.

"All right, all right," he croaked from the bottom of the pile. "I don't know if they are ready for this, but both of you are going to the same outfit—the 88th Armor."

The resounding yell of "Eya-hoo, tanks by God, we're in business!" could be heard from one end of Camp Enari to the other while the two tankers vented their pent-up anxiety.

Epstein had seen the orders being printed and insisted on the privilege of delivering them personally.

But he cautioned against the night of celebration that was being planned. "You don't have time to hit the 'O' club, gents. Check the times on the orders; they want you over to their base camp at 1830. And their executive officer and the sergeant major will be flying out to their forward base at 1900 hours. You've got just three zero minutes to get signed out and over there."

"Gentlemen, I'm Sergeant Major Hagerty. Welcome to the 88th," said the gray-haired NCO. He guided them into the well-lit frame building that served as the Battalion's orderly room.

Looking around curiously, they could see the military memorabilia of past conflicts, as well as souvenirs of the troopers' participation in the war at hand. The 88th seemed to have a long history.

"Lieutenant Franklin?" the noncom queried, checking the roster.

"Uh—that's me, Sergeant Major," Franklin said, taking a short step forward.

"Sir, you're being assigned to Bravo Company,

First Platoon. Their rear detachment is located two doors down, on the left.

"Lieutenant Hawke, you're assigned to Headquarters, and I believe the Old Man has something special in mind for you.

"If you two will get signed in with your new units, we'll get you some field gear and weapons, and be on our way to the forward base."

Shortly, the three of them were standing in the gathering gloom at one side of a steel-planked helicopter pad. The Sergeant Major carried a dispatch case and an ancient Thompson submachine gun, while the two lieutenants wore shoulder-holstered .45s, each carrying their worldly possessions in a rubber bag and carry-all.

"I think I should fill you in on some of the basics before the chopper gets here," Hagerty said. "Can't hear yourself think in one of those things.

"The Battalion forward base is about fifteen klicks west of here on Highway 19. It's a mud 'n' dust bowl called the Oasis. It's about halfway between Pleiku and the Cambodian border, smack dab in the middle of Charlie's main infiltration route into this area. We've been running search-and-destroy missions, along with reaction force and convoy escort duty. Usually, our line companies are scattered from here and gone—OPCON (Operational Control) to some outfit that has no idea of what the hell to do with armor."

The old soldier shook his head ruefully. "I'm sure you've already seen some of our raggedy-assed tanks. They got that way busting jungle, running roads like armored cars and bailing out some company of grunts that bit off more'n they could chew. Tanks are supposed to be turned in for total rebuild at five thousand miles, right?"

At Hawke's assentive nod, he jolted them back on their heels. "Ain't no tank in this Battalion got *less* than five thousand miles on it, and the average is more like twelve thousand! These are the best damn tankers on God's green earth, sirs—otherwise every damn vehicle in the outfit would've been scrapped long ago.

"It's no secret that I'm a tanker, gentlemen, and this kind of crap really gets under my skin. We spend more time making roads with our tracks than we do fighting the bad guys. When we do get a shot at them, there's always some damn restriction or other tying our hands.

"Goddamn politicians are getting our people killed through sheer stupidity! Ever see one of them sniveling, vote-sucking bastards out where he can get shot at? Hell no. But they sure as hell know what's good for old G.I."

Hagerty's voice had almost descended to a growl, as he punctuated his remarks with a shot of tobacco juice onto the helipad. "Sorry to get bent out of shape, sirs, but I've got over thirty years and three wars in this man's army, and I'm getting awful tired of seeing good kids shot up because some piss ant politico wants another vote."

"No problem, Sarge," Hawke replied. "I couldn't believe all the layers of command that just had to get into the act when we had that firefight at the Charm School."

Hagerty's stony face cracked into a big grin. "So you were in that bust-up. Was one of you the 'butter bar' that shot an NVA off a tank with no fenders?"

"That was me, Sarge," Franklin volunteered.

"Of all the weird coincidences. Those three were comin' in from a convoy escort, and they're the only three running tanks of the platoon you're to take over, sir. The tank commander whose ass you saved is named 'Gator' Scruggs, and he said he owes you a case of beer or a fifth—whichever you prefer."

Further conversation was forestalled while a Huey slick hammered its way down to the pad.

"I thought the Exec was accompanying us out forward," Franklin said as they swung aboard the idling chopper.

"He was, sir, but the Old Man wanted him to expedite some Battalion business, so he stayed on. But don't worry, you'll have *plenty* of time to make his acquaintance," Hagerty said.

They lifted off the pad into the setting sun, which had just broken through the cloud cover. Once the ship had gained enough altitude, the view of mountains along the border with Cambodia became spectacular—the irridescent green hills were gilded by the red-gold sunset. Their route west followed Highway 19W, over several tiny villages and a tea plantation called Catecka—the largest in the world, and still administered by the French.

There was still considerable civilian traffic along the road, but military transport had already sought the safety of firebases or laagered up in defensive perimeters for the night. With the sunset would come the "Shadow Government"—VC tax collectors and NVA raids on local government.

Numerous hulks of burned out and mangled vehicles of all types could be seen scattered along the edges of the partially paved road. The only armored equipment that could be seen was a couple of old Greyhound Military Police cars that had come to grief many years ago.

"There's the Oasis," the Sergeant Major yelled over the noise of the turbines. He pointed to a broad, livid red scar slashed out of the deep green of the jungle. "The Battalion TOC (Tactical Operations Center) is set up on that ridge to the rear of the camp. Because we're armored, we've inherited the most dangerous segment of the perimeter—the top of the ridge, sloping down to the foot of those hills, to the southwest over there."

It'd begun to rain again as they landed at a chopper pad near the center of the sprawling camp, and they hastily slipped into their new ponchos. A G.I. with the everpresent three-quarter ton truck met them, and soon they were deposited at the TOC, a rambling sandbag structure that seemed to have grown up out of the red earth. This was actually the case. The sandbags had been filled with a mixture of cement and dirt from a huge excavation, then stacked around the hole. The resulting bunker was half sunk into the ground, with only three feet of height protruding above.

An armored unit is intended to be commanded from moving armored vehicles, so gaps were left in the bunker wall for all of the command tracks—high-topped APCs (armored personnel carriers) which were backed into parking slots in the walls. Radiating out from the operations center was a maze of slit trenches, and surrounding it was a mix of sandbagged, framed tents and small bunkers.

Along the outer perimeter of Oasis, they could see bulldozed combat positions for whatever tanks happened to be in at any given time. Daylight was fading, but they could see a few tanks, and the ungainly bulk of a VTR (tank retriever) silhouetted against the clouded red line of the setting sun.

Shouldering their gear, the two officers followed Hagerty into the baffled entry of the command bunker. The sandbag walls had been painted white, and illumination was provided by at least a dozen naked light bulbs. They glanced around, somewhat bewildered. The bunker seemed bigger from the inside, and it took a minute to realize why.

The command tracks had their ramps down, providing extra space, adding their bit of light to the interior. A variety of radios occupied the insides of the modified personnel carriers, providing instant communication with all levels of command. Jeremy looked at all those radios with a sense of foreboding, and Franklin muttered something about Big Brother.

"Welcome to the 88th." A muscular blond major greeted them, offering his hand. "I'm Carlisle, Battalion S-3; come on into the op-shop and meet the rest of the staff. You're in luck, we're just about to have a briefing by the colonel involving a series of upcoming operations which will certainly include you two."

Entering the rear of the track, Carlisle introduced the staffers in turn, including the S-5, Captain Dawson, the Civil Affairs Officer, with whom they'd be doing quite a bit of business. Last, was the Senior Motor Officer, Mr. Larsen, whose baleful gaze seemed to be warning them not to tear up his charges.

"Ten-hut," barked Sergeant Major Hagerty.

"At ease, gentlemen," said the colonel, a smallish, graying man who radiated an immense energy. Giving the situation map a cursory glance, he said, "Is this current, Top?"

"Yessir, updated as of 1800, sitrep and statcom from next higher," Hagerty responded smartly. The colonel gave him a quick thumbs-up.

The colonel seemed to almost bound into the operations vehicle. "Welcome, gentlemen, I'm Colonel Barksdall. I understand you two handled yourselves quite well during your rather rude arrival to the Division. That's just an indication that Charlie doesn't go to sleep during the wet season . . . You've been introduced to the other members of the staff? . . . Good, then let's get on with business."

Following briefings from each member of the staff, attention again focused on Colonel Barksdall. "As you know, the Battalion has been on a constant round-robin of reaction operations and OPCONs which've resulted in the detachment of even our smallest sections to other units. I'm sure you've all heard the term '88th rent-a-tank,' being batted around."

There were several wry chuckles as the colonel went on. "This has continued to the point that there's now no cohesive armored force in this area. Someone up at Brigade finally noticed this, and the decision's been made to let the Battalion run its own operation."

This pronouncement was followed by a loud cheer from the assembled officers, but Barksdall raised his hand for silence. "We still have normal commitments to meet, so we're going to have to create this reaction force out of existing troops and hardware. I'm now going to implement the reorganization that we've been contemplating for some time. We can't create new tanks, but perhaps we can conjure up some ACAVs (armored cavalry assault vehicles).

"As you know, our mortar tubes are worn out, and the personnel carriers that carry them have been diverted to road patrol. Our alleged ground radar unit has proven less than effective in jungles and it, too, has been doing road duty."

Hawke and Franklin stared at each other while the more experienced men nodded their heads. The lieutenants were wondering just what their part would be in this reorganization. They soon found out.

"Effective immediately, the mortars and the ground radar element are combined as the Battalion Recon Platoon." Pausing, Barksdall turned to the Motor Warrant Officer, a secret grin on his face. "Mr. Larsen, this will of course require the modification of the affected tracks to ACAV configuration. You will begin preparations for this immediately. Of course, you will have the assistance of all the men assigned to the new unit, and of its new commander, Lieutenant Hawke."

"All right," Jimbo said, enthusiastically pumping his friend's hand and clapping him on the back in congratulations.

Other members of the assemblage looked on with mixed emotions while the colonel continued to speak. "There's no way that ACAVs, no matter how well equipped, can handle all operations. We've learned this the hard way, as have all the other armored units. Therefore, we are detaching one platoon from Bravo Company and assigning it to work closely with the scouts in combined ops. The designation of this new reaction force is TASK FORCE PUMA."

A shiver of anticipation and apprehension ran down the backs of the two lieutenants when the colonel designated Franklin's line platoon to be the heavy segment of Puma. What the future held in store could not be foretold, but it would test them to the utmost.

"There is a lot of work to be done with these men and machines," Major Carlisle warned. "The tankers lost their lieutenant in one hell of a firefight. They won't be receptive to a new officer yet, but we think that being part of the new task force will bring them around to their old fighting trim. Let's put it this way: your lives will depend on their being a cohesive force. One good thing is that the three groups have been doing much the same duty, and they're used to working together."

Barksdall ended the meeting with instructions to the motor officer. "Larsen, several of our local Cav units have offered to ship us some ACAV kits; but they won't be enough. I'm sure you understand that in addition to being agile, hostile and mobile, we're also most resourceful. Just don't get caught," he said, directing a broad wink to the assembled staffers.

With the briefing completed, Hawke and Franklin left the bunker with Captain Dawson, walking out into the sudden full darkness of the tropics.

"Kinda looks like you two newbys stepped right in it, up to your green necks. . . ."

Pop-Pop-Pop . . . Overhead the sound of incoming sniper fire, followed by a cry and a curse, broke the silence of the camp.

"Hit the deck! Shit! Somebody caught one," Dawson shouted. They dove into the sandbagged tent which had been their destination. "Goddamn, this is the first time anybody ever took a hit!"

"You mean this has happened before?" Franklin asked.

"Yeah, but usually during the day. Night sniping just recently started."

"That sounded like a U.S. carbine. Hasn't anyone tried to take that guy out?" Hawke asked incredulously.

"Oh, sure, but no one has even come close to hitting him."

"Well hell, he can't be too far away if he's using a carbine," Franklin said. "Plus, in order to shoot into this dark of an area, he must have a sniperscope. Ya know—one of those rigs you see demonstrated, but never used."

"Yeah, I know what you mean, man," Jeremy said. "Might have pinched it off the ARVNs."

"Hey, Jer, you thinking what I'm thinking? If that sucker's using IR (infrared), we can see him too," Jimbo said.

Hawke caught on instantly. Nudging Dawson, he asked, "Hey, Captain, is there a tank on the perimeter?"

"Oh sure, over at maintenance, but it's deadlined. Won't do you guys any good."

"No, but its infrared binoculars will. How do we get there?"

"Straight ahead, about fifty meters. You'll run right into it."

"Let's go, Jimbo," Hawke said, as he disappeared through the tent flap into the darkness.

Two and three round bursts from the sniper continued to harass the camp as Hawke and Jimbo sprinted through the unfamiliar murk of the darkened base. They found the silent bulk of the M-48 inside the open front of a large tent being used as a shop. Scrambling up to the turret, they dropped into the belly of the monster. Flipping an overhead switch, Franklin flooded the turret with red light.

Hawke had already begun to search behind the radio racks. "A-hah, here they are," he said, holding aloft the peculiarly shaped case containing the battery-powered binoculars. "Now, let's go find something that'll shoot."

"Hawke, Franklin, are you in there?" It was the voice of Captain Dawson, who'd followed them to the disabled tank.

"That's us," Hawke said. "You're just in time. Where can we find something with a .50 on it?"

"The tank retriever is sitting on the perimeter, over by the mess tent. They use it for sentry duty, just like all other vehicles."

Hustling from maintenance over to the mess area, they easily spotted the massive wrecker. "I got a hunch that's where we're going to find our little buddy," Hawke said, pointing to a clump of trees at the side of a stream that paralleled the wire, some fifty meters out. "It's the only place he could find cover close enough for the effective range of that IR rig I think he's got."

As they climbed up the front of the boxy iron monster, they were challenged by a sharp voice. "Halt! Who's there?" accompanied by the "snick" of a safety being released.

"Captain Dawson, with two new lieutenants," the S-5 said hastily.

"Okay, sir. But be careful, it's not too safe here with that dink poppin' away out there."

Squatting down beside the sentry, who was seated on a couple of sandbags behind the heavy machine gun, Hawke stared out into the dark in front of the barbed wire. "Have you been able to see where the fire is coming from, soldier?" he asked.

"No sir, I just got up here myself. We're only

supposed to man this gun if any hostile activity takes place," he replied, with a noticeable quiver in his voice.

"Jer, let's give the specialist here a little break. Go ahead, troop, let this ol' butter bar plop himself down behind the iron while Lieutenant Hawke takes a look-see at what might be skulking around out there," Jimbo said.

Franklin changed places with the man while Hawke scanned the area all round with the IR glasses. Through the eerie greenish-white optics he could clearly distinguish brighter spots, caused by nearby heat and light sources, readily discernible from the normal background haze.

"Jimbo, I'm going to rest my chin on your head. Make sure that your head is exactly aligned with the forward direction of the gun. I'll guide you with my elbows on your shoulders," Hawke said.

Again, he began scanning in front of them, guiding the following movement of the gun with pressure from his elbows. His vision was suddenly blinded by an intense beam of light, filling his binoculars. "Damn, got him!" Hawke exclaimed.

"He's scoping the area, Jimbo. You should be pointed right on him. I can still see his light. He's not being too smart by holding that thing on for as long as he is."

The hammering blast of the Browning shattered the night, lighting up the surrounding area with its deadly flame. With an iron hold on the spade grips of the weapon, Franklin liberally hosed the vicinity where Jeremy had indicated he'd spotted the sniper. As if it were alive, the gun continued to reach into the night, seeking its fragile prey, like an extension of Franklin's will.

"Hold your fire! Hold your fire!" Hawke shouted into Jimbo's ringing ears.

With the deafening roar of the fifty over now, only the tinkle of the expended brass steel belt links broke the silence. They'd run over seventy-five rounds of ammo through the gun, which should have torn up anything hiding in the light cover afforded by the sparse vegetation along the streambank.

"You think you got him, sir?" the young soldier asked curiously.

"Well we sure scared the living shit out of him, if we didn't," Franklin replied, stretching up to a standing position behind the gun mount.

The firing brought the rest of the area to life. Armed shadows scurried everywhere. Several approached the VTR.

"Who's doing all the shooting up there?" came an authoritative shout from below.

"Lieutenants Hawke and Franklin, sir," Jeremy responded, recognizing the colonel's voice.

"I'm up here too, sir," added Dawson.

"Well, what's going on?" Barksdall asked.

"Sir, we thought that if that clown was using a carbine at night, there was a good chance that he had one of those IR sniperscopes to go along with it," Jeremy replied. "We commandeered some IR binoculars from the deadlined tank and went looking for some red light. Figured that the fifty was the best way to get at that sucker if we found him."

"Good thinking, gentlemen," the colonel said. "He hit one of the cooks in the tail with his first few rounds. Might have gotten a few more of us if your guess is right. He was getting on my nerves.

"You know, you two have seen more trouble in two

days than most of us see in weeks. You use your heads and respond well," he said in a complimentary tone. "I think that the faster we can get you hooked up with your new commands, the safer we're all gonna be.

"Sergeant Major, have the Scouts sweep the perimeter at first light. Let's see if the lieutenants were right."

Chapter Four

THE FIRST RECONNAISSANCE PATROL RETURNED FROM ITS dawn sweep around the Oasis perimeter just as the staff was going over the morning Sitreps. Its squad leader, a curly-haired, burly individual who walked with a soft woodsman's gait, ambled over to the command track and asked for the Exec.

"The XO said for you to make your report to your new boss, Lieutenant Hawke. He's over in the mess tent finishing breakfast," said Captain Dawson.

Saluting smartly, the blocky NCO spun on his heel and left the command bunker, heading across the compound to the mess tent.

"Who is Lieutenant Hawke?" he inquired of the few stragglers remaining in the open air mess hall.

"That's me, Sarge," Jeremy said, standing up from a bench near the door.

"I understand you're to be the Scout Platoon leader, sir. I'm SFC Riley, your new platoon sergeant."

"Good to meet you, Sarge," said Jeremy, shaking the man's hand. "This is my partner in crime, Lieutenant Franklin. He's commanding the line platoon that'll be working with us."

"Sirs, I thought you'd like to see this before the goddamn G-2 REMFs got their hands on it." With this, Riley produced an extremely battered, but still whole M-2 carbine and sniperscope. Looking the weapon over, the two lieutenants developed a pair of self-congratulating grins—their guess had been dead right.

"I'll take charge of that bit of scrap, Sarge; I think I can salvage . . ." Franklin stopped talking as he cocked his head to one side, listening. Somewhere, heavy armor was moving, sending that unmistakable vibration through the ground.

"That'll be Cap'n Marks bringing Puma's tanks up," Riley said, as the two officers rapidly finished their coffee.

"Let's go find the troops, Jimbo, and see just what we've let ourselves in for."

The two of them followed Riley out into the compound and down to what passed for a tank park. At one side of the clearing, a mud-spattered jeep was leading a smoking, jerking, clattering column of five tanks into the Battalion Motor Pool. Four and three-quarters tanks would have been a better description. Only three of the battered machines were under their own power. One, smoking violently, was running free, but the other two each had a cripple connected to it by crossed tow cables.

With a stricken look on his face, Franklin said almost in a whisper, "THAT is my tank platoon? Those junkers look like candidates for controlled cannibalization, not combat."

Riley, acquainted with most of the crews, stood up for his friends. "They're good troops, really, sir. They're just in need of some stand-down time. Like the mortar and radar tracks, they've been run so hard for so long, they've not had time to pull maintenance."

"Well, if you say so, Sarge: I'll go meet them," Franklin said. Putting unwilling feet in motion, he walked toward the jeep while a small, Banty rooster of a captain got out and began directing the tanks into a line.

"Sarge, I hope the PCs aren't as bad off as the tanks," Hawke said.

Riley grinned. "Worse, sir. And most of 'em are out in the hills, limping along on half-ass suspension. All we've got here are the hopeless cripples." He was pointing to three tracks at one end of the park, where a group of men, moving slowly in the early morning heat, were unloading mortar and radar equipment into a series of shipping containers. One was being retracked while the other two seemed to have attracted every available mechanic. Mr. Larsen had obviously given top priority to the new project.

Walking over to the deadlined PCs, Riley gave Hawke a quick rundown. "We've got eleven tracks assigned to us, sir, plus one medtrack. Most of 'em are armed only with 7.62s but there are two .50s in the group, and the paperwork's gone through for the rest of our weapons. There's two tracks out on bridge security, and two escorting one of our inbound convoys—those're the ones with the .50s.

"The last one is out with a medic track, winning the hearts and minds of the Montagnards."

Noticing Jeremy's blank look, Riley explained. "Medical Civil Action Patrol. They send the medics and an intelligence officer out to the remote villages. The pill rollers hold a sick call for the hill people, while the intel types try to gather some info on activities of the local VC—some of whom have been blackmailed into the cells because their kids have been kidnapped for 'duty' on the Ho Chi Minh Trail. Communism sucks, Lootenant.''

Coming up to the trio of PCs, Riley was about to introduce Jeremy to the crews when a man who'd been on radio watch atop one of the vehicles hastily addressed them. "It's hit the fan again, Sarge. The medics got jumped, their PC's taken a hit in the running gear, and they've gone sixty-nine with the gun track in that clearing south of the junction." A heavy, steadily increasing rumble behind them announced the arrival of Franklin's contingent, and Hawke turned to Riley.

"Get full information, Sarge, while I find out how much we can get rolling . . . er, just how far is that junction?"

"Ten klicks west on 19, sir, then five more on a trail we made—the gooks took it over for their own road. Fairly firm going till just before we get there."

Riley climbed up to the top of the PC, and Hawke strode over to where Jimbo was getting a final blessing from his new CO. "Those're damn fine men," the captain was saying. "They were a damn hot outfit once, and they will be again if you treat them right. And you better do just that, mister, or I'll have your hide salted and nailed to the back fence—with you still in it!" The man stalked back to his jeep and drove off.

"Whew," Franklin said. "What a hard case; I'd hate to be working for him full-time."

"You may change your mind after today," Hawke

replied. "We've been hit, and *we're* the official reaction force. How many tanks have you got effective?"

Franklin raised an eyebrow, turning to his top NCO, the craggy, lantern-jawed "Gator" Scruggs, whom they'd seen briefly in their first firefight.

"Just two, sir," Scruggs said with a voice like a running gravel crusher. "The rest need one hell of a lot of work, but the ones that can move are hot and reliable. We cannibalized the two cripples into them —we even got full crews." The man, who resembled an aging second stringer for a pro football team, said this as if it were quite an accomplishment.

Just then Riley jumped down from the PC. "I got the sitrep, Lootenant. They're in a hole under deep jungle, sir, and there's no way choppers can get in there. We gotta do it the hard way." His eyes met with those of Scruggs, and an old soldier's knowing look flashed between them. Two shavetail butter bars were on the hotseat.

Jeremy's mind had been working furiously. He had a half-formed plan, but just as he was about to say it, he spotted Carlisle coming at a jog-trot. "We got the word over our own radios, Major, and two tanks are all we can move right now. How close are the two tracks on convoy duty? And can you release one or both of those on bridge security?"

"I was just coming to tell you—the convoy's fifteen minutes out; they only had to come from Pleiku. And you can have the track from Bridge 17—we can see that one from here."

"Right, that's all we need. Thanks, Major."

Carlisle hurriedly left to go about his own business, and Hawke turned to Franklin. "Two tanks, three PCs and two of those with Brownings—that should do for starters. Give me a lift to Bridge 17, and I'll use that track for a command vehicle. By the time we get lined up, the other two will have caught up with us."

"Right Sarge?"

"Right, sir," Riley said crisply. "I've got the signals book and I'll get 'em on the horn on the way out."

Franklin had already mounted up on his battle-wagon when Hawke and Riley, having quickly acquired a pair of M-16s, climbed aboard. The sergeant dropped into the turret, alongside the loader, and rapidly got into communication with the rest of the PCs.

He stuck his head out of the loader's hatch. "The two on convoy are breaking loose at full throttle, Lootenant. There's a couple of MP gun trucks to babysit the freight drivers for the last few miles. And the one on the bridge is warming up; he'll be ready when we get there."

The tanks rolled smoothly westward, and the two officers could see the bridge coming up. They could also see a pair of PCs coming up fast behind them—at a speed considerably in excess of regs.

"GM diesels," Riley explained. "The mechanics put civilian injectors in 'em and change the rack timing slightly. Most of your new tracks'll clear fifty, and the one we're comin' up to has been clocked at sixty—downhill." Hawke responded with a happy smile that told Riley all he needed to know about his new boss.

Riley, who knew the road from long experience, sat with Jeremy in the lead PC. They raced westward, then turned south on a side road that disappeared into a tunnel of thick foliage. The chatter of automatic weapons, oddly softened by the intervening jungle, drew steadily nearer. Jeremy developed a giddy, clutching feeling somewhere right underneath his heart, something halfway between fear and excitement.

Glancing sideways at Hawke, Riley swung his intercom mike up out of the way, and said, "The butterflies're always there, Lieutenant. Bullets run 'em off for awhile, but they'll be right back." Hawke noted the fact that his new top soldier hadn't used the intercom and decided that he was being broken in by an old pro.

"I'd put one of the tanks ahead now, sir. The PCs are good enough for lead duty on the roads, but we may have to smash something out of the way down here in this thick crap."

"Right, Sarge." Keying his radio, Hawke got in touch with Franklin. "Put one of your big boys in lead, Jimbo. They're what we need for breaking and entering."

"That's a roger, Jer," Jimbo called back.

As Jeremy's driver slowed down, the tank Ballbuster clattered by. Its TC, the hell-sergeant Gator Scruggs, lifted a hand in half salute.

Now they were close enough to distinguish the sound of individual weapons. Jeremy got in touch with the two embattled PCs, getting an update and ordering them to fire everything they had, to mask the sound of their tracks.

The sound of firing nearly trebled as the column punched its way through the heavy tropical vegetation. Then the line of vehicles halted as Ballbuster stopped short of the edge of the clearing, its long ninety roaring like an angry dragon.

The loader must have shells under each arm, Jeremy thought. Cannister shells smashed the foliage to pulp on each side of the trail, and a continuous wall of sound tortured his ears. Those guns can't fire that fast, he thought again, as the column jerked into motion.

Entering a tree-roofed, cathedral-like clearing that seemed much too beautiful for war, Jeremy gave his first combat order. "Puma Force, form assault line, tanks to the center, and advance." That must not have been quite right, for Riley was giving him a worried look. He soon realized his error.

He'd been imagining the pair of personnel carriers surrounded by a swirling cluster of assailants—like a covered wagon train. Instead, they were sitting nose to tail in an old Montagnard village clearing among the old foundation poles, sniping at muzzle flashes in the surrounding treeline. The enemy would have to be rooted out or driven off.

Hawke hastily modified his order. "Tanks cut left and right, beat up the treeline. PCs 4-5 and 4-3, pair up with the closest tank and cover their backs."

The tankers, old hands at this game, each took one side of the clearing and rumbled slowly forward, punching out a mix of cannister and HE (high explosive shells). As they systematically rolled up the resistance, the flicker of AK-47 muzzle flashes began to fade away.

Jeremy glanced at Riley.

"That'll work, Lieutenant. All we have to do is set here for a bit, and then go check out those two PCs in the center of the glade."

The two trapped vehicles were sitting side by side in the center of a small clearing that was completely enclosed and covered by triple canopy rain forest. A single road led into and through the space, and three dim trails wandered off to the south and west.

Riley's long-range assessment of the situation had

been right. Out here on the border under deep jungle, helicopters couldn't get down to the ground, and artillery was of limited value. This was a primitive slugging match, gun-to-gun and, if need be, blade-to-blade.

Methodically, the tanks ground down the enemy lines, followed by the PCs who picked off the few survivors. Hostile fire diminished to a few diehards, and then faded off to nothing.

Puma's first combat hadn't even lasted ten minutes!

Jeremy's driver, a large Cajun named Dubois, pulled up to the pair of ambushed tracks to find that what few wounded Puma had sustained were already patched up—and vehicle repairs were being started. Riley and the rest of the noncoms were going competently about their after-battle chores, and Jeremy remembered a choice bit of advice from his grandfather who'd ridden into Mexico with General Pershing.

"Goddamn it, boy," the old cavalryman said. "You're goin' to be an officer, just like your great-great-granddaddy back in the Confederate Army. The one thing you gotta learn, in addition to command, is when *not* to command. Sergeants are the backbone of any army—all the way back to Sumeria. If you want something done, tell the sarge what, not how . . . If he's already doin' it, shaddup and look intelligent."

Jeremy looked around him and wisely shut up, and at least tried to appear as if he knew what was going on.

When Puma's few mobile machines rolled into base late that evening, the motor officer, Larsen, had a pleasant surprise for them. Striding up as they swung into a parking line, he announced, "Your command tank, Franklin, can be repaired quite easily; all it needs is tower seals on the cooling fans. We'll have them in by tomorrow noon. The other two, though, will need to have their power packs pulled."

Larsen motioned to where a wrecker was pulled up between the pair of battered machines. "One has a stripped-out steering clutch, and the other has about four cylinders trying to jump out of the hull. Since one is engine problems, and the other is a blown transmission, we can split up one spare pack and get all tanks running in two or three days."

Franklin grinned and began to congratulate him, but the old, prune-faced warrant officer held up a hand and said, "Not so fast, son. We've been getting a lot of bad rebuilds lately, and we've got to dang near retorque everything that comes in. Blow those replacements and you'll be grounded for a *long* time." Franklin promised to ride herd on his drivers, and the master mechanic turned his attention to Hawke's problems.

By now, the three of them were taking a break from the heat, sitting in the relatively cool motor office. Larsen reached into a small Japanese refrigerator and produced a six-pack of Korean beer.

"Combat always creates a thirst, and the inner man needs lubrication, like machinery. Now, Mr. Hawke, we got problems. I could only get four ACAV conversion kits, so we're going to have to improvise; in other words, steal. The guns for all vehicles are no problem —they're on the way. In fact, you'll find plenty of extra hardware stashed in those tracks already— damn troopers've got magnetic hands.

"The sore spot is gun mounts and the armor shields. I know you've got some pretty slippery troops in those tracks you're inheriting, because I've had to protect my own parts inventory from that batch of thieves. My suggestion to you is that you have a platoon meeting and 'develop' some sources—outside the 88th, that is.

"I have a few connections that will help; Sergeant Major Hagerty has some more. And I can always release a couple five-tonners for anything that won't fit in a jeep."

The two lieutenants rose to leave, and Larsen added one last caution. "The reason most of your PCs are down is transmission breakdowns. They're not caused by excessive speed, but by the weight of those layers of sandbags they carry to soak up mine damage. If you can figure a way past that problem, you'll have made a real contribution to the war."

Hawke thanked the man for his advice, and he and Franklin went to catch a belated supper and do some constructive plotting. Puma was a paper reality, and had been blooded, but they had a long way to go before it could be called combat ready.

A few days later they caught Hagerty in the NCO segment of the Headquarters mess, and laid out their dilemma. "We're short of nearly everything, Top," Franklin said. As junior of the two lieutenants, he'd automatically inherited the job of Exec/Motor/Supply Officer for Puma, while Jeremy became the CO/Weapons Officer. Riley and Scruggs were "staff."

"Most of the men have ratty field gear," Franklin continued. "Would you believe one gunner was issued a helmet with a bullet hole in it? And half the tankers are still wearing stateside fatigues that the mama-sans patch for them."

"He's right," Hawke said. "I've got a couple PCs

down on bridge duty just to get close enough to a female to get their uniforms mended. And there've been threats to hold up a convoy and take supplies at gunpoint. The supply system just isn't working properly because we're a composite unit, and neither parent company wants to support us entirely."

"It's causing some loss of morale, too, Sarge," Franklin added. "These troops have been orphans for so long that they take the lack of support as a personal insult. At first, when we got all five tanks running, it generated tremendous enthusiasm, but that died off in a few days.

"How can they respect officers that can't even get new clothes for them? All these men know is jungle, dirt roads and baling wire—they're starting to count days till port call. We've got some damn fine men and some absolutely top noncoms, but they're beginning to get stale. If we don't do something pretty quick, we might as well put Puma back on the shelf."

Hagerty shook his head, reaching for his notebook. "This job never stops. Even when I sleep, I'm scheming where to get the wherewithal to keep the tanks moving.

"I know both Bravo and HQ Company's top soldiers. Those two owe me favors going clear back to Inchon and the Chosin Reservoir. Also, I've recently found an old friend, Major Kameha up in Brigade, whom I soldiered with back in '44, when he was a shavetail and I was a PFC. If you'll get me a list . . ."

As if by magic, a half dozen sheets of legal paper appeared before him.

"I'll lean on those two First Shirts to make supply requisitions, and if one or both of you gents will go introduce yourselves to Major Kameha, explain your predicament and mention that Hagerty from the old Americal Division would take it as a favor, we'll get something faked up."

Hawke and Franklin were beginning to feel some of the weight come off their shoulders as one of the prime operators of the Green Machine went smoothly to work.

"One more thing, sirs," Hagerty added as they prepared to leave. "You'll have to assign an NCO for the pickup run, and I'd suggest Dubois. That boy'll make a fine top soldier one day, and it's time he learned the ropes."

Major Kameha was a short, sparely built Hawaiian who'd first served in the American-Caledonian Division back in the Pacific during World War II. He received the two armor officers graciously, promising immediate action for their problem. His predecessor had the soul of a bureaucrat, and had been miserly and dishonest with his supplies, which explained the situation that Kameha had acquired.

"You may assure my old friend, Hagerty, that I will be most happy to aid him," the major said in precise, textbook English. "However, I am experiencing some troubles that slow my efforts."

The major's troubles, it turned out, were that he had to supply literally dozens of small LZs, firebases and even Special Forces camps. He too was spread far and wide and couldn't always be sure of armed escort for his trucks.

Since part of Puma's reason for existence was to be the protection for small convoys of this nature, the three officers immediately set about making arrangements that would benefit all concerned—provided, of course, that no regulation-happy staff officer got wind of the informal arrangement. A fast call to Captain Hensch at Division Communications resulted in the assignment of a special radio frequency—and Puma's web acquired another strand.

Four days later, shortly after Dubois and a detail had gone off with an ACAV, Gator Scruggs called Puma together in his most diplomatic manner.

"All right, you meatheads, front and center, every swingin' Richard of ya. I want a formation of all crews in five minutes. No excuses and no goof-offs." He picked up a fist-sized rock and caromed it expertly off the red cross on the side of the medic track. "And that means you pecker mechanics and that sorry-ass excuse for a driver, too!"

Five minutes later, he had Puma's half-hundred men lined up in front of him, some half-dressed and still half-asleep, having been up most of the night working on battered machines.

"We're finally gonna get resupply," Scruggs told the unbelieving soldiers. "I want each of you to go back to your hootch, tent, track or wherever you keep yer gear stashed and start inventorying. Dig out all the worn-out crap for accountability, and we'll make up a legal-lookin' combat loss list for the rest.

"When you hear Doobie's track and a pair of six-bys comin' in the gate, reassemble right here. Fall out!"

The shocked but happy men scattered to their various crashpads, and the tank commanders gathered enthusiastically around Scruggs.

"What happened, Gator?" asked a short, wiry individual. "I thought we'd joined the Foreign Legion and had to get our supplies through Bizerte!"

"We got officers now, Jenks, and things are gonna be

different around here. If we're gonna be a task force, we'll need the equipment . . . So the lieutenants leaned on the Sergeant Major, and he came up with a connection. There's gonna be some radical changes made around here—you can bet on that. Now go get yer own shit together, so you can at least try to set an example for the troops."

"Hep Sarge!" the noncoms chorused, and split for their respective quarters, talking eagerly about how much pressure this mysterious new source could stand before someone clamped down the lid.

Late that afternoon, the distinctive shape of Dubois' track, "Rebel Rouser," slid through the front gate of Oasis Firebase, leading a pair of shiny base camp five-tonners, driven by a pair of obviously excited rear-echelon types. Dubois shepherded them over to Puma's isolated corner of the perimeter.

Hawke and Franklin had requested that the newly formed task force be set up in its own area, in order to help develop a sense of cohesiveness. And the Battalion CO, knowing that a certain amount of extra-legal maneuvering must necessarily accompany the operation, had consented, over the objections of several of his book-bound staffers.

When Dubois swung his track into the parking line, giving an ecstatic "V" sign to the men, the two trucks pulled up side by side. Grinning Brigade supply personnel rolled back the canvas tops, revealing an incredible array of goodies to the astonished men of Puma.

Kameha jumped from the cab of the lefthand truck, acknowledging the salutes of Hawke and Franklin, who'd just walked up, attracted by the rattle of Rouser's tracks.

"My predecessor must've been part squirrel," Kameha said. "When I put my crews to taking inventory on the mountains of supplies he left, I could see that he was more concerned with his inventory than with the comfort of the troops."

Hagerty strode up. "Aloha, Major," he said, referring to a memory the two of them shared.

"It's been too many years," Kameha responded softly. "How long do you have left in this tour?"

"About six months, sir; plenty of time to catch up on recent history. We can get something cold over in the Battalion Forward Club, if everything here is under control?"

"No sweat, Top," Dubois said, walking up in time to read the signals that were passing between two old warriors. "These specialists of the major's are a good bunch, and Gator's got things moving real fine."

Kameha smiled gratefully, startlingly large teeth flashing against his brown face. "So, if the lieutenants are not needed here, perhaps they could join us at the club?" he asked, looking in their direction. The two of them saw the process of reoutfitting Puma moving smoothly and wisely decided that any detailed supervision would only slow down the operation.

When the four prime movers had left for the Battalion watering hole, the flow of goods was getting into high gear, and Dubois smiled at Scruggs. "Good thing the wheels got out of here. You ain't gonna believe all the stuff that came to light in those warehouses. The previous Brigade supply honcho must've had something illegal going on. Come look!"

Camouflaged poncho liners, actually lightweight quilts, were a new issue item in the Vietnam War, and consequently in scarce supply. Someone had discovered, however, that if a number of them could be sent to a local tailor, several excellent, saleable cool weather jackets could be made out of one of them.

"Look at that bale of 'em," Dubois said, as one of the supply techs was issuing the somewhat illegal garments to an eager line of men. "We ripped off enough for the whole task force—the officers, too."

The prosaic mind of Gator Scruggs, however, was more interested in the stream of vital "housekeeping" supplies coming off the trucks. Jungle fatigues, hammocks, jungle boots, first aid kits, Coleman lanterns, canvas cots, tank tarps, squad stoves, five-in-one rations, Lurp supplies—the list seemed endless. Scruggs and Riley patrolled the line of vehicles, clipboards in hand, endlessly checking every detail. No one knew when such another bonanza would materialize, and they were taking no chances on being caught short.

The medics came in for special treatment because it had been found through painful experience that the ubiquitous Dustoff chopper couldn't always be called up out on the border. A helicopter couldn't batter its way down through triple canopy jungle, so the rolling aid station needed to be close to a combat surgery.

A surgeon could be let down on a sling, and a sufficiently expert crew could get a stretcher cage up and out. The only prerequisite was that the doctor have adequate equipment at the combat scene. So Puma's Iron Angel carried enough supplies to stock an aid station, and was manned by medics that were trained as surgical assistants.

The medi-track was armed with twin, M-60 machine guns, and was dangerous in its own right. Unlike enemies fought in other wars, the Communists had signed no Geneva Convention agreement, and considered the red cross on a medic's arm to be one more target. Armor medics not only defended themselves, they'd been known to smash their way into wounded G.I.s, creating enemy casualties in the process.

Over the course of the war, several medics had been wounded while patching up enemy casualties after battle.

By the next day, the Task Force's little corner of the perimeter had been altered radically. The varied tanks, ACAVs, trucks and jeeps that'd been slowly acquired for Puma's use were parked in a pair of neat lines, combat vehicles facing outward, with the thin-skinned machinery protected behind armor. Beyond these were a pair of tents, a general purpose medium and a smaller, so-called officers' tent that had been set up as a headquarters.

Antennas were being erected, and waist-high sandbag walls were being constructed around the tents. The stowing of newly acquired gear was proceeding rapidly, and the troopers, all dressed in new uniforms, were moving much more briskly. Puma was coming alive.

Around noon, Hawke called a meeting, taking this time because it would be one of the few times he would have a majority of his men in the same place at the same time. Since both he and Franklin had seen combat—both as infantry and with the embryo Puma —their acceptance into the select combat fraternity was quicker than most. As a result, he could talk "business" with them as soon as he could gather them in and lay it on the line.

"This is how we're going to set it up," he told them as they gathered in the still-cluttered GP tent.

"Franklin's Bravo First Platoon will be called the heavy element. The ACAVs will be the maneuver element and will do much of the light patrol and escort work. However, since all the scattered, uncontrolled sections are now under uniform command, there'll always be a reaction force of tanks someplace around.

"We now have five fully operational M-48A3s, and by running them relatively slowly, we'll keep them that way. On short runs, for instance, the ACAVs will proceed at convoy speed, while the tanks tag after, at about twenty. That way, the tanks will stay in the most probable ambush zone without blowing their engines, and still be on call if some group of Cong gets tricky and pulls off an ambush close to a base.

"When we get hit with a long-range escort, say down to Chio Rio or out to Mang Yang, we'll naturally send at least a light section of tanks with the convoy."

Hawke went on to designate Scruggs as combat top sergeant, and Riley as rear area and reaction force noncom. Then he turned the meeting over to Franklin.

"Lieutenant Franklin, in addition to being a platoon leader, is going to wear several more hats—he is also our working Exec/Supply/Motor Officer."

As Jimbo stood up, Riley said sardonically, "You're going to wish you'd been born twins, Lieutenant."

"Now we've only been able to get four full ACAV kits," Franklin said. "All the fifties and M-60s are in, and we can get the mounts welded up easily enough. The problem is armor, transmissions, belly protection and running spares. I've got some feelers out, but do you have any suggestions? Anything goes, except an armed raid on the ordnance park down at Qui Nhon."

When Puma's sticky-fingered, magnet-palmed soldiers found out that they were literally being asked to scrounge, they licked their chops in anticipation. It was as if Jimbo had opened up a floodgate, and he had to hold up his hands for silence. He picked out a staff sergeant who'd been whispering with a pair of Sp4s.

"How about you, Jenks? What can you and your cohorts get us, without going to the stockade?"

"Well sir," Jenks said, setting his beer down. "Camp Enari's got a controlled cannibalization point where we can go to scrounge parts off wrecked machines. That's where we've been getting all our track spares, road wheels and such. What nobody's ever done, is to go in there with a cutting torch and cut up the hulls themselves."

Jenk's intensely blue eyes flickered with a sudden glow. "I lost a damn good buddy on one of those half-assed reaction missions, sir. So if you'll let me have a truck, one shield kit for a sample and a few warm bodies, I might could get us the rest of our armor."

Franklin immediately spotted a possible flaw. "The PCs are made of aluminum, and you'll need a heli-arc."

"No sweat, Lootenant," an SP5 piped up. "The Engineers back at Enari are loaded with metal working equipment and just begging for something to work on. I met an SFC on one of Jenk's scrounging trips who said his whole platoon is doing make-work on showers, fire gongs, piss tubes and the like."

A lively buzzing was issuing from the assembled troopers, and Franklin told the two men to come see him after the meeting. After that, the conference, in true American style, became a free-for-all with one noncom after another volunteering to handle details. Puma was falling into place quite nicely.

In the weeks that followed, sergeants with small work parties tagged their trucks onto convoys or got escort from inbound PCs, which often returned with homemade gunshields on top, and transmissions and running gear inside. The new task force couldn't just sit in Oasis and work on machinery, though; they had their normal commitments, plus whatever else Battalion thought they could handle—and the inevitable surprise raids on small outposts.

In desperation, Franklin came up with the idea of putting crippled but runable machines on stationary duty, such as bridge guard or hilltop strongpoint. Such measures, the two officers knew, could easily lead to casualties and court-martial, but they felt they had no choice. Sometimes only genius-level troop juggling saved the day, such as having a tank with its long ninety on a high ridge . . . specifically, SSG Kim, a staff sergeant of Korean descent in Puma 1-5 "Bearcat."

"What's the external security status?" Jeremy asked Dubois who, taking a break from driving, was handling one of Rebel Rouser's tail guns, navigating, while the other tail gunner kept tabs on the radio.

The bulky buck sergeant turned to where Hawke rode the .50 turret and answered. "About as screwed up as usual, sir. The track on the bridge we just crossed is the last one in line for conversion, and he hasn't got his shield yet. Kim's 1-5 tank is settin' on that rise up ahead with a fried turret motor and a blown alternator. All he's good for right now is direct fire artillery."

Hawke and a section of three fully converted PCs were escorting one of Kameha's running columns which delivered much-needed supplies to small combat bases. The convoy, half empty, was barreling along, headed for the next customer, a fortified relocation hamlet, where several Montagnard villages had consolidated and armed themselves against the depredations of their Communist brethren—Montagnard Vietcong.

The village, north of Highway 19W, consisted of a football field-sized barbed wire compound filled with native housing. Guard towers covered the corners, and the natives themselves manned bunkers when under attack.

"We oughta be about a half hour out of the hamlet at this speed, Lootenant," the other tail gunner said. "I heard the Puffs have even got a bar set up . . . AMBUSH!!!" he shrieked, his voice rising two octaves in alarm. He opened up with his machine gun, firing short, savage bursts into the roadside brush.

Their ACAV had been in the lead and was allowed to pass through the kill zone unharmed. Two trucks behind them, a fuel tanker had been blown by a command-detonated mine as it slowed for an unusually deep pothole. Now a ripple of RPG rounds leaped out of the brush toward a five-tonner directly behind them, swiftly enveloping it in fire and black smoke.

Hawke brought the fifty into play, raking the undergrowth along one side of the slightly curved dirt road. He couldn't see the outside of the curve, but his other two ACAVs had pulled off on that side, adding their firepower to the fray. Hawke's driver turned and backed in the road until Jeremy's gun could cover the convoy, while the two M-60s stabbed the nearby brush piles. This segment hadn't been adequately cleared of foliage, and there were plenty of places for hostiles to hide.

Looking up, Jeremy saw the bridge guard track coming over the hill behind the convoy, its fifty hammering into where the NVA reserve should be. A fire-spitting crash erupted from its right track. The PC rolled helplessly off the tread, the driver using the other tread to brake, swinging the PC out into the brush where its attention was drawn to survival—not aid to the convoy. Things were turning into a downhill shit-throw, and Jeremy, now convinced that he'd been jumped by something larger than the usual harassment ambush, decided to call in some outside help.

"Meadowlark 6, this is Puma 6, we are in a kill zone four kilometers south of the relocation village of Plei Djerang." He ran off the grid location down to eight places and was assured that aerial rocket artillery ships were on the way, along with close-in gunships. Switching frequencies, he apprised Battalion of his problems, ending with "All Puma elements not committed, rendezvous this location."

Returning his attention to the immediate vicinity, Jeremy saw that the enemy commander had decided to concentrate on the tracks first, wiping out the sheepdogs in order to have a free hand with the flock of trucks. It almost seemed as if they intended to steal, rather than destroy. But his own immediate problem concerned a determined assault on his ACAV by a group of khaki-clad men with AKs who were trying to clear the way for an RPG team that would certainly take out his entire crew.

Dammit, Jeremy thought, where are those gunships? This is too close quarters for artillery . . . By God, those're NVA, he was thinking, when the offending group vanished in a medium-sized explosion—about what could be expected from a light artillery piece.

Jimbo Franklin's "Big Bastard" and another tank commanded by Sergeant Alveretti prowled cautiously through a mixed forest of scrub, jungle and second-growth hardwoods south of Highway 19W. The region had been clear-cut once, as the few remaining giant stumps attested, but now nature was slowly reclaiming the land, aided by a chaotic political situation that kept human traffic to a minimum. Monsoon had temporarily broken, and the two tanks, carrying three squads of infantry between them, moved side by side out of a clump of brushy woods into a clear meadowland, under a brassy hued sky.

This was the first time that Franklin had been out on his own, and he was still under the tutelage of his NCOs in some matters.

"You got to watch these woodlines," his gunner, Krause, said. "Charlie knows that ol' GI will relax out in the open . . ."

Franklin spotted movement in an isolated clump and grabbed his override control.

"Contact," Jimbo snapped. "Get in the hole!" Krause dropped and twisted past the breech in a maneuver that a gymnast would have envied, peering anxiously through the view panel in his periscope, while Franklin swung the turret.

The lieutenant had seen movement and was taking no chances. His instincts had been correct—the sudden swing of the turret panicked a trio of VC who were lying in wait.

One stood up with an RPG launcher, while the other two sprayed the tanks wildly, in hopes of hitting an infantryman. No such luck, Chuck. The GIs, part of a highly experienced infantry platoon, hit the ground, shooting at the first motion, filling the air with 5.56 zingers.

"Driver, hard right, grind 'em under," Franklin ordered. The fire-shot backblast issued from the anti-tank launcher, and instant heat wash seared his bare arm, the suction of a close miss lifting him in the turret, while the muzzle blast of the ninety shoved him back down. When the tank surged forward, it sank sickeningly to one side in a hidden patch of soft mud. Old Charlie had chosen his site well, and positioned himself where the surface of the gently sloping land met the water table. Big Bastard was helpless.

"1-2, I'm stuck, flank his ass," Franklin ordered. His running mate obediently moved around the soft spot, running over a hidden mine in the process. A tiny puff of smoke swirled from under its left tread, and the track began to roll off the rollers.

Both nineties had already pumped a couple cannister shots each through the offending brush, and the infantry were probing carefully toward it, waiting for a follow-up. The gunners, old hands at this, each took half the horizon, traversing their turrets, eyes straining into the underbrush through ten-power sights. Through whatever was to come, their vigilant eyes would never leave those optics, and the turrets would never cease to move.

After a tense quarter hour, Franklin dropped off his rear fender to join the infantry command group behind his hull. "It'll be a while before we're mobile again, Owens," he told the platoon leader. "You might as well set up a perimeter and let 'em chow down."

"Yeah, I see," Owens said, nodding to his top

soldier, who trotted off to a waiting cluster of squad leaders. "Some of my boys have been armored infantry and know tracked vehicles. Do you want me to stir up a work party?"

"Damn straight I do. That would help a lot," Franklin said, focusing his attention to his own predicament. First, he'd have to put men to work cutting a large log to chain to the tracks of the mired tank, so that it could lift itself out, using the log as traction. Then the damaged tread would have to be patched with a few spare track blocks and rerun over the sprocket.

Of course he could put both crews on track repair, and then use the 1-2 tank to haul Big Bastard out, but that would take more time; and he didn't particularly like the way this day was starting. Better to get both tanks up as soon as possible.

Fortunately, the two tanks were close together, and Jones had set up a loose perimeter around both of them. Extra men were at work on the broken track, and Franklin, after looking the operation over, saw that he could be of no use there and went over to the wood-cutting detail. The men were obviously willing, but just as obviously city boys, chipping away ineffectively at the ten-inch trunk.

"Let an old farm boy have that axe," Franklin told a very surprised PFC, and proceeded to expertly lift an ordered series of chips out of the tree. He'd cut the felling notch and was taking a breather when Lieutenant Owens walked up behind him.

"I'll finish the job, Jimbo. Take a break and go look important for awhile."

Noticing the amazed expression on Jimbo's face, Owens explained, "I grew up in a logging camp, I'll finish this off and limb it out. Go find some shade."

Less than an hour later, both tanks were free and running, the two crews having taken the simultaneous breakdowns as a race, to see just who would be "up" first. Franklin and Owens were now deciding whether to continue the sweep or try to trail the ambushers.

"Hey, Lieutenant, Puma 6 is on the horn—he's got his ass in a crack," Krause yelled from the turret.

In a series of leaps, Franklin was on the turret, cramming a commo helmet on his head to hear: "Meadowlark 6, this is Puma 6. We are in a kill zone south of the relocation village of Plei Djerang." Hawke gave a string of numbers and Franklin saw that not only were they on the same map, but were fairly close. Hawke had been on the long-term convoy escort, and Franklin hadn't known his boss's whereabouts for almost a week.

"Require ARA (Aerial Rocket Artillery) from the south ASAP, and close support gunships if available," Jeremy ordered in a steady voice. Only the background of intense small-arms fire gave any indication of combat. Franklin could visualize the gunships lifting off from distant Camp Enari and again checked his map. Technically, he was committed to the sweep, and Jones was senior officer, but . . . Switching to Puma internal frequency, he heard: "All Puma elements not committed, rendezvous this location, 6 out."

"Sounds like your boss has got more action than we do," Owens said, climbing up on the hull beside him. "How long will it take to get to the party?"

Franklin thought about their recent encounter and asked Owens, "What are the chances of that bunch we just busted laying a mine or two on our inbound trail?"

"About 100 percent!"

"Well then, we'll have to make a new road out past your LZ at Plei Duc. Load 'em up and we'll curve around this contour line to 19, and haul ass."

While the riflemen were mounting the hull, Franklin radioed to Hawke. "Puma 6, this is 5, we are in some green crap one zero klicks south of you, but will rendezvous your location ASAP, over." With Jeremy's terse acknowledgment, he again heard the intense hail of gunfire in the background and gave the order to move out.

"Say Lieutenant," Krause said, "Kim's 1-5 is settin' on a hill not too far from that village. You suppose he can see the action?"

Thinking for a moment, Franklin mumbled to himself, "Idiot, of course he can," and reached down to switch frequencies. "1-5, this is Puma 5, over."

Kim immediately answered, informing Franklin that he could indeed see the action and requested instructions, volunteering the information that his turret motor was still dead, but that he could shoot on manual.

By now, the two tanks were plunging at high speed through the young forest, and Franklin needed all his attention for his own situation. He ordered Kim to assist by fire, but to inform Hawke first.

"Please to keep head down, Lieutenant-san," came Staff Sergeant Kim's sing-song voice over Hawke's radio. "One each Bearcat gonna kick ass, but mebbe shrapmetal get a little too close."

Jeremy scoped out the hill behind him, awestruck as Kim's gun began a death roll, high explosive plastic sizzlers dropping on alternate sides of the embattled convoy. Well, that was what he was there for, Jeremy had to admit, but the man's gunnery was superb as his explosive fingers walked through the ambush.

"He's got to be shooting that gun himself—on manual—using his whole crew as loaders," Dubois guessed, as the twentieth round in less than four minutes slammed home.

That comment catalyzed a plan in Hawke's mind, and he keyed his mike, interrupting the young Korean-American's roll. "Kim, this is 6, keep your hits on the inside of the curve, the western side of the road. You copy?"

As soon as he was assured that Kim understood his plans, Jeremy ordered his driver to pull out into the brush on the outside of the curve. "Tracks 2-2 and 2-3, this is 6. I'm coming down the outside, flank me as I pass, and get on line."

"Roger 6," the other two echoed. In less than a minute, the three were rolling up one side of the ambush in a tight line formation. Swinging wide of the kill zone, they made another pass, farther into the treeline, and were still flushing hostiles when the lead ARA ship got on the air.

"Puma 6, this is Meadowlark 4-6, we have your convoy in sight from the south, and a commotion in the green line to the east. Where do you want our fire?"

Oops, Jeremy thought to himself, those buggers aren't too accurate. Aloud, he transmitted a slight delay. "Meadowlark, the commotion is us, wait one, break; Puma elements, get back on the road NOW— driver, hard left, put us on the road at the head of the column."

During the next few minutes Jeremy was busy vectoring the arriving gunships in, designating one segment of the road as a combat LZ, and securing it with ACAVs. Shortly, helicopter borne infantry were sweeping the ambush site, leaving Hawke free to survey his own casualties.

Dismounting at the mined track, he found one badly concussed driver being littered off to a waiting chopper, and a medic patching minor cuts on two more. The remainder of the crew had been joined by several men from the other ACAVs and promised to be ready to roll as soon as the truck remains were off the road.

The scene around the ambush site had changed from one of strife and bedlam to one of orderly consolidation and evacuation of wounded; and Hawke clambered back up into his gunmount and ordered Dubois to take him back to the LZ. Choppers were busily arriving and departing while wounded and dead were lifted out, and military investigators dropped in. He could see groups of information specialists moving right behind the probing infantry, searching NVA packs, cutting off unit patches and writing voluminously on clipboards. This may be a war of hit and run, he thought, but it's also a war of information.

Jeremy saw a U.S. medic tending to a short row of wounded enemy, and he thought again. It's also a war of cruel extremes. First we blow them up, then we patch them up, while they take our wounded off, untreated, to hang in cages up North.

While he watched the trees being smashed down by Big Bastard's rattling treads, Jimbo mentally inventoried Puma's assets, coming up with zero. Kim was on deadline but perched on a ridge nonetheless. Gator had two tanks on convoy headed toward Kontum,

Riley and three tracks were stuck on bridge guard, and Jenks and two more tracks were bringing a supply convoy from Enari to Oasis. The two in shops at Enari couldn't be counted yet. If Kim and the gunships weren't enough, it was now up to him.

The trees disappearing under his treads began to thin out into bushes, and suddenly he was in a clearing, taking intense small-arms fire.

"UNASS! GET ON LINE!" Owens screamed, and the riflemen literally vanished from the decks. Jimbo's hand clutched convulsively on the override, and cannister belched out of the muzzle, wiping out a group of VC who'd been trying to set up a light machine gun.

Sims, Big Bastard's giant, black loader, looked up, his eyes questioning, and Franklin commanded, "All cannister, leave the co-ax switched on."

Alveretti's Bronco had pulled up alongside him after dumping its infantry, and the two tanks stopped at the edge of an almost circular clearing and took stock. They seemed to be at one side of a normal Montagnard village, except that armed men were scurrying everywhere, weapons flickering from under all of the post-mounted houses. Peeking out jack-in-the-box style from his open hatch, Franklin noted that the infantry had gone to ground level with the tanks' drive sprockets, and were firing methodically.

Directly behind him, Owens and his command party—the platoon sergeant, radioman, medic and interpreter—were crouched, surveying the scene, too. "You ready, Owens?" Franklin asked.

"Anytime," came the terse answer, and the two tanks began to roll into the hidden village, machine guns probing.

A clatter of AK fire from the rear caused a simultaneous chorus of "Medic, medic!" from the infantry, and Jimbo saw men falling like corn in a high wind. Owens had come around in a low, firing crouch as the platoon sergeant fell, blood spurting from a line of holes in his chest.

Franklin's turret was already swinging when the first hostile face came aboard, followed by a muscular pajama-clad body. He was reaching for his .45 when three more appeared in his peripheral vision.

"Five, button up, yer buried," Alveretti said over the radio, and Franklin dropped, pulling the hatch down with him. He heard a high-pitched scream and saw bloody fingertips fall into the turret with him as a grenade went off on top of his hatch. A quick drumroll of tinking sounds pattered over the side of the turret while Alveretti scratched his boss's back with machine gun fire.

Bronco also was covered with enemy, but Alveretti was an old hand at this. He had his driver peel the uninvited passengers off by driving through a burning hut, throwing flaming thatch in all directions, working his co-ax all the while. Jimbo saw a group bringing an old B-40 launcher up behind Alveretti, and vaporized them with a load of cannister, opening his hatch at the same time, .45 at the ready.

"Wait a minute, Lieu . . ." Sims said, but Jimbo was already face to face with the inevitable holdout whose eyes instantly went dark as Sims, firing from his hatch, shot the man "right in the bung hole," as he would later describe it.

Motion close-in caught Jimbo's attention, and he and Sims hastily armed and dumped a half-dozen grenades off the hull. Alongside, he caught an occasional glimpse of what appeared to be dozens of two and three-man infantry skirmishes as American riflemen hunted through the now flaming village, flushing bands of pajama-clad guerrillas from under burning huts.

Bayonets had been fixed on both sides, and Jimbo saw one grizzled old sergeant cross blades with an AK-armed youth. The kid came in low and fast, and the American caught the charge, parrying deftly, driving the M-16s butt through his opponent's jaw. Pivoting left, the old sergeant dropped his next assailant by a simple high port block and a boot in the nuts. Breaking his foe's neck with a stomp, the man turned and began to round up his squad, disappearing into the smoke.

The two tanks were littered with bodies and blood was dribbling down the turret sides, dripping into the hatches as they paused to "clean house," shoving carcasses off the hulls and chucking out empty shells. Sims, an unemotional veteran of dozens of these fights, dumped machine gun brass, and then reached into the external beer cooler, found a trio of undamaged beers and silently handed them around. Franklin took one swig and then wedged his beer can into a grenade box—the taste was like bile in his mouth.

The local battle was over, and Jimbo could see Owens sitting on the ground crying unashamedly, the platoon sergeant's head in his lap. "Dammit, I loved that ornery old coot," Owens said, the words coming low and clear through the engine's rumble.

An unarmed, aged Montagnard ran up to the interpreter and chattered away for most of a minute, tugging at his sleeve and pointing down a dim trail. When the two natives got Owens' attention, he was abruptly galvanized—all business again. "They tell me that the VC are holding half the village captive out in the jungle, using them as hostages to make the rest keep up a front. There's a chance we can save 'em. Can you split up and give me one tank?"

That was going against all doctrine, but Franklin said, "Yeah, this one, if you'll leave two squads back here with my sidekick."

"Right," Owens answered. Turning back to his squad leaders, he put one in charge, leaving the radioman with him.

The first squad and their lieutenant mounted Big Bastard's hull, and Franklin gave Alveretti orders to set up an LZ and secure it for medevac. Almost as an afterthought, he switched to Puma frequency and got in touch with Hawke. "We ran into a hot one, Jer, and it ain't over yet. I won't be able to get to you till I don't know when."

"Roger five," came the relaxed reply. "We just wrapped this one up, with the help of Kim and the choppers. But I can't get down there either, so keep your butt down, buddy. Over."

Franklin acknowledged, and then concentrated on the old man who sat his turret top, gesturing down a trail which Big Bastard's treads were rapidly converting to a road.

Franklin's driver, Dean, was the first to see into the clearing ahead because he was able to see under the foliage, and his shocked tone put both officers on high alert. "Holy fuck, Lieutenant, kill 'em quick."

When the remaining branches were whipped out of the way by the long ninety, they gazed upon a scene from hell. A line of villagers were tied to stakes, and VC were systematically going from one to the next, slitting the throats of old and young alike; a rocket team was standing between Franklin and the mass of the group. Any weapon used would surely kill civilians as well as the gunners.

An inarticulate scream came over the intercom and then the tank's engine was wide-roaring open, the hull almost dancing across the clearing as pivot-steers threw the gunners off. A rocket cut a new gouge in the turret, and the rocket team was smashed, the infantry shooting and slashing the executioners.

"God-damndest thing I've yet seen," Franklin told Hawke next morning. "Dean went semi-berserk for a few seconds and ran that gun crew under the treads . . . yuck! Anyway, we saved over half the civilians and trampled out a combat landing zone in the middle of that village." He paused, taking a long drag on a cigarette, pointing to a nearby chopper pad. "The poor sods are being choppered in and will probably wind up in a relocation village like Plei Djerang."

The two officers of Puma Force were sitting on top of Hawke's ACAV just inside the Plei Duc MI station gates, at the junction of Highway 19 and the Plei Djerang cutoff, taking a breather and comparing notes. Hawke had brought the remains of his convoy back down from the village, while Franklin, after providing overnight security for his combat site, had broken out the relatively few kilometers of heavy jungle to the station. There was now a new road back into the undergrowth and infantry patrols were already using it.

Hawke had sent one tank and a truck up to resupply Kim and give him a battery charging. A supply chopper, later in the day, would drop off a new turret motor, which the crew would install. And Larsen promised to have a new alternator in by the end of the week. Right now, though, the two sections, a pair of tanks and three PCs, were taking a well-deserved break, waiting for Gator and his section to come in off the convoy run and take over patrol duty.

"You wouldn't believe all the supplies and general munitions we found out in the bushes around that one village," Franklin said. "The grunts are still operating a search pattern, and there are trails radiating in all directions from there. The place must have been a major supply base, with only a company of security troops."

Hawke nodded his head in agreement. "Heavy armor seems to make the VC nervous, and they do things that ordinarily they'd avoid—such as jumping you yesterday. If they'd let you go on down that long ridge to the south, they'd have got off scot-free. As it is, we've cost them heavily and gotten beaucoup info in the bargain. Nobody can say that Puma isn't working for a living! By the way, anything new around Oasis? I haven't been back for about a week; we've been living off Kameha's convoys."

Franklin's face clouded. "Almost no good news, Jer. First off, that triple-damned, book-happy Battalion XO has figured out our little deal with Kameha. He's put in a squawk about 'nonreg private armies,' which 'Barky' Barksdall is politely ignoring—for the time being, at least.

"Second, Alpha and Charlie tank companies are being reconsolidated and sent to the north and south ends of the Brigade AO. Something doesn't smell right about that, but it keeps the staff busy. I'm going to visit Epstein and see if he has any hot skinny for us peons out in the hills, next time we draw an inbound convoy."

Hawke had been listening intently as Franklin talked, and now he drew out the stubby pipe that'd replaced his cigarettes, stuffing a rag mixture into it. "Something is damn strange out here all right. We're getting more and more NVA, with newer gear and better weapons. Also, some whole truckloads are being *stolen* from ambushes!"

"Uh-oh, that *is* strange," Franklin replied. "Now I know for certain that we better go see Epstein. Say, remember that discussion we had about finding our own LZ?"

"Yeah, I've been thinking about Plei Duc here. It's under-utilized, undermanned and closer to the action. Why bring it up now?"

"Because Cap'n Marks has been given the Oasis-Enari security mission, plus Oasis base security itself. And if I've got that prick figured out right, he'll be angling to reabsorb this platoon—and/or Puma."

Hawke was silent for a few seconds while he thumbed a kitchen match alight, firing up his pipe. "We've worked too hard for this, Jimbo, and no sawed-off banty rooster is going to steal it," he said quietly. "I may only be a butter bar, but the Hawke family has been military clear back to the American Revolution. Let me think a bit, and maybe I can talk to old Barksdall and make the status quo look good from his side. He's a career soldier, and his ultimate record is more important to him than the temporary happiness of a self-inflated OCS escapee."

Chapter Five

SERGEANT ELIAS BENTEEN FELT DISTINCTLY OUT OF PLACE in Division Headquarters and walked self-consciously down the waxed corridors of the huge, H-shaped building. Three hours before, a spiffy, polished jeep had pulled up outside the Ranger Platoon base compound, and a slightly mystified courier had walked delicately through the chaos of returning LRRP teams, asking for Sergeant Benteen.

Identifying himself, Eli had been ordered to report ASAP to DivIntel, Lieutenant Epstein's office. Striding up to a busy, attractive WAC typist, he cleared his throat loudly, and when she looked up, asked the way to Epstein's office.

"Through that door to your right, down two on the left, and knock, loudly, in case he's concentrating," she said, eyes widening as she took in the tiger fatigues, headband and magnetic gray eyes.

"Thanks, miss," he said, addressing the brown-haired Sp5 as a woman, rather than a soldier. He disappeared through the door, leaving one very intrigued female behind him.

"Come on in and sit down, Sarge, we ain't too formal around here," Epstein said. "This is a workin' soldier's office."

"Yessir, what can I do for you, Lieutenant?" Benteen asked, putting on his best official soldier manners.

"Come off it, you fucking barbarian," Epstein snapped. "We've kicked ass together, remember? I've got your combat reports here, and you've personally got more kills than most teams. I got a problem, and I need the Ponca—not the E-5."

"Er, just what did you need, Lieutenant?" Eli asked, jolted out of his formality.

"That's better," Epstein began. "I got your debriefing reports here, and like I said, your kill record is impressive. You seem to be able to get closer to Charlie, unnoticed, than any other team in the platoon. And once you get in there, you're a cold berserker."

Benteen thought for most of a minute, a variety of emotions flickering through his mind, while his face remained impassive. "We were a small tribe before the white man came, Lieutenant, and my ancestors had to out-Indian tribes like the Cheyenne and Commanche. When I go into those trees, I'm home, like Brer Rabbit in the briar patch." His grin vanished from his face and his gray eyes hardened like chips of flint.

"As to the killing, sir; have you ever seen a weasel on a slaughterin' binge in a chicken coop? And have you ever seen a mother on her knees beggin' an NVA not to take her only son for porter duty for the liberation? And then get shot by the local VC? Have you ever gone into a VC camp and found a GI who'd had his ears, eyelids and testicles cut off—and had to put him out of his misery yourself?" Benteen's eyes showed a deep, abiding flame, far back in his soul. "He was a medic, sir; they tortured him to death. Those people are animals. Lootenant, they *need* killin'!"

Epstein had read the reports, but he was nevertheless shaken by the intensity of the Ponca's emotions. His own family had fled Russia in 1917 to escape Bolshevik persecution. Now here he was, facing another tentacle of the Communist monster.

Automatically, the con artist buried deep in his psyche analyzed the man before him and came up with the correct approach for what he wanted done. "Sarge, you're hurting them, no doubt, but you're only nibbling around the edges. If you'll volunteer for a project of mine, I think we can cut off a big chunk of the buggers and send 'em straight to hell—wholesale!"

"Kind of a big job for a buck sergeant and a buck lieutenant, ain't it?" Eli asked.

"That's just it," Epstein said. "I'm seeing a pattern I don't like. I think the NVA are pulling a sucker play, hitting hard north and south of here, drawing all our forces away from Highway 19."

"That squares with what I'm seein' and what comes over the grapevine," Benteen said. "The Lurps're getting less action around here than up north. Anyway, my feelers don't run too far south."

"Mine do, and the pattern's the same. But my problem is that a second looie just ain't supposed to be that smart. I think we're about to be had by another full-scale assault, but I need proof! And to get that proof, I need my own *eyes* out there. If we can spot whatever it is they're plotting, we can nip it in the bud."

Benteen became a bit diffident. "Er, with what, sir? Meanin' no disrespect. But with all the heavy shit moved outa here, how much force can a second looie move?"

Epstein shook his head sadly. "Just one little task force, I guess. I know the commander and exec of this new hotshit Puma 88, and they're as slippery a pair as I've ever met. Matter of fact, you know them too."

Eli, whose acquaintances in the rarified atmosphere of command numbered exactly zero, was baffled and said so. "Lieutenant, I don't recall ever meeting no armored task force commander."

Epstein's huge smile practically met at the back of his head, as he said, "Remember that little get-down when the school patrol got nailed a couple months ago? Hawke and Franklin run Puma."

The Ranger couldn't resist that one. "Well I guess you've got yourself a new bunch of seein' eye dogs, Lieutenant. I'll go talk to the boys. It was gettin' dull around here anyhow."

Jeremy came awake instantly when the runner called his name. "Lieutenant Hawke, the colonel wants you and Lieutenant Franklin at the TOC—there's an operation going down."

"All right, we're moving, we'll arrive in five."

As the soldier left, feeling his way to the next tent with a shaded flashlight, Jeremy and Jimbo hurriedly finished dressing. They'd learned to change clothes in the evening and to hit the sack mostly dressed. All they required was a few minutes to lace their boots, find their weapons and leave. Not quite fully awake, they beat the runner back to the operations bunker, picking up cups of hot, black coffee on the way in.

The staffers were already assembled, along with a strange lieutenant, when they arrived, and Carlisle quickly laid out the situation, standing, pointer in hand, in front of a large-scale map.

"A LRRP team, code named Mongoose," he began, and Hawke gave Jimbo a sharp nudge as Franklin hastily thumbed through his SOI, "has seen a large group of hostiles headed toward Bridge 26. They have a party of MVC (Montagnard Vietcong) scouts, roughly a battalion of NVA, and a quote 'humongous bunch of bearers carrying all kinds of junk,' unquote.

"We're planning a night-blocking ambush, using a combined force operation. The Lurps are tracking the party, and we suspect that they'll be turning south at this stream that flows north into the Tonle San River, following it to 19W. This is about the only place they can safely bypass the local bridge garrison without being spotted."

Carlisle's pointer stopped at a mark on the highway. "They can cut under the wreckage of the old French railroad bridge, and not be seen. If they can accomplish this, they'll be able to resupply a large part of the central highlands—and we'd just as soon that didn't happen. We expect them to have already planned an ambush between their crossing point and the bridge guard force, so as to interdict Puma's bridge guards."

When Carlisle said this, Jeremy broke out in a cold sweat. That bridge was guarded by a tank and a broken-down ACAV. The lighter vehicle had an oil leak in its blower; and if that engine was cranked, it could easily run away, out of control. The crew had the parts and a mechanic on board and work was progressing, but . . . He returned his attention to the operations officer.

The pointer had moved again. "We plan to set up a two-company ambush here, north of the road, where they'll hit the streambed and turn south. The infantry have been choppered out to a release point and are moving quietly on foot. You'll note that the ambush position is within gunshot and tank searchlight range of the bridge. Lieutenant Hawke, is your tank on the north side of the bridge?"

At Jeremy's assentive nod, Carlisle continued. "As soon as Mongoose informs us that the majority of the NVA are in the kill zone, several things will happen, hopefully simultaneously.

"First, the infantry will open fire, releasing parachute flares. This will be the signal for the bridge tank to commence IR searchlight illumination and take targets of opportunity. Naturally, the load bearers will immediately stop and shit themselves—and Mongoose will call in artillery on them. All guns in this camp are now plotted on the coordinates—all that's necessary is the marker round."

Exclusive of their own problem, Jeremy and Jimbo liked what they were hearing, but what was planned for Puma? Virtually the whole outfit was in the area, and Carlisle would have figured out a role for them. Their half-whispered questions were soon answered.

"The firing of the ambush and the arty barrage will effectively mask the sound of moving armor," Carlisle said, "and when release is given, Puma will split into its two segments. The tanks will move up with the ground troops. Lieutenant Hargreaves, here, is from the light infantry concerned, and he'll ride with you, Franklin, as liaison with his men."

Franklin and Hargreaves immediately left to confer while Carlisle continued. "Mr. Hawke, you'll take your ACAVs and rush west to that side road north of the junction cutoff, as soon as Franklin's nineties open up. You're to follow the north fork off 19W, and link up with the Special Forces CIDGs (Civilian Irregular Defense Group), who Captain Torrion, the local A-Team leader, is bringing down on a forced night march. Once you've met up, you're to load the CIDGs on board, carry them with you, and set up a secondary ambush along that track. Any questions?"

"How about an interpreter, sir?" asked Jeremy. "Most of the line companies have one or two, but Puma's been on the list for weeks now. We'll really need one for this op."

"Sorry, forgot to mention that," Carlisle said, motioning toward a corner. "Loo, come on out here and meet your new boss."

Startled, Jeremy looked over his left rear shoulder, and liked what he saw. The man who stepped out of the gloom was short, compactly built and of undetermined parentage. Dressed in worn but neat tiger-patterned fatigues and armed with a U.S. carbine, he appeared quite competent.

"I am Chinese Nung, sir," the man said, stepping forward and saluting. "Loo Ky my name, and am speaking Viet, English, French, three 'yard dialects and Chinese, sir; enough of each for soldier."

Hawke returned the salute, glanced at Carlisle, eyes questioning.

"He's a Nung mercenary," the major informed

him. "Captain Torrion has got a company of them to back up his CIDGs. We made a deal with him, and we can have all the interpreters we need, in return for extra protection."

Hawke was now thoroughly used to these informal deals and, the briefing obviously over, he led his new recruit outside and found Franklin. Puma's exec had already passed the word to the troops, and when the command party got to the side of the tank park where the two rows of murder machines stood, the silence and darkness had been shredded by scurrying feet, metallic clinks, assorted thuds and muffled curses. Hatches had been thrown open, and the eerie glow of red combat lights was added to the firefly tracery of hooded flashlights.

Their arrival had been noted, going through the grapevine, and the TCs were already assembling around the open ramp of Jeremy's track for their orders. Jeremy barely had time to lay out the plan, when the auxiliary radio set to Mongoose's frequency spoke forth with Benteen's well-remembered voice.

"Okay Foxglove 6, they're in the bag," the ranger said. "They're all yours, I'm switching to Redleg. Mongoose out."

Flipping a radio to the infantry internal frequencies, Hawke could already pick up the excited commands to platoon and squad leaders, backgrounded by a steadily increasing stutter of small-arms fire.

"All right, Puma heavy, crank 'em and roll 'em," Hawke ordered. And with a muted thunder of engines and a clattering of treads, the line of carniverous iron dinosaurs moved out, rapidly increasing speed. It'd been less than an hour since a runner had awakened Hawke.

While Franklin's line platoon moved out to link up with the grunts, Jeremy had time to look back and survey his line of ACAVs. Of the eleven tracks currently assigned to Puma, only four had "Made in USA" conversion kits, and they would be the first to go in harm's way.

Jeremy's own track had been the first converted, and he now sat inside a half-turret of ballistic steel, behind a fifty caliber machine gun. On either side of the crew compartment behind him, were two men with smaller shields and 7.62 machine guns. Down inside the ACAV were thousands of rounds of ammo, auxiliary weapons, food, water and maintenance spares.

Behind the four original conversions, came six more tracks, in various states of alteration. All had their guns mounted, but the armor was patchy, having been made in Engineer shops at Camp Enari. Bringing up the rear was the medic track with its illegal, twin 7-six deuce mount. The original mortar FDC track would remain behind as a communications base.

With white parachute flares lighting up the western horizon, and the heat lightning flicker of artillery dancing through the valley, Jeremy's radio finally came to life. "Puma 6, this is Big Thunder 6. Your heavy element is now in place. Move out and execute stage two, over."

"Roger 6, wilco, out." Switching back to internal frequency, he ordered, "Roll the tracks, head west, cruise at three zero miles under red light." The line slid forward, engines rumbling gently, with the drivers using infra-red headlights. Hawke picked up his IR binoculars and looked behind him, making a headcount of nine pairs of greenish-white headlights.

Bringing his attention forward, he could now hear the steady roll of Franklin's guns.

Good, he thought, all that commotion will mask us completely . . . If I can just get away with a fast halt at the bridge.

His noncoms knew full well that their boss had to pull off a fake at the bridge, and maintained thirty miles per hour, as Dubois pulled out all the stops, easily drawing ahead of the column, engine screaming into the night as the treads clawed the dirt road that served as a major highway.

When they'd topped the last hill, the sight below them reminded Jeremy of a cauldron. The bridge tank had its Xenon searchlight on infra-red, and a brilliant green beam appeared in Jeremy's binoculars, playing on the far shore of the stream. The enemy soldiers were lit up like daylight, and didn't know it. Overhead, a shape flitted across the starlit night, and for a minute, he could hear the friendly noise of Wright Cyclone engines. A dragonship was on the prowl.

At intervals, the bridge guard tank would fire, but most of the damage was being done by the four that Franklin had brought down into the infantry positions. Farther north and west, the 105s from Oasis were walking their fiery footprints up the side valley. To the right of the bridge, the sparkle of small arms fire twinkled up and down both sides of the stream.

"How's it goin', Jimbo?" Hawke asked, keying his radio mike.

"Just fine, Jer. Regular turkey shoot so far, we've got 'em falling back, and we're about to begin pushing. Scruggs and Kim have each found fords in the stream and we're loading grunts now."

That suited Hawke just fine; with the valley full of

activity, no one would be watching the bridge too close. His driver skidded to a halt between the tank and the injured PC. Jeremy vaulted from his turret and the vehicle's ramp came down. Two men appeared, carrying a rocket-damaged engine hatch, and trotted over to the PC, using the intermittent muzzle flashes of the tank cannon for illumination. Jeremy and one of his gunners rapidly pulled out a matching spray shield and followed.

"Switch 'em and store the good parts," Jeremy ordered the young tank commander, "and hook up to the tank with tow cables. If it gets hot here and you have to be towed in, there's your alibi."

"Right, sir," the staff sergeant said, "but we might have those bearings and seals replaced by morning."

"True, but it never pays to take a chan . . ." He was interrupted by a rattle of AK fire right over the hill to his rear, which was immediately squelched by an unholy roar as eight fifties and sixteen M-60 machine guns pounded an ambush into dust and shattered flesh. The ACAVs rattled through a would-be kill zone like an angry freight train.

The local VC had been expecting something else entirely and the sudden, speeding appearance of Rebel Rouser out of the night had taken them totally by surprise. They'd barely gotten set for this new direction when Puma had swept through them, able to see their would-be adversaries by IR light. Anxiously, Jeremy counted headlights through the IR binoculars as they came over the crest. "All present and accounted for, roll it Doobie," he said. With a lurch and a growl, they picked up speed and again took the lead, leaving the battle behind them.

Easing the column's speed to twenty miles per hour,

Jeremy led them through the night. There was no particular hurry now, because the NVA, in total disarray, would be stumbling through the dark, desperately trying to get back across the border. Cordoned off by American and ARVN posts on 19W, and Franklin's tanks in the Tonle San valley, they would be, hopefully, beaten through the weeds, trees and bushes into the guns of Puma and the CIDGs.

Pressing closer to the border, the column passed through innumerable villages, and as the moon rose to give its wan light, Hawke could see pale faces staring out of unlit houses. "What do they think?" he wondered, these people of a war-torn land, who are hosting yet another generation of warriors, would-be conquerors and half-assed allies.

He'd studied history and knew many of the causes of this war. Food was one of them. The rich rice bowl of the Mekong could feed all of Southeast Asia, if the farmers were left in peace. But the impoverished dictatorships of communism couldn't find the cash to buy the rice. The Russians eyed the strategic location of the peninsula, and supported Uncle Ho, in hopes that he and his people would do the dying for them. Rice in return for ports.

His thoughts were interrupted by a tiny red light in the road up ahead, and a thick southern drawl in his headset. "Puma 6, this is Viper 6. Welcome to the border; y'all might jest as well shut 'em down and pull ovah, y'all are right smack in the middle of us."

"That's Georgia, for sure, sir," Dubois said, identifying the accent; "thick enough to butter cornbread."

Torrion had been standing in the center of the crossroads with a pair of American noncoms and a group of his Montagnards, and Hawke quickly directed his armored force into a tight circular laager around them, dominating the area with the outward-facing fifties.

Taking off his intercom helmet, Jeremy picked up the latest result of his friendship with Hensch—a squad leader's helmet radio. No larger than an AM-FM transistor radio, the high-tech device was clamped to the side of a standard GI steel pot, giving him constant communication with the tracks, even though dismounted. Dropping the electronic wonder over his head, he picked up his CAR-16 and slid off the hull to meet the A Team leader.

The Special Forces captain was not a man to waste words. "I've got one hundred men," he said. "Can you haul 'em all, Lieutenant?"

"Yessir, if we load some on top of the medic track too. How far in do you think we'll need to go?"

"About six miles in. There's a place that the NVA'll be comin' down at a dead run—if they're comin' at all—and that's where we'll have to set up. It's their best shot home, and we can set up a standard 'L' while I send out a fan of scouts."

Jeremy instantly caught the "if." "You mean there's some doubt, sir?"

"First off, don't waste breath on 'sirs' out here in these hills. And yes, there's about a 50-50 chance the buggers will use a back door north out of that valley. You ever been up this trail before?"

With Jeremy's negative answer, Torrion volunteered to guide the lead track while Jeremy controlled the column from farther back. At the captain's command, the cluster of natives behind him faded into the jungle, and groups of CIDGs began coming out, to be divided and put on the tracks.

In a surprisingly short time, the column was again underway, moving slowly up the heavily rutted overgrown trail. Loo Ky sat on the hull behind Hawke, acting as "talker" between the squads of 'yards and Nungs perched atop the line of ACAVs. As the line of troop-covered armored machines left the road, the terrain gradually sloped downward, then leveled off, opening up into a narrow, brushy glade. At one side of the open space, a stream burbled its way down rocky stairsteps.

"That's a solid crossin'," Torrion said, while the two officers stood at the head of the column. "And if they come at all, they'll be trottin' down that streambed in about an hour."

Jeremy could see the captain quite clearly in the moonlight, and asked, "You still figuring on a standard 'L,' parallel to the stream?"

Torrion nodded and Hawke reached up, pushing a helmet button, apparently speaking into thin air. "Puma, this is 6. Riley, put one on each side of the stream. Doobie, take Rouser and lead the rest of the platoon up the treeline and back 'em in. Medics stay back with the Special Forces reserve."

Before he'd finished speaking, the line of PCs was in motion. The CIDGs were dropping off, filtering cautiously into the dark jungle, carefully keeping out of the moonlight.

"What in the hell did you use, a Dick Tracy radio?" Torrion asked, fascinated with the possibilities.

Jeremy took his helmet off, showing him the miniature radio. "The Air Cav down on the coast has been using them, but they're strictly line-of-sight. Division is running a test to see if they're worth a damn up here in the hills and jungles."

"Well, what kinda range do ya get?"

"About 300 yards on average. Sometimes I just don't have to yell; other times I get damn near half a mile."

"Well, what do I have to do to who to get a few of those for us to test?" Torrion asked.

"Oh, I've got a pretty good working relationship with a signals captain who controls the test, and I'll try to get you a few, since we'll probably be working together off and on."

"Ah'd appreciate that, and you call me Frank, out here."

"I'm Jeremy, or just plain Jer," Hawke replied, and the two shook hands. During the next few hours, as the ambush became an obvious "dry hole," they discussed their views of the local situation, becoming more and more apprehensive as their information began to dovetail into a sinister pattern.

Torrion reported increasing pressure on his camp, up to and including determined assaults that had required artillery support and U.S. infantry. "There's two main infiltration routes through here," he said, "one of them good enough to take heavy trucks, and we're sittin' astride both of 'em. Ah've got a pretty good force here—'yards and Nungs—and between 'em we've really been getting under ol' Chuck's skin. Worst thing of all is, some of my patrols have been reporting tread marks . . . There's tanks over there!"

Hawke was intensely interested, but not in the way Torrion had anticipated. Instead of alarm, a predatory hunter's gleam shone in his eyes, and Torrion could see a look of eager anticipation spreading over the lieutenant's face. Whatever he'd been about to say, though, was interrupted by the distant clatter of treads, as Franklin's four heavies topped a hill. The captain was suddenly apprehensive, but Jeremy quickly reassured him.

"Relax, that's my other half coming up the far end of this counterfeit road."

"That wasn't in the plan. The tanks were supposed to just beat up the NVA and let 'em find their own way over the hills; I didn't even know armor could get *in* here. What have you got, M-41 lights?"

"Wait and see," Hawke laughed, reaching up to try the helmet radio. "Puma 5, this is 6, over."

Franklin answered right back, "I have you weak but clear, Jer, I'm about a half klick from your estimated location, over."

"I'm using the Mickey Mouse radio, Jimbo. That's why the signal is weak. How was the jungle bashing?"

"Fair. We found a blue line (stream) with a hard bottom, and used it part way. Picked up a hitchhiker, too."

Naturally, that triggered Hawke's curiosity. "Five, who the hell would be way out here . . . ? Oh yeah— Mongoose."

The noise of treads had been joined by the deeper pitch of diesels, and now the four battered war steeds emerged from the jungle into a growing dawn light.

"Main battle tanks, way out here," Torrion said in wonder. "Well ah'll be teetotally dipped in shit." The more excited the captain became, the thicker the cornpone accent got. After introductions and commiserations about the failed ambush, Puma mounted up the SF troops and gave them a ride back to the compound, exchanging experience and knowledge on the way. The tankers were very impressed by the woodsmanship of the native soldiers, and Benteen, who out in "his" jungle, talked easily with officers, added his impressions to the discussion.

Torrion and his noncoms, for their part, were very interested in the concept of heavy tanks in jungle combat. They'd been on the downhill side of their war; and tanks are the world's greatest levelers. The speculations were still continuing when radio calls for Puma to escort convoys, chase phantoms, bust jungle, pull stuck trucks, et cetera, began coming in.

Chapter Six

BENTEEN, IT TURNED OUT, WAS NOW BASING HIS OPERA-
tions out of the Military Intelligence compound at
Plei Duc, so Puma gave the Lurp and his men a ride
back from Torrion's remote camp. The Ponca and
Hawke shared a common view of war and the ways to
win a guerrilla conflict, and fell into a professional
discussion as the miles rolled under Rebel Rouser's
treads. They'd just begun discussing the use of captured enemy equipment when the radio interrupted
their conversation.

"Puma 6 or 5, this is Big Thunder 6, over."

"Uh-oh, that's Barky, wonder what he wants,"
Hawke said as he reached for the mike. "Big 6, this is
Puma 6, over."

"Puma, what is your present general location, and
do you have Mongoose leader with you, over?"

A blank, now-what-the-hell look passed between the
two as Hawke coded his approximate road position

and answered affirmative for Benteen, whose radio operator was three tracks back.

"This is Big 6. His principal employer is here and needs his latest report. Bring him in with you; we will arrange return transport."

"Puma 6, wilco, out."

Benteen had a somewhat embarrassed expression on his face as Hawke replaced the mike. "I, er, forgot to tell you, sir, that Lieutenant Epstein got me to volunteer for this AO. That's probably him at your base. The combat reports comin' in from this area have got him mighty curious. He thinks the NVA are trying to pull a fast one."

"Could be, Sarge, could be," Jeremy admitted. "The patterns have been changing in just the few months we've been in-country."

Benteen, with over half his tour behind him, had seen even more of a change, from determined assault to an even more determined effort to get massive supplies into the country. "Whatever it is, Lieutenant, it's gonna be bigger than anything we've seen so far."

Epstein and, unexpectedly, Barksdall and a new lieutenant were waiting as Puma swung smartly into its parking line in the Battalion motor park.

Hawke and Franklin gave hurried instructions to Scruggs and Riley, making sure that the overworked tank crews all got stationary duty for the next two days. Then they turned to face Colonel Barksdall, who returned their salutes and introduced the new officer.

"Gentlemen, this is Lieutenant Benjamin Weiss, our new assistant S-2 officer. He flew out with Lieutenant Epstein, who has brought us some rather alarming news. Please follow me—you too, Sergeant Benteen."

Barksdall led the group, which now included a very

bothered Eli, not to the TOC, but to his private office/trailer. On the way, Jeremy had a chance to pass some small talk with the new officer, and to get some impression of the man. Weiss was a well set-up man of medium height, an intelligence type and a West Point grad who had "future general" stamped all over him.

Barksdall, who had picked up some of the commanding general's mannerisms, reversed a chair, straddling it and resting his arms on the back. "Perhaps you'd better just lay your suspicions out, Lieutenant Epstein, and let us shoot at them."

"Well sir, let me ask Sarge Benteen a few questions first, then we can let him off the hook. Would you mind?"

The colonel gave his approval, and Epstein addressed the Lurp. "Sarge, you get all over this side of the AO, and I've asked you to get info from your other teams, Ermine, Ferret, Fisher and Wolverine. Have there been any raids, extortions, or large-scale ambushes lately?"

Benteen had been expecting this question. "No sir; oh, a few small-scale operations that we suspect are VC training exercises. But the Northerners are mostly escorting supply convoys like last night's, and then vanishing. Sometimes we find a base camp and call in a strike, or Brigade sets up an operation, but an awful lot of 'em are simply vanishing. At least as far as we're concerned, one platoon of Lurps ain't enough for a Division—beggin' your pardon, sir."

"What kind of supplies, Sarge—normal infantry/guerrilla equipment, or maybe something more sophisticated?"

Benteen now saw why he'd been brought here, and gave the expected answer. "The normal amount of guerrilla stuff, sir. But also radio spares for sets we know the locals don't have, but the main force NVA does. Also, truck ignition parts, fuel in cans, stashed in the jungle, heavy caliber ammo, like 120mm mortar bombs." He saved the zinger for last. "And 76mm tank ammo, sir."

During the silence that followed that comment, Epstein let the ranger off the hook. "Thanks, Sarge, that'll be all. I think you'll be able to find the chow hall and the club, and my chopper will drop you off at Plei Duc on the way back to Enari. Be at the pad at 1600."

After Benteen had left the room, Epstein went on. "As you know, pressure is building at both north and south ends of the Division area—"

"Well I, above all, know that," Barksdall said in an acid tone. "Half the time I can't even *find* Alpha and Charlie Companies; continue, Lieutenant."

"The current scenario at Division is that the NVA will harden up one of these pressure points as a feint—then hit with everything he's got at the other. On the other hand, they could pull a double feint and come back on the first one with their full weight. There's a lot of shit hidden out in those jungles and we have no way of knowing where they've got the majority of their supplies stashed. Supplies are the key. The NVA are weak on mobility and transport, so wherever their stash is, that's where they'll strike hardest."

"Makes sense," Barksdall agreed. "But what's that got to do with us here in the middle?"

Epstein replied with another question. "You know the routes between the border and the coast, sir; what would a hostile armored force be able to do, loose on Highway 19, with all our heavy armor committed to Dak To and Ban me Thuot?"

"I see," Barksdall said reflectively. "And just how much force does Division give this theory?"

"Less than 30 percent, sir. But it has to be covered, just in case. There is a possibility and we should have some kind of a contingency plan."

Barksdall stood and said, "I see that the possibility has to be covered, and the mention of those 76mm shells adds validity to the theory. For the time being, I'll leave this in Puma's sphere of influence.

"Lieutenant Weiss, you'll work closely with Puma, and keep in touch with G-2 through Epstein. Now, I've got business elsewhere." Turning to leave, he caught Jeremy's eye. "Lieutenant Hawke, see me later in the day, when you get time; I'll be here all day."

Barksdall led the way out of his quarters, cutting off toward the operations center, while the four lieutenants headed for the sandbagged tent that served as their quarters and Puma's office. Settling down in canvas folding chairs, the two Puma officers looked suspiciously at the West Pointer, not sure of his bona fides.

"Well go ahead and talk," Epstein said to Jeremy. "Aw, he's as dishonest as the rest of us, I gave him a full briefing and he's convinced."

Franklin popped open a beer, sipping appreciatively, and glanced sideways at Epstein. "Kinda stretched that one a bit, didn't you, Ep. Just how much of that line does Division buy, anyway?"

"Almost none, but my boss gives it enough credence that he's decided to back me to the extent of putting out a few feelers and warnings."

"Well, we've got most of the bugs worked out of Puma," Jeremy said, "and given a bit of a warning, we can pot PT-76s all day long."

Weiss, a taciturn, analytical type, had been sitting and listening, but now he put his finger on the pivot point. "The NVA have several battalions of T-54s, some manned by Russians. Can you handle a company or two of main battle tanks?"

After a shocked moment, Hawke answered. "Down in our jungles, we could eat them alive and the PTs for dessert. Out in the open, it's up for grabs. If they open up at long range, they're dead. If they get within 500 meters or so, we're in deep shit."

"Why the range difference?" Weiss wanted to know.

"Range finders and gunnery computers," Franklin put in. "Every tank the United States owns has full ranging/computing gear; the Russians issue one range finder per company. But Lord only knows what these poor sods down here get."

Hawke had been thinking while this interchange was going on, putting two and two together, coming up with six. "Jimbo, I see what Weiss is getting at. If the Lurps start finding 100mm shells in those jungle caches, we're in trouble."

That deduction got the four lieutenants into a serious tactical conversation that lasted until Hawke finally got his nerve up for whatever it was his colonel had up his sleeve. "Well fellas, it's been nice knowing you, but I'll die of suspense if I don't find out what Barky wants me for." Pushing his chair back, he stood, straightening his worn patched uniform, and headed for the TOC.

After being informed at the TOC that Colonel Barksdall was in his quarters, Jeremy approached the sandbagged trailer with some trepidation. His hesitant knock was answered by a gruff "Come in," and he stepped through the door, saluting. "Sir, Lieutenant Hawke reports as ordered."

Barksdall looked up from behind his desk, owl-eyed with fatigue. "Come in, grab a chair, Hawke," he replied, returning the salute without rising. Shuffling through a thick sheaf of papers marked "Secret," he said, "I asked you here for a couple of reasons, and if you'll bear with me for a few minutes, I'll be set. There are times when I'd rather be shot at than smothered in paperwork."

Placing the offending forms in a safe, he said, "Okay, first and most important, I want to be the first to congratulate you on your promotion to First Lieutenant." A friendly grin spread over the old colonel's face as he offered his hand to the amazed Hawke. "For some reason, promotions always get hung up on some paper shuffler's desk, and don't get passed on to the troops until thirty days too late. Anyway, it's long overdue and certainly well deserved, young man. You have more than borne out my initial confidence in you."

"Thank you, sir. I'm glad it came from you. The promo, I mean. I really appreciate the confidence and won't let you down," Jeremy said, somewhat embarrassed at the older man's praise.

Barksdall pushed away from the desk, leaning back in his comfortable swivel chair. "I also wanted to get your impressions of the Puma assignment, now that its had some operational time, and anything else that you feel needs discussing, relative to its mission."

"Maintenance, sir." The word jumped unbidden from his lips. "I think you already know how happy I am with the people and the assignment, but we're being run ragged. Franklin's genius-level scheduling is the only thing keeping us going. My tracks can only take so many convoys and shorthauls to Enari. I'm just afraid that when it comes time for us to tackle a really big mission, our vehicles will have been worn out to the point of uselessness.

"It almost seems, sir, that of late, some of the

Battalion staff have been misusing us to facilitate good relations with every Tom, Dick and Harry in the Division . . . I've even been hearing that old '88th rent-a-tank' again." Hawke saw Barksdall wince when he heard that one and decided to continue.

"I understand the problem out here, especially with the Tenth Cav spending so much time chasing phantoms down south. However, the necessary escort missions west of Oasis could very easily be run on a more organized level. We get two, and sometimes three, five and six vehicle escort jobs per day between here, Plei Djerang, Duc Co and the Cav base. Wouldn't it be more efficient if those convoys were combined and run together? Right now, with my tracks scattered from here to Duc Co, should a real nasty situation arise, we wouldn't have the hardware to create any kind of decisive force."

The colonel, nodding his head reflectively, yet affirmatively, left the desk and seated himself in an easy chair opposite Hawke, and continued to listen to the outpourings of the Puma leader.

"I wouldn't want to seem to be criticizing staff or operations, sir," Hawke said carefully, "but we, Lieutenant Franklin and I, believe that Puma could be much more effective and responsive to our primary missions if we could have more personal control over scheduling of our escort missions and if we were in a base more central to what has become our primary AO, somewhat west of here.

"Right now, we can't even get out of here in a hurry. Since First Brigade HQ moved in here, there's just too many trucks, jeeps and trailers clogging the tank trails. Plus, the Mech Infantry tracks are everywhere. Why couldn't they be put to work doing some light escort duty between here and Enari?"

Rising and walking over to the large operations map on the wall, the colonel asked, "Where do you see your unit setting up for maximum effectiveness? Come on over here and show me."

Hawke picked up a grease pencil and drew a circle around a pronounced hill on the topographical map. The hill was west of Oasis and nearly to the Cambodian border.

"This is the MI (military intelligence) detachment camp located just west of the village of Plei Duc. As you can see, it's situated right in the middle of Charlie's infiltration routes. It's only a couple of klicks off the main road, and it has a distinct defensive advantage. The hill on which it's located is a bald knob, dropping away on all sides to shallow valleys. There's almost no dense vegetation around it, and what there is can be flattened by tank treads. Access is via this little hardpan trail here." Using the pointer, he traced out the trail and the salient features of the site.

"There's a village here, connected to the camp by another hardpan trail, and both Captain Dawson and the MI officer tell me the locals are trustworthy.

"Sir, this location would put us in an excellent reactive position, both to the main road and to the border camps. It would reduce the mileage on the combat machines, and cut reaction time significantly. Right now, we're taking over an hour to react to Duc Co. Like that probe last week—Charlie was gone by the time Scruggs got out there. Also, we can get jumped on that section of switchbacks west of Thang Duc. But here, we'd be west of the hairy part of the road."

"Sounds like you know more about this than poop

picked up from just a map recon," Barksdall said, one eyebrow raised in question.

"Yessir. Jimbo and I have been over the area with Lieutenant Epstein a couple of times. And naturally, we use it for a way station if one of our little fire brigades is in the area overnight. Of course it'll need a major facelifting, but a dozer can take care of that in a day or two. We put together a 'wish list' of equipment and supplies that we'd need from the engineers to get the job done," Hawke said, handing a folded piece of paper to Barksdall.

"Your assessment sounds solid enough, Hawke, but what about getting all this done and still keeping up with mission requirements? You know we're getting more and more little probe actions and snipings along that stretch of road. We can't afford to let Charlie get too rambunctious or effective."

"Well, being closer to the action will help immensely, sir. As you know, there's a platoon of grunts rotated in there most of the time, and with some of the road pressure off our tracks, we would be free to load up a couple of squads and go down in there and keep Charlie off balance. He's a lot less likely to be pulling anything cute with half of Puma running around loose in his Papaya patch.

"Also, the villagers have been providing Lieutenant Jones, the MI officer, with quite a lot of good info; and I'm sure they'd open up even more if they felt more secure. And the plan would put a solid buffer between here and the border."

Barksdall stood silently gazing over the map, thinking about the idea while Hawke fidgeted. Finally, he relented.

"I'll go over your list, Hawke, and discuss it with

Carlisle and Dawson. You're right in your observations that it's too crowded around here. I've had to face down some five-ton driver nearly every day, trying to get in or out. Sometimes I wish I could get the entire Battalion out of Oasis to some place of their own. Every time the gooks fart, somebody else thinks they need armor to cover their ass. Nobody ever thinks of our primary mission."

Venting his spleen in front of a subordinate was not at all like Barksdall, but he felt an uncommon closeness to this young lieutenant, so like himself in his first wild combat command, back in '44. God, had it been that long?

Few young officers that Barksdall had met in three tours in Vietnam had made the positive impression that Hawke had. There was an honest, unpretentious manner in the way he approached military problems and life in general. He simply thought an issue through and got the job done without frills or hang-ups.

The young lieutenant's integrity, vision and perceptiveness were as yet unclouded by the dirt and smokescreening of service politics. So far, Puma was in good hands. With any luck at all, Barksdall could run behind-the-scenes interference and shield the task force from outside meddling.

Barksdall would have to smooth the ruffled feathers of his staff and those of the other company commanders—should they take umbrage to the enhanced status of Puma. Captain Marks, in particular, would need some distraction . . . Politics, for Christ's sake, just to get a necessary job done.

Old Barky was oddly distant toward the end, Jeremy reflected as he stumbled across the dark firebase. Maybe he was just very tired. But God, what a load that man must carry.

Jeremy was on an actual high over his new promotion, and the colonel's obvious interest in the new plan as he entered their tent. And for a moment, he didn't even hear Jimbo or Scruggs, who'd been waiting anxiously for the word.

"Well, dammit, man, how'd it go?" Franklin asked for the second time in as many minutes.

"As you were, Butter Bar," Hawke responded in an artificially officious tone. "I would expect a little more deference to an officer of my rank and station."

"Oh hell, don't tell me that I have to put up with a 'senior leader' now," Jimbo snorted. "And how was the First Lieutenant's meeting with the colonel?" he asked formally, popping off an exaggerated British-style salute.

"At ease, stumblebutt," Hawke kidded, "or I'll have your ass escorting the garbage wagon for a week."

"Congratulations, sir," Scruggs offered slyly. "It's nice to have a *real* officer around now."

"Traitor," Franklin squawked. "I'll have you toting those honey buckets for this—with a dummy stick."

Suddenly, they were all serious. "Will he let us move, Jer?"

"He said he would sleep on it and get back to us in a wake-up," Hawke answered. "I'm sure that he sees our arguments and the advantages of having us closer to the potential action. Also, that new intel that Epstein laid on us this afternoon has to have had a positive effect on his reasoning processes. He does have some politicking to do, though. You know he's going to get static from your boss, Marks, and from the Battalion Exec—just on general principles.

"Start to prime the troops, Scruggs. But keep a low

profile; no use lighting any fires under our REMF detractors."

For most of a week, affairs in the dangerously overcrowded Fire Support Base percolated on several levels. Puma, keeping low and quiet, rotated its tracks and tanks through Larsen's homemade refit facility. Roadwheels, torsion bars and support rollers were replaced. Two tanks required engine or transmission replacement. RPG hits were plugged, new plates were welded on holed ACAVs, supposedly bullet-proof vision blocks were replaced and the snapped-off radio masts were repaired.

Hawke and Franklin, hoping that Barksdall would see his way clear to free Puma from the confines of what was fast becoming a major support facility, made their plans and hoped. Puma's troops had gotten the word through the inevitable grapevine and were gradually making ready to break up housekeeping.

As always, non-portable goodies, such as private refrigerators, went up for sale to the new occupants of bunkers; and bunks and tables were broken down for travel. Most important, though, were the transferring of the "connections," without which no military unit can function. Puma, if it moved out, would be shifting into a new world, almost disconnected from its conventional GI network, but plugged into a new, exciting para-military environment.

Barksdall deftly manipulated his staff and company commanders, easing them around to his way of thinking, ensuring their cooperation in what would surely develop into an innovative, extra-regular situation.

Bravo Company's Captain Marks, for instance, was

properly bent out of shape at not being able to reabsorb his errant platoon. He'd been charged with road security from Enari to Oasis and was having a time of it with just two platoons and his less than adequate HQ tank section. The colonel defused that particular situation by informing Marks that, for operational purposes, he would be acquiring the use of the Battalion HQ tank section—an addition of three tanks to his ten.

Barksdall gave Marks a few minutes to gloat over this, and then informed him that, in return, the company dozer tank was being transferred to Puma. Marks started to blow up, and then, with a crafty gleam in his eye, volunteered to throw in his own "6" tank as well.

That particular machine was notorious throughout the outfit as "Old Crip." No one had ever been able to evict the jinx that'd kept it in base camp since the time a company commander had been shot off its cupola during a night ambush. In fact, there'd been un-founded rumors of a shadowy presence that kept the more superstitious members of the 88th out of the tank entirely.

"Oh, no, not the jinx!" was Franklin's automatic response when informed of the swap by Larsen.

"Don't sweat it, Jimbo," Larsen said. "I've got plans for that sucker. I've never met a tank yet that I couldn't straighten out. Technically, it's yours; but in fact, that junker will set up here at Battalion till I'm ready to release it—even if I have to have the chaplain in to hold an exorcism."

As an afterthought, he added, "Oh yeah. You haven't got the word yet, but I was up at the TOC this morning, and your move is official. Puma's got its new home."

By the time he finished speaking, Larsen and the dozer's crew were alone; Franklin and every Puma trooper within hearing had gone to spread the word.

"Now what the hell have we gotten into?" the dozer crew wanted to know. . . .

Chapter Seven

No one, not even Hawke and Franklin, who had built Puma out of spare parts and leftovers, quite believed the size of the armored column that lined up at the Oasis' gate next morning. Lead tank, as usual, was Ballbuster, with salty old Scruggs sitting tall in the turret. Behind the tank came a pair of ACAVs, then another tank, until the whole force of six tanks and twelve PCs had been accounted for.

Following the combat machines came a line of trucks, some of which would stay with Puma for the duration of its life as a task force, and some which were only loaned for the move. Swelling the number of cargo vehicles, was one of Kameha's "Flying Serials"—portable supply depots—which would have to be escorted on its rounds. Moving day for Puma was also another working day.

Something odd about the column had been bugging

Hawke, along with a few sneaky grins among the troops that he couldn't quite account for. Then it hit him. They all had the same identical flags on their antennas.

Normally, American armored vehicles flew a variety of banners—anything from Old Glory, through the Confederate battle flag, to the Jolly Roger. Now, however, each tank and ACAV sported a foot-square green flag with a tawny-colored cougar's head in the center.

"All right, Jimbo," Hawke asked, chuckling, "whose idea was the flags, and where'd you get them?"

"The men came up with that one themselves," Puma's exec answered with a laugh. "Seems they like being a part of this jackleg outfit. They took up a collection to have some mama-san run 'em off. Once we get out of base, take a look at the back of the poncho jackets—there's cats on them too."

There was a small lump in Jeremy's throat. Yesterday, he'd been Lootenant Hawke, but now he was the Old Man. Self-consciously, he swung up into Rouser's cupola, dropped his helmet on, keying the mike. "Roll out PUMA, let's go get Victor Charlie."

To the inhabitants of the MI camp at Plei Duc, the arrival of Puma was a measure of salvation. The lonely post had been understaffed most of the time, serving only as an information collection point, and as a patrol base when needed. Its only full-time denizens were a military intelligence section, which was now Benteen's home in the outback, and a mortar platoon, detached from 2/8 Infantry. Normally, one could expect to find an infantry platoon from the same battalion in residence. But that couldn't always be counted on, since the grunts could be airlifted out for any one of a variety of reasons—leaving the camp dangerously vulnerable.

Physically, the LZ was perfectly circular in shape, having been laid out with a mortarman's aiming circle, a device much like a surveyor's transit. Originally, it had been no more than a large circle of triple-row concertina wire. But over the years, various people had haphazardly added to the defenses so that now the perimeter was marked off by an uneven, waist-high earth wall. Outside of this were two rows of concertina, with a thin line of mines in between them.

Inside the gate, an observer could see a random defensive layout, which had survived more due to quick reinforcement from outside than for any other reason. Spaced ninety degrees apart around the perimeter were squad bunkers, each topped by a sand-bagged LMG emplacement.

A rough circle of "amenities" formed the center of the compound. A visitor, facing right from the gate, would see a thatch-roofed mess hall, manned by Army cooks. Behind that, one would usually see a hodge-podge of trucks, and as the eye passed left, the inevitable latrine/shower combination. On the higher side of the hill, above the town and the station, a partially fortified artesian well supplied both settlements with water. Scattered around the area were a collection of old bunkers, ratty thatch awnings, and a few squad tents—inhabited by rodents as well as soldiers.

The camp sat astride an old French logging trail, the origins of which were somewhere to the west, inside Cambodia. As a result, the weakly defended M.I. base had the nervous distinction of being the camp most likely to be overrun in the event of an NVA offensive. And by now, it had to be obvious to the Communists that this small base was providing valuable information to the allies about VC and NVA movements in the critical border triangle area, bound by Duc Co, Plei Me and Plei Duc as its three points.

The infiltration of critical specialty units, such as sappers, and badly needed war materials into the highlands had been delayed by information that had been gathered at Plei Duc. Fierce American strikes and highly effective Special Forces raids by unsuspecting resupply convoys on previously safe routes and sanctuaries had hurt the enemy badly—and the few residents of the M.I. station had been expecting annihilation.

The reinforcement of the area by the now-famous Puma armor would come as a great relief to the occupants of both the base and Plei Duc village. The presence of heavy armor would threaten the already weakening hold of the VC on the Ia Drang/Chu Pong infiltration corridor. Consequently, Hawke knew that they would be tested early on. He did not know just how early.

Plei Duc village was located a couple hundred meters to the east of the camp and subsisted on local and provincial logging business—and the traffic associated with it. The presence of some sixty G.I.s inevitably brought considerable revenue to the village in the form of laundry, sundry trinket and souvenir businesses and the everpresent boom-boom girls and their motorbike pimps.

Of course, the settlement had acquired its share of Communist-oriented American-watchers, and right now, several very interested pairs of eyes were counting the arrivals and departures. Since Kameha's column had to be protected, and infantry sweeps required "backbone," more vehicles left than stayed and the local VC came to the erroneous conclusion that nothing out of the ordinary was going on.

They sent word to their comrades out in the jungle that the planned attack was still on, and to continue preparations. Their plan was to "blood" several companies of freshly trained recruits on a toothless outpost and impress the villagers with their growing power.

Once the dust of departing wheels and tracks had settled, and what few combat machines remained had been allocated around the earth-bermed defensive wall, Jeremy and Jimbo set out on a tour of "home."

"Kinda gives you a queasy feeling, doesn't it, Jer?" the exec asked as they walked the dusty perimeter road that circled the camp between the central cluster of installations and the alleged defenses. "We're supposed to make something of this God-awful, rat-infested mess."

"It may be a mess," Hawke replied, "but at least it's *our* mess. And we've now got our own dozer tank. Three guesses as to what's going to happen to most of those unoccupied bunkers and hootches."

"Gotcha, bossman. Better to start from scratch than try to fix pure shit."

"Right, and you just became our prime contractor. I found out from the M.I. people that the man to see is Nguyen Van Loc, who's the local subcontractor type. He's got contacts all over, and he can get you the thatching specialists to build us above-ground roofs and the work parties to do the sandbag work."

From there, the conversation wandered through a maze of technical considerations while Franklin, once given Hawke's intended direction, took the ball and ran with it. LZ Plei Duc would be given a facelift and a security boost, starting next day—and the residents would benefit from the work provided. Hawke looked forward to a period of relative peace and quiet, since the communists were known to be concentrating on laying in supplies, instead of raiding . . .

"Incoming, incoming, hit the bunkers!" yelled an infantry squad leader, running through the starlit night, rousing his men and dodging mortar bursts.

Puma had barely settled in and had just two tanks and three tracks in the perimeter. Jeremy, bounced out of a light sleep behind Dubois' ACAV, heard the mortar sergeant calling for star shell.

"MORTAR CEASE FIRE!" Jeremy roared across the firebase, in a voice that, while not loud, carried an incredible distance. Grabbing the nearest soldier, he gave him a message, "Get to the mortar position, tell them no illumination till I say so; we're going to use infra-red."

As the man ran off, Jeremy turned toward the ACAV, and then resolutely controlled his instincts. He was now in charge of the strongest force in the base, and his place was in the commo track. Eyeballing the mortar pattern, he judged that there were only three tubes working on them, so he ran for the last burst, angling off that shell hole to the commo vehicle. Skidding to a halt behind it, he pulled open the rear door, stepped inside and was instantly in control of the situation.

Puma had inherited a number of radios and operators from its various contributing units, and Jeremy's communications center could monitor a rather large number of activities at the same time. "Tanks scanning on IR," reported one radioman. This was followed by reports from all units on the perimeter. The mortars and the American infantry checked in, and even the cooks, wired in by field phone, reported ready.

The mortars continued thudding randomly into the LZ until finally one of the tanks reported activity at the maximum reach of its searchlight. "Looks like about a hundred VC walkin' up, fat, dumb and happy, like on a Sunday picnic," Kim's Bearcat reported.

Hawke, remembering the savage battle in the clearing, wasn't so sure, and set up a communications link between the tanks and waiting mortars. "Zero your mill counters and feed bearings and ranges to the mortars," he ordered the tank commanders.

In a short period, no less than five separate, small groups of VC were being plotted. And while a tank's range finder won't work on IR, the TCs had fed cross bearings to the mortars, who computed the ranges for them.

"Puma 6, this is Big Thunder 6. What is your situation, and do you require assistance?" the voice erupted from the auxiliary radio set tuned to Battalion frequency. A radioman automatically punched in a transmitter and handed his boss a live mike.

"Negative, Big 6. We've got 'em on IR, and we're going to give the buggers a lesson in manners."

"You sound confident, Puma. We will monitor, over."

"Roger 6, I have to get back to work, out."

Knowing that the Battalion was now figuratively breathing down his neck, Hawke began to sweat a little—more from professional worries than from hostile intent.

The mortar sergeant came in on the land line that'd been wired into the track. "All five groups have now been ranged, sir, and we've recalculated our concentrations. Their mortar hits are still random, so they're just trying to keep our heads down for their assault troops. When do you want us to open up?"

"Can you hit all five concentrations simultaneously?"

After a few seconds' pause, the man answered, "Give me a couple minutes to refigure and I can hit the closest two groups, then the other three."

"Okay, two minutes. Fire on your own time, I'll get word to my troops."

Jeremy's half-baked, hip-shot plan looked to be about to function. He sent a runner to the tanks with a message to switch to white light, high explosive quickfuse when the mortars started hitting—and then sat back to watch. After loading his pipe and deliberately taking his time to light it, he slid up through the track's overhead hatch to check out the results.

Franklin, perched in Big Bastard's cupola, had been watching the events develop and could almost read his friend's mind. By using the capabilities of the tanks and the mortar platoon in combination, Hawke had instinctively set up a classic mousetrap.

"Man, I wouldn't be a VC tonight fer nuthin'," Krause commented from the gunner's seat, where he'd been watching the happenings with professional interest. "This is goin' to be like drowning kittens."

So it proved to be. When the hollow booming sound of the 4.2 mortars reached Franklin's ears, the attackers' doom was sealed. A series of flashes less than 500 yards out was followed by semi-daylight as the tanks switched over to 75 million candlepower white light, and the mortars threw up a series of star shells. A dozen 90 millimeter rounds per tank later, Hawke ordered a cease fire. And in the utter silence that ensued, the cries of wounded could be heard, faintly drifting in on the night breeze before the nocturnal insect chorus resumed.

Breakfast the next morning was served in the open-air, thatched mess hall and was surprisingly good, considering the conditions. At one end of the pole-supported native thatch structure, were the components of a G.I. field mess hall, presided over by three army cooks rotated out from the same infantry battalion that supplied the grunts.

The field cooking ranges and serving line sat on a long, low bench of local construction. The benches and tables for the troops were also obviously local, and with the Vietnamese KPs and waitresses, it gave the impression of a native eatery rather than an American mess hall.

Hawke and Franklin, sitting at the far end, as distant as possible from the commotion and kidding of the armor troopers, grunts and mortarmen, had been discussing the pitiful state of the defenses, when the incredibly young-looking military intelligence lieutenant walked up, steaming mug in hand.

"Boy, are we ever glad to see you guys around here," he said enthusiastically. "Those mean mothers of yours saved our butts last night!"

"You ain't just whistlin' Dixie there, Pard," replied Jimbo, still shocked at the dilapidated state of the camp's defenses. "How'd you ever keep the gooks from throwing you off this hill, with those sorry defenses? A bunch of pregnant mama-sans could've bounced you out last night, if they'd known enough to hit on that sorry-assed north slope."

"Jimbo has a habit of speaking his piece, when the situation warrants it," Hawke interjected, trying to keep the peace, while supporting Franklin's assessment of the camp's condition. "Lieutenant Jones, I—"

"Call me Jonesy, everyone else does," the man interrupted. "And no offense taken about the state of the defenses. M.I. expects the infantry to take care of them, and the grunts aren't permanent anyway, so it looks like Puma's commander just inherited base command. What would you suggest we do with this place, Lieutenant Hawke?"

That, in a nutshell, took care of the diplomacy, Jeremy had to admit; and the kid was smarter than he appeared. In a very few words, he'd solved any seniority problems and cleared himself to continue his main task—the extraction of information from available sources.

"Call me Jeremy, or just Jer," Hawke said, and then got down to brass tacks.

"Jonesy, if you've got any pull, we're going to need a real bulldozer in here ASAP. The tank dozer can only do simple work because it has no blade tilt, and it's just too damn big for most work. We can start with it, though, and get those old, half-ass bunkers flattened and filled in. The first order of business is going to be to lay out a totally new defensive perimeter outside of this one.

"Jimbo, get Scruggs in here, and have him set up a new layout with spaces for all combat vehicles, just in case we accidentally get them all in the same place again. Have the dozer tank push a new outer berm up—man high—and then get busy flattening the existing counterfeit defenses. Barksdall promised that we'd have all the concertina we'd need by this morning; and Jenks just radioed in that he's got the trucks under escort now."

The three lieutenants worked on the details of the

perimeter defense plan for over an hour, walking the area, siting vehicles, gun and MG positions—even down to individual rifle pits. New bunker sites were laid out and additional wire entanglements, claymore and fugasse (flame bomb) positions were added to the diagram.

Once their preliminary survey was completed, they gathered the two senior noncoms from Puma, along with representatives from the camp's regular inhabitants, and went over the plans in detail, assigning areas of responsibility and zones of fire to all concerned.

Finally, maps and diagrams in hand, they climbed atop the soon-to-be demolished central bunker to survey the layout. Hawke and Franklin were satisfied with progress so far, but Jones was utterly flabbergasted. "I didn't know the work could go this fast," he said. "That dozer tank has made five passes around the outer rim while we've been talking; and now it's pushing a new defensive wall, and two PCs are laying wire already."

"Yeah, Jonesy," Franklin replied. "It's coming along, and with our firepower, Chuck would be nuts to try a ground assault, especially after last night. We could pick him off before he got to hand-grenade range. Right, Jer?"

"Sure, Jimbo, but I'm still worried about the village being so close. The dinks could sneak up through it and be within two hundred meters of us before we knew it. We've got to come up with some way to reduce that threat."

Switching his attention to the M.I. officer, Jeremy said, "Jonesy, you've told us a little about the local situation. What say we adjourn to your hootch and you fill us in on this Nguyen Van Loc and his people?"

Jones's explanation took longer than either Hawke or Franklin had expected because there was more to the small settlement than met the eye . . . a lot more.

Plei Duc looked like any other village in Vietnam, and a casual traveler would have categorized it as another wide spot in a narrow road. Due to its function as part of the logging industry, there were several logging trucks based there, whose owners struggled to stay in business despite the war that sputtered on around them. The presence of the trucks naturally created business for some small shops and followers of the mechanical arts.

Besides the soldier-oriented establishments, there was a single food and drink cafe, providing restaurant services to the villagers, as well as catering to the beer and soft drink needs of the troops. The owner of this business was an enterprising and quite slippery Vietnamese. His less than forthright business practices, however, were far overshadowed by his value as a keen observer and covert operative for the allies. His simmering hatred for everything Communist dated back to the early 1960s, when the Viet Cong "liberators" had murdered his parents and sister as examples to the villagers of the danger of following capitalist ways.

Usually that VC plan worked to perfection, intimidating the villagers into submitting to the extra Shadow Government. But in the case of Plei Duc, they'd miscalculated. First, the remote village hadn't been stripped of all its military-age males by either the Saigon government or the VC, and it had the wherewithal to decide its own fate, to an extent, if effective leadership was provided.

The Cong's second and worst mistake was that they'd only succeeded in galvanizing Van Loc. His father had been a venerated elder who'd fought against both the French and Japanese; upon the old man's decapitation, the son had taken up the sword.

Since that horrible day, Nguyen had hunted down each of the seven VC cadremen and one woman who had participated in the murder. Each of them had appeared mysteriously next to the gate of his home village, impaled on a bamboo stake. Last to appear had been the VC cell leader, a man of some local repute. He'd been found sitting astride his own severed head, in front of a house which he'd expropriated from a village elder.

"Nguyen Van Loc is kind of the titular leader and spokesman for the people of the vill," Jones advised. "He keeps a live screen of kids around the town, as an early warning system."

"Sounds like somebody we want on our side," Hawke commented. "Let's go meet the man. I can see why he cozies up to the G.I.s; he must be Public Enemy Number One as far as the Commies are concerned."

"Yeah," Franklin added, picking up his carbine. "If an invasion is planned for this area, they've probably got orders to wipe the camp *and* the town off the map!"

"I'm sure that one of Van Loc's minions has already informed him of our approach," Jones said, as they neared the village. "You can be sure that he'll be waiting for us when we get to that row of bushes near the first hootch."

True to the lieutenant's forecast, a group of civilians scurried onto the pathway into the village. In their center stood a stocky individual, attired in gray shorts, tiger stripe shirt and red baseball cap. His broad grin and shiny white teeth were visible from a hundred meters, and he was waving for them to come on in. The half-dozen children surrounding him were at a position of attention. The women demurely held a position of respect a few steps to his rear. This had to be the man's family, which meant that his greeting was serious.

"Welcome, welcome, my American friends. Welcome to our humble village. Plei Duc is honored and proud to have you with us. We are at your disposal, sirs." With wide open arms and a series of bows he ushered them into the shade of a large, free-standing thatch in the center of the village.

More children and mama-sans came out of the surrounding hootches, and the area began to fill up with curious people. Many women carried babies, and the children seemed happy.

"Lieutenants Hawke and Franklin, I would like you to meet the Honorable Nguyen Van Loc, his wife, Lin Mai, and his children," Jones announced in his most formal manner.

Removing their hats and bowing slightly at the waist, both lieutenants shook hands with Loc and nodded recognition to the pleasant-looking woman standing to the rear of the children.

"You are most welcome, sirs. We are most anxious to extend our hospitality to you and your men. Please be seated and have a cool drink with us. We have Coca Cola or Ban Moui Ba beer."

Selecting a Coke, Hawke settled in one of the plastic bound aluminum lawn chairs and waited for the man to continue. Long ago, he'd learned that a talkative man will eventually tell you all you want to know, and then thank you for the privilege.

"I will not ask you gentlemen any of the usual,

unnecessary questions that my counterparts in other villages ask. I will simply say how happy we are to have you here, especially now. We have many reports of major NVA and VC movements into our region, and I know they will be coveting our hamlet."

"We thank you for your candor, sir," Hawke responded. "Puma Force will be headquartering in the camp. As you can see, we are already at work making some major changes in the defenses. We want you to be aware of the changes and of the added security measures that will affect your hamlet as well. We have some fears regarding the potential access to the compound that would be gained by VC who sneak up through the town, and we certainly wouldn't want this group of dwellings caught between our guns and those of the attackers."

Hawke's statement was taken in by the Vietnamese with no apparent change in his demeanor. The broad smile and nodding head remained while the man digested Hawke's words and built a response, having to translate both the question and answer in his mind before he spoke.

Rising from his chair and motioning for them to follow him, Van Loc started heading for the eastern end of the village. "Gentlemen, if you would walk with me, please, I may be able to set your minds at ease."

Following the man, Hawke could see that the trail through the center of town did not continue out beyond the eastern limits of the hilltop. Instead, it bent southward, leading into a steep defile. The area fronting the edge of the inhabited part was open for almost two hundred meters, with few dips or clumps of scrub where enemy could hide. In fact, the section surrounding the village was as clear of concealment as the free-fire zone around the camp itself. And Jeremy was thinking, "If guns were mounted here, I could hold this as part of the camp."

"As you can see, lieutenants," Van Loc said, "there is very little cover for an attacker to hide in. We also have set up our own surprises for the invaders. None of our people use this field for any purpose. We have heavily booby-trapped the hill, out to more than two hundred meters. Anyone walking blindly up that slope will injure himself very gravely, making a loud noise in the process."

"Sir, how's that possible?" Franklin asked, politely, but skeptically. "There are no claymores or wires showing at all. What kind of traps do you have out there?"

"Lieutenant, please throw your coke can out as far as you can—it will better answer your question."

Grasping his half-empty can like a grenade, Franklin hooked it out onto the open hillside. Just when it was about to strike the ground, it seemed to disappear. Then a sharp explosion rent the air, spraying shards of can into the air.

The two officers stared in amazement, and Nguyen explained. "That, sirs, is what we call a rice paper trap. We fill a pit with punji stakes and what you would call toe poppers, and cover it with rice paper. Little animals can run over them, but not people."

Jeremy flinched inwardly at the effect the trap would have on its victim. An intruding foot would be shattered, and then held in place by the bamboo stakes . . .

Obviously drawn by the explosion, a small, bald, tanned man trotted up, and Van Loc addressed him. "Doan, Dem chao toi bay no eh-thuoc no;" and the man smiled, picked up a paper bag, easing gingerly out on the field.

"Le Doan is a former VC sapper," Nguyen said. "I asked him to replace mine and booby trap materials and repair trap. He knows by heart where all are placed."

As they watched, Doan moved over the treacherous ground like a spider, his hands and feet seeming to sense the stubbled surface before they touched it. Within five minutes, the place looked as if it had never been touched, and Doan was on his way back.

"We could use this man's services in our own perimeter," Hawke said. "Mr. Van Loc, you've been described to us as the man to see for materials and work parties. We are virtually remanufacturing the camp, and will require much labor and materials. And now, it seems, the services of Le Doan would be of value to us, as well."

By now the sapper, all smiles, had emerged from the death zone, and Van Loc turned to him, grinning. "Doan, cam o n ong," he said, bowing. "I have thanked him," Nguyen said to the Americans. "Like me, he lose many family to VC. Very loyal to Saigon now—no more family to lose to Northerners."

While they talked, the group began walking back toward the thatched town center, which evidently served as a market/meeting square. And Hawke and Van Loc fell into an intense business discussion, leaving Franklin and Doan to struggle along on each others fractured Pidgin version of the two languages.

The conversation was interrupted by the rumble of heavy machinery, and Franklin glanced up to see his own Big Bastard coming toward them, leading a pair of Riley's PCs. Van Loc looked on with evident interest as the iron monsters approached, but Doan stopped in midstride, staring at the lethal metal with a hungry fascination. "Perhaps he's been on the receiving end?" Franklin guessed, and then had a sudden inspiration.

"Mr. Van Loc, please ask Doan if he would care to take a ride on one of our vehicles and maybe look around inside it. He seems quite curious?"

"I am sure that he would be most honored, sirs. I will ask and, if it would not be too much trouble, I also would like such a ride."

"No problem at all. In fact it would be our pleasure," Hawke answered, flipping the radio helmet out from under his arm, keying its tiny transmitter.

"Puma 5 Charlie, 2-4 and 2-3, this is 6. Hard left, right now, and meet us at the edge of the village."

Even as he spoke, the three machines pivoted and rolled toward the group. Hawke had no way of knowing it, but this casual yet complete control of such awesome fighting machines impressed Van Loc and Doan much more than the slaying of the night raiders. Vietnamese were more used to autocrats than Democrats, and Jeremy had just unconsciously displayed the power of a warlord.

When the hulking M-48 ground to a stop, both Vietnamese were assisted aboard and chauffered around the perimeter of the camp, affording them a good view of the working dozer tank. Each was outfitted with a commo helmet, and Van Loc was planted in the commander's hatch, while Doan sat cross-legged on the turret next to him.

Again, Hawke had unconsciously done the right thing. Vietnamese thrive on "face" and status, and putting Nguyen in the TC hatch had made a friend for life out of him. It was obvious to all that they were thoroughly enjoying themselves—grinning widely and babbling animatedly to each other as the tank roared by their families and the villagers.

Suckers for kids, like any other G.I., the Puma troopers put nearly all the townspeople aboard tanks and PCs, including a half-dozen stoic old mama-sans, creating an impromptu parade. Even the old matriarchs were grinning from ear to ear, squatting in the inimitable Vietnamese way on the turret tops, waving to those remaining on the ground.

At the end of the day when the two Puma leaders made ready to head back to camp, Van Loc drew them aside. "Gentlemen, I cannot thank you enough for what you have done here today and on the hill last night. My people get little chance or reason to laugh in these times. You have made many friends here, and we will not forget your thoughtfulness. We will speak more of repairing the camp later, and Doan's service will, of course, be available to our common security."

As the two lieutenants walked up the hill heading back to camp, Jeremy said, "Talk about a lucky guess; that was an inspired idea, Jimbo."

"Yeah," Franklin laughed. "I figure we did a year's worth of PR work for about 25 gallons of diesel."

Several days later, the two Puma officers were comfortably settled in the outdoor patio of Nguyen's French-style restaurant, after arranging for the extra native labor that reworking the camp would require. "Y'know this is a picturesque little place . . ." Franklin was saying, when Van Loc's voice sounded behind him.

"Lieutenants, I would like to present to you my daughter, Tien Lin. She is the greatest gift to me, and bears the beauty of my wife."

Both officers swiveled their heads and hastily stood

up, bowing courteously, tongue-tied at the heart-stopping beauty of the young woman standing before them.

She was tall by Vietnamese standards—perhaps five and a half feet—and the traditional white Aodai and black silk pajamas fell in breathtaking curves to her bare feet. Her glistening raven hair fell nearly to her hips, accentuating the lushness of a young, vibrant body.

James Franklin was out of it. As far as he was concerned, this girl's lovely face could launch every junk and sampan on the South China Sea. She was the most breathtaking female he'd ever met. For him, the beauty was in the tranquility of her features and expression—soft and yet utterly sensual and provocative.

It was Hawke who first acknowledged the introduction and then introduced the befuddled Franklin to Tien Lin. "We call her Ti, as in tea," her very proud father was saying, when another, older Viet walked up, smiling ingratiatingly. And now the happiness of Van Loc's face was replaced by a mask of formality.

The man was possibly in his late forties or early fifties, with a ferret-like face and small, narrow eyes. His hair was nearly white and hung down his back in a long white braid. And he wore an irritating smile like it had been issued to him. Franklin, somehow, was as aggravated by the man as he was attracted to Tien Lin, and he examined him closely as Van Loc spoke.

"This, gentlemen, is Vo Nguyen Thuot. He was displaced from his home in upper Darlac province some months ago, and has been our barber in the village since then. He is also a noted trader among the merchants' stalls of Pleiku and Ban Me Thuot."

The old man bowed formally to the officers, and in a

tinny, grating voice, welcomed the Americans to the village. Then he went into a lengthy diatribe on his preference for G.I. equipment and food, during which Tien Lin and her father quietly left, Van Loc shrugging politely as he backed into his kitchen. Hawke, unmoved by the girl's beauty, seemed to be listening interestedly to Vo, but Franklin's warning system had just snapped to red alert.

After the man left, Franklin confided his worries to Hawke. "Jer, I know we should be giving all kinds of slack to our little brown buddies, but I gotta tell you—there's something about that Thuot character that ain't Kosher. The first sight of him sent my hackles up."

"I noticed," Hawke answered wryly. "And I also noticed how that young lady plunked your magic string. Better watch yourself there, pard. She's one hell of a beautiful woman, but I'm sure that old Loc holds a tight rein on her . . . God, she is something out of a picture book, though."

Chapter Eight

FOR MOST OF A WEEK, THE DOZER TANK REARRANGED THE top of the bare hill on which the town and camp perched. When each new bunker site was scooped out, a gang of native workers descended on the resulting dirt pile, bagging and stacking. Other teams, subcontracted out through Van Loc, who always got his cut, built pole and thatch awnings over the bunkers, providing living and working spaces. Gradually, the M.I. base was increasing in livability, even while its defenses were being improved.

An additional barrier of triple row concertina wire was laid outside of the earth wall by the infantry platoon, supervised by their own NCOs and surprisingly, Le Doan. The wiry Viet mine expert not only placed his own brand of booby trap, he lent his expertise to the Americans as well. In front of each combat position, a beaten zone was dozed, raked smooth and mined. Claymores, surrounded by native

Vietnamese mines filled the death strip between the earth wall and the outer wire.

Camp building and improvement went on for nearly three weeks, and with the continued association of the villagers and the G.I.s, social barriers began to fall. The locals became quite friendly with the armormen, sharing supplies of ice and soft drinks while they worked on the base defenses and on the village's own homemade security system.

A heavily wired corridor now replaced the vulnerable path that'd been the village's only link to the LZ. In case of attack, the people could now retreat to the security of the hilltop fort—at the cost of abandoning their homes to almost certain destruction.

Franklin, under whose responsibility much of the work fell, supervised most of the construction. And he had not failed to note the regular trips that lovely Tien made to the newly cemented well bunker, now firmly embedded in the defensive entanglements. He was literally mesmerized by her elegance and unpretentious aura of class—as well as the effortless, fluid motion of her derriere as she made her daily water trip.

Finally, he built up the nerve to wander over to the well early one morning before Ti was due to appear. He only nodded when she approached and simply filled a canteen and a G.I. canvas shower bucket. On the way out of the unlighted bunker, he tripped over his own feet, spilling the bucket. Ti did her best not to embarrass the American lieutenant and strangled an amused twitter behind a friendly smile.

On their second meeting, he broke the ice, managing to get out a controlled "Good morning," to the apparently friendly Tien Lin. Answering in the same good English that her father used, her musical voice reached into Franklin's very soul, completing the captivation that her appearance had begun.

As the days of construction went by, Franklin never missed his morning water run. And he began to notice that if he was delayed for some reason, Tien extended her visit to accommodate his schedule. Gradually, their conversations and meetings lengthened, and they began to find more common ground, even though from widely differing cultures.

On another level, the cultural gap was being bridged even more rapidly. The G.I.s, on their frequent visits to Van Loc's restaurant and other less reputable establishments, provided an unending source of entertainment for the children. Drawn naturally to kids, some of whom were homeless waifs, the troopers began to share their care packages and gifts from home with their young allies.

The children showed an endless curiosity about the ways of the big men from a fabulous, faraway land, and the soldiers responded as American soldiers always do. Footballs, soccer balls and even a badminton set appeared, along with the usual PX goodies. And soon the older boys organized teams to challenge the larger Americans. "Damn, those little suckers tackle hard!" more than one man was heard to say.

Village women had expanded the services of the laundry, adding light starching and ironing to the washing—thanks to the "souveniring" of three electric irons and various electric appliances from the G.I.s. Old Van Loc had engaged the services of a traveling electrician, who sold the services of an ancient, diesel-powered 5kw generator set. For a continuously variable fee, the clattering mechanical dinosaur could power up the village for several hours each day.

This amenity, of course, led to a need for other conveniences, such as electric lighting for the restaurant where Van Loc had "Americanized" the menu. Hamburgers and french fries were now featured, although the soldiers called them "Buffaloburgers," cautioning one another to check for legs and feelers.

The dozen tables were tended by the elegant Tien Lin, whose quiet beauty seemed to have a sedative effect on the normally boisterous soldiers. There were never any loud or off-color remarks made during the evening meals, nor did the G.I.s ever quite allow themselves to get totally drunk. This, however, was as much due to the continued existence of the VC as to the mannerisms of the girl. No sane man will allow himself to become helpless in the presence of the enemy. And the local customers of the establishment must surely include some who were hostile to the continued presence of the Americans.

Vo Thuot had been able to entice the men to visit his barbershop, providing an excellent haircut and shave for a nominal fee. The Vietnamese version of a haircut usually included a masseuse and manicure that naturally left the troopers in a relaxed mood, desirous of even more female services, which Vo could provide for a little more currency. As a result, a visit to Vo's Cathouse/Clipjoint became a weekly practice for most of the contingent of Puma base.

Despite the growing confidence in the man, Franklin remained suspicious, asking Doan to keep a very close eye on the comings and goings of the barber. Doan, as an ex-VC, had spotted a familiar pattern in the barber's movements and shared Franklin's feelings about the venerable Vo.

Franklin also found out that Tien and her parents shared his and Doan's suspicions, making that an excuse to escort her home in the evenings whenever his schedule permitted. Surprisingly, Nguyen did not object at all to his daughter fraternizing with an occidental, so their relationship continued to ripen.

Intelligence was coming in bits and pieces, indicating that the NVA and the Viet Cong were infiltrating large groups of men and supplies into the highlands, carefully avoiding any major contact with allied troops. LRRP and SOG recon teams, working deep in the enemy sanctuaries, reported massive buildups of men and material, including artillery and armor.

Exactly when and where these troops would cross from Cambodia and Laos into Vietnam had become the 64-million dollar question by the middle of the dry season. And the intelligence analysts at all levels of command could only guess at the enemy's ultimate plans.

Lieutenant Jones, working out of Plei Duc, was most junior of all the diviners of Uncle Ho's intentions. But his crystal ball was closer to the action than anyone else's. Since the arrival of Puma, and the addition of Epstein and Benteen to his sources of information, a pattern was beginning to emerge. When it finally jelled in his mind, he sent a messenger off to find Hawke.

Jeremy, curious as to why Jones had found it necessary to send a runner for him, stepped into the cool interior of the M.I. bunker and saw that one entire wall had been taken up with a new map.

"Lookee here, Jer," Franklin said excitedly. "We've just got our intelligence matrix laid out—and it's already a shocker!"

Jeremy scanned the oversized situation map that

included not only the 88th/Puma AO, but a large segment of Cambodia, north and south of Highway 19.

"What we've done," Jones explained, "is to plot everything we could find that applies to Epstein's theory. And as far as I'm concerned, it ain't a theory anymore. We're gonna get hit! The NVA own most of northeastern Cambodia, and 19 extends all the way in to Stung Treng, across fairly level ground. It'd be easier to move supplies from here than either of the crossings by Dak To or Ban Me Thuot. Logic aside, look at the pattern.

"Franklin's plotted all the sweeps that Puma's been on; also your ambushes and the debriefing reports from the crews. That's in green, and the numbers refer to file references. The letter code tells whether any significant data was acquired. The blue notations are from my files on native interviews, and purple are debriefings from the infantry platoons. Yellow is from the Lurps, and Benteen is in Pleiku right now, getting copies of the other teams' reports. Torrion's on his way in too, with whatever his S-2 noncom could dig out."

As Jones's exhilarated rush of words ran down and he paused for breath, Franklin cut in. "Check out the number of little 'S's Jer. Those are the ones where we've caught some bunch hauling supplies. The 'C's are caches like that village a couple months ago, where I got boarded and Alveretti had to scratch my back."

The number of reports and incidents involving military supplies was indeed impressive, and Hawke asked, "Well, how does this compare with the same period last year?"

"About quadruple," Jones replied. "In fact, from

records my predecessors left back at Division, the only comparable buildup was back in '65 right before the Ia Drang invasion."

"Well, doesn't all this convince Division that we're sitting on a powder keg out here?"

"No, they're still convinced that the big thrusts will come where the current pressure is. If anything, they think all this is just supplies for a diversionary 'spontaneous uprising.'"

"Shit," Hawke said contemptuously. "There wasn't any uprising in '68, and there won't be one now. You know the attitude of the villagers here. They've damn near become part of the base defense force, and they're actually beginning to pester us for captured weapons. They've got a few old MAS-35s, AKs and whatnot—and they've actually run off some local VC."

Looking back at the map, Hawke said, "That's a right smart bit of work. Epstein is going to want a copy of that. He'll probably be out here for updates, which will keep us plugged into DivIntel."

Pausing, he looked at the map again. "It appears that there's a few holes where we don't have any coverage at all, and where Torrion's CIDGs don't go."

Hawke let a slow, conspiratorial grin spread across his face. "You know, we've got a temporary breather. Marks and Bravo Company are covering the road from Oasis to Pleiku, and 10th Cav is taking a lot of the escort load off us. In fact, we've got some tracks caught up on maintenance and semi-idle. Right?"

"Right," Franklin said. "We've got three ACAVs and one tank in base now, with the crews fifty percent on pass in town, armed of course."

"Barky didn't really say so, but I get the distinct impression that he wouldn't complain if he found out that Puma had taken on itself the task of probing those empty grid squares."

"Well, where are we going to get the infantry to ride the decks?" Franklin wanted to know. "We have enough trouble keeping one platoon in here on a steady basis."

Hawke had been in the process of lighting his pipe when the question was asked, and he pointed the stem toward the chopper pad where a "slick" was depositing Torrion and one of his sergeants. "Their company honcho just landed, Jimbo. I've already had his Nungs on the tracks, and they adapt real well."

Torrion didn't require much persuasion. He'd already checked his own map as he dug the requested information out of his rudimentary files—and the picture hadn't given him much cause for joy. He and his intelligence noncom had stood in silence as the map was explained to them, eyes slowly enlarging. "Jer," he said at last, "that map is jest one big arrow pointed right up mah tail end.

"Y'all couldn't put a pair of tracks up my way? . . . No, I suppose not," he said, shaking his head. "But gunships don't work too well down where I am."

Hawke saw his opportunity and jumped. "We don't report all our finds, you know. And if you don't mind using Russian hardware, we could fix you up with a pair of 12.7 MGs, DShK 38-46s to be exact, and a few cases of ammo. Also, I think the men have got a few captured RPG-2s and 7s stashed."

Torrion smelled "deal" immediately and smiled, raising one eyebrow. The two had grown closer as they worked together and understood the sub-rosa method of the Army perfectly.

"It's like this, Frank," Hawke told the A-team boss.

"Barksdall will look the other way if Puma decides to probe those unexamined areas, but finding U.S. infantry to ride the—"

Torrion was one of the fastest men on the uptake that Jeremy had ever met, and he raised a hand and turned to the E-7 beside him. "The Mike Force troops would be better for this. Pull about half of them off patrol and send out the best Puffs we've got instead." The man nodded and Torrion turned back to Hawke.

"Off the top of mah head, I'd guess we can provide two, mebbe three, squads of Nungs at any given time. But if we get hit . . ." This time it was Franklin who interrupted. "Whoever jumps you will have a large, hairy cat in the middle of his back."

"Y'know," Hawke said, "if you rotate those Strikers of yours so that they all get experience in armor/infantry cooperation, we'll have more than doubled our separate strengths. And I've got a feeling that in the next month or so, we're going to have to hold a line while Division gets its shit together."

Jones, long used to being out on the end of a string, had a much better description. "More like a kid with his finger in the dike," he said quietly.

Alveretti's Bronco and Kim's Bearcat, the 1-2 and 1-5 tanks, had been out on lone patrol for three days. They'd spent the past night back to back on a brushy hilltop, while their three squads of Mike Force Strikers sat in ambush over the most likely approaches to the armor position.

The standard operating procedure was for the tanks, which were almost impossible to hide anyway, to be bait as well as back-up for the trap. Any VC who were tempted to sneak up on the two tanks would trip a Mike Force ambush, which would then be able to call on armored firepower and a searchlight. Sometimes the trap worked, but word had been getting around, and tonight there'd been no takers.

"Daylight, Sarge," Alveretti's loader said, reaching out and shaking his boss, who slept directly on the armored steel deck of the tank. With a muffled curse, Alveretti lifted his head, looked around and thanked his God for another night, marking off another day on the tiny calendar that was pasted inside a pocket-size New Testament.

Slowly, the hot, muggy night became a hotter, muggier day, and the comforting bulk of his running mate, Bearcat, changed from a silhouette to a dust-shrouded, mud-encrusted olive green M-48. Once the light had increased to the point where a sniper could no longer sight in on any point of brilliance, one of Kim's crewmen, a giant Norwegian, easily twice the mass of the diminutive tank commander, began the section's daily ritual.

Reaching into a wooden box wired to the turret cargo rack, he pulled out a white, putty-like stick of plastic explosive and pinched off a golf-ball sized chunk. Taking a pot that was handed him by another crew member, he jumped down between the two tanks and inserted the ball of explosive under a previously laid tepee of sticks, lighting it with a battered Zippo.

Once the brilliant flare of the C-4 plastic had gotten the sticks ablaze, he hung the pot on a wire stretched between the two tanks and filled it from a rusty five-gallon can. By now, all of the crew members were awake and each, in turn, scratched his initials on a C-ration can and dropped it in the pot. This one container of water would provide coffee, shaving water for those who cared, and hot food for all six tankers.

Both of the tanks, due to personnel shortages, were running with three-man crews and were training one of the Mike Force troops as an emergency loader. The Nungs, their ambush having turned up dry, were filtering up through the bushes, each group seeking out its tank and digging out their own rations from the packs stored on the hulls.

The senior Mike Force squad leader, Wu Sung, and Alveretti shared a fatalistic religious attitude toward war and had developed a soldier's friendship. Now Sung came up to Alveretti, rice bowl in one hand, an ancient Garand in the other. Silently, he squatted beside the low rock on which the American sat, rifle cradled across his loins while he deftly manipulated a pair of pointed Viet chopsticks.

Understanding more English than he spoke, Sung listened while Alveretti laid out the day's plans. "Lurps have tracked several parties to the village at the far end of this ridge," he said. "And we're to be the probe. We're already out here, and they won't be as suspicious as they would of some outfit who just left the road and came straight on. They're probably lying low, hoping we'll go on by—which we'll do."

He took out a map and laid it on the ground for Sung. "We'll cross this ridge, and the next one," he said, tracing the projected route on the map, stopping at the dotted blue line that indicated an intermittent stream. "This creek is now dry, and passes close to the village. We'll turn south here and run back to it, very fast."

Wu Sung nodded his head slowly. "Two ridges turn south, follow stream back. I tell men." As they both stood up, they understood that men would die, and a silent salute passed between them.

"There's a company of infantry cooling their heels at Oasis," Alveretti told the crews as they gathered around him. "And 175s can reach this place, so we're not alone. To quote the Old Man, 'Roll 'em, let's go get Victor Charlie.'" Tense, yet cheerful, the two tank crews and their Striker infantry moved out, watched by hidden eyes in the bushes.

"That's about enough fakery," Alveretti said two hours later. "Kim, I'm turning now, follow me down this creekbed, and we'll see if it worked."

With Kim's affirmative response, he then switched to Puma frequency and got hold of Franklin. "Puma 5, this is 1-2. We are at the approach line now, over."

To anyone not familiar with U.S. tactical terminology, that conveyed nothing at all. But to Hawke, the simple comment was sufficient to put a complex plan into operation, involving many factors . . . and at least one layer of deception.

The alleged village picked out for the day's operation was ideal for several reasons. First off, Hawke's usually accurate local sources told him that there'd been no village there for many years. Second, the Lurps had tracked several supply parties out of Cambodia directly to that location. And the houses, while carefully constructed so as to look old, were, on close inspection, new. Mongoose had gotten inside the actual village perimeter, and it was Benteen's opinion that it was a brand new cache, guarded by ill-trained troops.

Third, and most important: the infantry on ready duty at Oasis was commanded by Lieutenant Owens, with whom Franklin had been in several firefights. His company commander had been killed in what should have been a fairly safe search and destroy mission by a kid with a grenade. The captain had held his fire a second too long, and dustoff had been a few minutes too slow. As a result, Owens was now CO in a three-officer company. He'd suffered a large number of rotations and needed a nice tame little firefight to break in a number of greenhorns. Also, he could be trusted to pull out quickly without asking questions.

Fourth—unless something went badly wrong, the only higher up intelligence types that would show up to examine the site would be Jones and Epstein. Everything seemed to be set to go. So Hawke gave the go-ahead to what he and Franklin called "Operation Robin Hood"—the resupplying of Torrion's ill-armed Mike Force Strikers with modern arms—courtesy of Ho Chi Minh.

Alveretti and Kim hadn't achieved total surprise, but the VC hadn't had much time to get ready either. The tiny bogus settlement was a circus of madly running people when they roared into it, spewing cannister at a rate that threatened to empty their ammo racks in short order. The Nungs dropped off the hulls as they entered the village, with orders to lay low till the tanks came back for the third pass, then get on line while they picked off any survivors.

In practice, there were considerably larger numbers of hard-core VC than expected. And while the first pass went as planned, when they turned around and separated by about fifty yards, the going got suddenly tougher—partially because they were under orders to cause as little damage as possible.

As they rumbled back through the half-wrecked compound, an organized defense appeared, with groups of anti-tank gunners moving purposefully into position. The Nungs, armed with American World War II weapons, were pouring steady fire into the area, keeping the defenders in a pincer. Kim saw several groups fall to an ancient Browning M1917 machine gun, fed by a man who hadn't been born when the weapon was made.

The crux came when Alveretti got boarded and had to button up. "Bearcat, this is Bronco. Cannister my back, Kim, one of those suckers has a . . ." Wham! Wham! . . . "a satchel charge." Two cannister rounds punctuated his request. . . . "Look out, Kim, there's an RPG . . . Oh shit!"

The shaped charge weapon exploded against Kim's upper bow, fortunately at a bad angle, and shattered his searchlight with shrapnel. Alveretti saw figures crawling over Bearcat's hull and carefully dusted his running mate off with the co-ax, as the two backed gingerly out.

"Piss on this shit!" Alveretti said, switching to Puma frequency. "Six, this is Bronco, the plan will probably work, but we gotta use Redleg, over."

Hawke radioed permission back from the chopper in which he and Franklin were rapidly approaching, and Alveretti switched to the 175s, requesting "concentration echo one seven, marker round and fuze V-T."

"That oughta thin the buggers out a bit," he muttered, after adjusting the second smoke round and giving the emotionally satisfying "fire for effect" command. For five minutes, huge 150-pound shells rained down out of the sky, exploding sixty feet above the defenders, killing men but causing curiously little property damage. The two tanks used the time to circle around and link up with their Strikers, just as the heli-borne infantry arrived, along with Puma's officers.

Wu Sung and his men, jealously guarding their privileged status as tank-riding infantry, stuck to the two M-48s like glue, some of them taking serious wounds in the process of nailing RPG teams. They, too, were under orders to avoid property damage. The American infantry CO got exactly what he wanted— a small, out-of-the-way, "tenderized" objective on which to break in his green troops.

"Hawke, I have to congratulate you," Owens said, after the last hostile had surrendered or been killed. "This was exactly what my replacements needed. Now they all feel ten feet tall."

He shook his head ruefully. "But now, I'll have to slow them down to keep them from doing something stupid."

Owens, after seeing the last of his few wounded medevacked out, lifted off with his last squad just as Epstein and Jones landed in a lightly armed Huey, whose pilot'd been working with Puma for some time. Finally, the coast was clear for Operation Robin Hood . . .

Hawke reached up and keyed his helmet radio. "All right, Frank, bring 'em out of the woods and let's count the goodies."

"That's a roger," Torrion answered, chuckling uncontrollably as he talked. "I feel like a kid at Christmas!"

In a few minutes, a procession of Strikers, accompanied by half the Special Forces team, marched out of the low-growing scrub and into their newly acquired supply depot. Uncle Ho's war matériel had just been redirected.

The Strikers tore into the hidden crates, cases and barrels with undisguised glee, seeing the captured munitions as their salvation in hard times to come. Most of them had been on cross-border patrols and knew as well as their bosses that an invasion was probable. Why the Americans chose this method of beefing up their weaponry didn't particularly concern them. If any thought about it at all, they wondered why this hadn't been done before.

Epstein and Jones, for their part, were ecstatic at being turned loose on a virgin site with no interference from Rear Echelon Puzzle Palace Commandos. They followed the Nungs, clipboards in hand, noting the type, age and condition of everything in the stashes.

"Oh, those stupid, stupid bastards," Epstein crowed. "Look at this!"

Hawke, attracted by the shout, turned to see Epstein holding a uniform shirt aloft—complete with unit patches. "65th NVA Regiment," he said. "We know where they are. And now we know where they will be. The only question is when."

Slowly, the pieces of the puzzle were falling into place. Every operation produced a bit more info and, if handled carefully like this one, more weaponry for Torrion's native troops and a few other provably loyal groups in the immediate area—such as the village militia at Plei Duc.

Group by group, the Strikers started up the trail heading back to Torrion's valley, each burdened with appropriated commie gear. Some of the bundles, however, had been made up with a carefully prepared shopping list in mind. They would be carried back on the tanks and distributed where they would do the most good. Any hostile tank force coming across the border would find the woods full of RPGs . . . in the hands of Southerners.

Within days of the successful completion of Operation Robin Hood, Hawke and Franklin had gotten word to Epstein that the border data collation was complete. And he took the first opportunity to ride out, hitching a lift with a supply-carrying Chinook.

On arrival, he was properly appreciative of the improvements around what was being referred to by the troops as "Puma Base." He was given the grand tour before being taken into the M.I. station and shown the mass of data.

At this particular point in time, Hawke was out with Van Loc and Doan in a pair of tracks, escorting a Medcap mission, using Puma's own medic track and interpreter. "Winning the hearts and minds of the people" had been a good concept, but Jeremy thought its execution by higher command left something to be desired. So he'd set out to "customize" his AO, leaving Franklin in base much of the time; a situation that the love-smitten lieutenant turned to his advantage. He found many excuses to visit the town, ostensibly to "cement relations with the locals."

"We're developing our own intelligence and support network out here," Franklin was explaining to Epstein. "We're operating on the basis that when, not if, the NVA come howling across the border, there may be little or no official warning. We may have to move at high speed, and at night. Therefore, we desperately need for all the tank commanders, and as many of the troops as possible, to know the ground like their own backyards—and to know which villages are safe."

"Also," Jones added, "we're developing a network of reliable VC spotters who will get the word to us when the nighttime tax collectors and recruiters come around."

"That's a bit risky for them," Epstein commented. "If they get caught"—he drew his hand suggestively across his throat—"it's curtains!"

"Yeah," Jones said, "but you wouldn't believe how much some of these people hate Communism. We've had little old ladies come and fink on mining parties —and ditty wagon drivers deliberately tip over just short of a kill zone. . . .

"Anyway, you mentioned something about prisoners, right after the hook lifted off, but it kinda got lost in conversation. Just what was it exactly that you needed?"

"Some virgin POWs," Epstein replied. "Those base camp assholes don't know interrogation from 'Twenty Questions.' They actually let hard-core VC know that they're going to be treated like gentlemen before they put the questions to them. I want some that are still coming out of shock, or even before the medics patch them up . . . Can do?"

Franklin thought a minute. "Er—yeah. It'll take a bit of setting up, though. It would have to be an operation that has ACAVs involved, so we can haul 'em inside and let the suckers vanish for a while. And then you'd have to be on call. Let me talk to Jeremy and see what we can come up with."

Gator Scruggs was working his Ballbuster cautiously through one apparently uninhabited arm of a wishbone-shaped village south of Oasis. The other arm of the village was the scene of a fitful, on-again, off-again battle that two companies of grunts had been trying to finish for three full days. The infantry, under the command of the battalion's operations officer, who'd been sent out to oversee a pair of inexperienced company commanders, had called for armored support, and Puma had drawn the task.

Jeremy, whom the men were now referring to as "The Hawke," had sent Scruggs and his running mate, Staff Sergeant Gutierrez, whose 1-3 tank, "Bandido," was the newest vehicle in the tank platoon, out to settle the issue.

Attached to the tank section was Riley's ACAV section, which included Dubois and Rebel Rouser. Just now, Scruggs and Dubois were easing through the apparently empty half of the zone, supposedly checking for hostiles—but really working for The Hawke.

Scruggs had volunteered for the mission because in his estimation he was the best man for the job. After thirty years in the military, fighting Asians from Guadalcanal on, and a quarter century of marriage to an extremely attractive San Francisco nisei, the craggy Floridian claimed the ability to "think gook."

Gator had his driver pull up in a clear area, halfway up one arm of the wishbone, motioning Dubois to come up beside him. Both vehicles kept their engines running, and the main armament manned as Scruggs and Doobie squatted on the tanks' fenders, plotting the next move.

"They'll be retreating slowly," Gator said, "now that a tank and three ACAVs have pushed the odds against them. Their honchos will be leapfrogging the defenses. They'll hold a line with half the troops while the rest set up a new line behind that. Then the engaged men will filter through the new line. Through it all, though, the HQ will be farthest back with its own guard of fanatics."

"Those are the apes we want," Dubois agreed.

"And the lieutenant wants them snuck out. How the hell are we going to pull that off?"

"It won't be easy. But the one advantage we've got is that for a while we control the pace of battle—until that major gets his defecation centralized. I plan to slip up to the head of the wishbone and get there before the defenders fall back that far and pick out the most logical spot for a last-ditch stand and command post, and just shut down and wait. If we're lucky, they'll walk into us. If we're not, we just beat up the rear of their line and look ignorant."

Dubois, who'd volunteered because the job sounded interesting, and who'd been accepted because Hawke wanted the biggest men he could find to go hand-to-hand with the NVA, wasn't convinced. "Granted, we can always blow them away. But how do we hide the operation?"

"Gunfire, and the extra frequency. No one in Division operates on that band. So I'll just have Gutierrez and the tracks open up and accidentally use some white phosphorous to set a few thatches afire."

Shaking his head, Dubois agreed, somewhat reluctantly. "This'll be one for the grandkids, if I ever have any."

Slowly, carefully, the two vehicles moved through the deserted habitations, whose occupants had obviously bugged out long ago, taking everything of value with them. Engines scarcely above an idle, running less than one mile per hour, they eventually reached the head of the wishbone.

Both armored machines went to full camouflage by the simple expedient of rolling through the back walls of houses, leaving the fronts of the buildings intact. Gator, bumping his skull in the process, clambered out of his turret, right under the thatched rafters of a small family dwelling, and trotted over to where Dubois had set up inside the remains of some kind of animal shed.

The worries of the giant Cajun Dubois had been lessened considerably by the situation. "This just might work, Gator. That house over there's almost perfect for a command post. There's a few small knolls in front of it, and you can see down that village arm, and the open space too—might have been the village potentate's house."

"Right—yikes! Keep yer head down!" Gator hollered as an errant burst cracked overhead. "They're workin' up this way."

Gambling on the tendency of NVA leaders to want to save their own skins and live to fight another day, Gator had picked the house nearest the enclosing jungle as the obvious location for the last-ditch stand. Next he'd positioned the two Puma tracks as close to it as possible. The gamble was whether there would be enough time for a snatch before the combat troops leapfrogged back to the new HQ.

They didn't have long to wait. The sound of firing grew closer, and then suddenly a small cluster of men in khaki uniforms trotted into view—not looking behind them. They were clearly headed for that oh-so-inviting house. Sure enough, three officers, identifiable by their red collar tabs, immediately set up housekeeping in the dwelling, along with two radiomen.

Outside, two machine-gun crews were setting up, and an RPG team was looking around for a likely spot, when the sound of Puma's engaged vehicles suddenly trebled in volume. Dubois' driver, spotting the command party, had passed the signal to Gutierrez and the tracks. The deception had begun. The steady thumping of Bandido's gun was the signal Gator had been waiting for, and he raised his hand so that his gunner, now commanding the tank, could see it.

From the front, the sound of a tank's main armament is nearly unbearable, and the sound of the ninety almost deafened them. They would have to work by signal and plan. Three cannister clusters, almost four thousand metal cylinders, swept all life from the front yard of the house. A pair of white phosphorous followed, obscuring the area from the direction of the infantry.

Gator and Dubois, safe on the other side of the enemy command post, lobbed a pair of tear gas grenades, and then slipped around to the back while the gas was spreading. Rouser's driver shot a couple of M-79 gas rounds in through a side window—just to make sure.

Quickly donning and checking their gas masks, the two tank commanders entered the house through a storage room, running for the front. The kitchen area, between the two sections of the dwelling, was deserted. But looking out of the kitchen doorway, they saw a half dozen men coughing and crying, helpless from the tear gas, and trapped by the M-60 fire from the track.

Gator shot two radio operators, and then holstered his .45. Stepping boldly into the NVA command party, he grabbed two ninety-eight-pound officers and crashed their heads together. Doobie shot a clerk, and laid the third officer out with a ham-sized fist that rearranged his features, putting his brain in "park."

Hastily binding the trio with extra shoelaces brought along for the purpose, they unceremoniously chucked their captives out the door. Doobie's ACAV, using that as a signal, rolled forward, dropping its ramp as it moved. Tired, dispirited NVA from the combat line were beginning to filter into the clearing, and the ACAV gunners barely had time to stack the captives on the sandbag floor of the vehicle before coming under fire.

The house which had concealed Ballbuster began to bulge, and the 52-ton bulk of the murder machine emerged from the front of the building, the doorframe hanging from its gun tube and bits of thatch roof cascading from its turret. Another cannister round sleeted death across the clearing, and Dubois abruptly emerged from the building with a radio and several leather briefcases. Diving into the track, he popped up in the .50 mount, chucking a flare into the thatch while swinging the gun to cover the hostiles. His crew, thoroughly pleased with the maneuver, were laughing as they drove off, making room for Gator's tank to pick up its boss.

"All right, let's eat out the back of their line and make it look good," Scruggs said as soon as he'd put on his commo helmet. "And switch back to the infantry frequency."

Almost without a pause, he switched to the infantry COs radio net and transmitted. "Rosebud three, this is Puma 4. We have completed the sweep, negative hostiles, but we're right behind your hostile forces. Suggest we roll them up from here, over."

After a few seconds startled delay, Rosebud came back, evidently very pleased. "Affirmative, Puma; most affirmative," the infantry major replied happily. "Let them have it!"

Scruggs, with Doobie trailing to his left rear, proceeded to do just that. Digging into the enemy rear with a vengeance, and with such good effect that, less than an hour later, they came out of a treeline to find Bandido and the other three ACAVs set up around a combat LZ with the usual horde of choppers removing wounded and prisoners and inserting wheels from HQ.

"I have orders to split up, sir," Gator told the major, after receiving effusive congratulations. "Puma 6 wants me to leave Gutierrez and two ACAVs here and take my section back to base. I think he's got another job for us."

"Well, I can well imagine that, Sarge. I've never even heard of heavy armor operating at close quarters like this; and I'll certainly be dropping by to see your boss up at Plei Duc—to thank him personally."

"Thank you, sir, and I'm sure he'll be glad to pass the word on to the troops," Scruggs said, saluting as he swung up to his turret.

After a quick conference with the other two tank commanders, he led the small column out, triumphantly bearing his prizes back to Puma Base.

The three NVA officers, after having been rudely kidnapped by the Yankee tankers, were bound hand and foot. Gagged with smelly mechanics' rags, they'd been thrown to the floor of Doobie's track like so much Viking plunder. Unceremoniously stacked in a corner, they awoke to find themselves in a portable Hades bossed by one of those impossibly huge Americans. Acrid battle smoke attacked their unaccustomed eyes, and the clatter of their comrades' bullets rattled across the armored sides of the ACAV.

The close, hot, smelly interior of a combat machine is a terrifying environment to the uninitiated. When the vehicle rocks and bucks through a battle zone, it's constantly in violent motion, battered by bullets and explosions, as it lurches unpredictably through the remains of a village. Sound and motion are abrupt and continuous, and the stench is overpowering. The oily stink of overheated machinery, the constant swirl of powder smoke, the stale odor of unconsumed rations, unwashed bodies, and the foulness of slopping urinal cans combine into an unsettling miasma which could overturn even a paratrooper's stomach.

Into this world the three captives returned to consciousness—a red-lit hell filled with unfamiliar sights and sensations. Fitful spears of sunlight penetrated the gloom, as the armormen kept three machine guns yammering with showers of hot brass cascading upon the hapless prisoners. Now fully conscious, they began to struggle to attain some semblance of balance, inevitably attracting hostile attention.

"Hey, Doobie," the loader shouted. "Our gooks are back in the real world."

"Well, lash the fuckers to the cargo rail, and make sure they don't get strangled on the rope. We went to a lot of trouble to get those dudes."

"Right," the man answered, picking up an NVA officer like so much dunnage as he spoke.

"You guys are lucky," he said as he worked. "You're gonna get special treatment."

One officer's eyes widened slightly, when he heard the English words and understood. That didn't go unnoticed, and the loader quickly got on the intercom with Dubois.

"Doobie, this little shit in the center, the one with the scar on his chin, understands English."

"Lieutenant Epstein'll be glad to hear that," Dubois said. "Hey, Scruggs is leadin' us out to an LZ. This fracas is about over. Be ready to pile ammo crates and the tarp on 'em if I give the word. We're supposed to sneak these apes back to Plei Duc, remember?"

"That's a roger," the man replied, as the track rumbled to a halt at one side of the cleared area. "I can always knock 'em back out if need be."

Shortly, the ACAV was again underway, and the crew, more relaxed now, went about housekeeping duties, refilling ammo racks, dumping cartridges and C-ration cans, and generally tidying the vehicle's interior. One of their normal battle rituals, however, had an untoward effect on the prisoners.

Weeks before, after a long, drawn-out battle, the dozer tank had been put to the task of excavating a mass grave for Northern casualties. In the process, six old skeletons were unearthed, and the skulls had rapidly disappeared into various tanks and tracks before the grave was covered up.

Dubois' crew had polished theirs to a high luster, put red flashlight filters in the eye sockets and hung it in one corner of the track. The finishing touch had been added when a pair of instrument light bulbs were set behind the lenses. But due to a bad connection, the lights tended to flicker.

A primitive animism underlies the Mahayana Buddhism which is the official religion of much of Vietnam, and one of its beliefs is the immutability of the body. Many Vietnamese believe that if the body is not buried complete, the soul will have to search for the missing components.

The trio of NVA were forced to undergo captivity with the presence of a body part that Dubois, in typical fashion, had christened: "Sergeant Yoric."

As the track bucketed along, the crew shared the usual after-combat beers, talking and discussing the day's events. Yoric, for his part, swung from the vehicle's roof, seeming to nod his head sagely when some trooper ended a monologue with "Ain't that right, Yoric?"

Finally, though, the trip ended, and the ACAV pivoted to a halt in front of the M.I. station at Puma Base, backing up to the thatched awning, dropping its ramp and letting in a gush of cool night air. The captives, though not tightly bound, had nonetheless lost most of their strength to fear, and when abruptly jerked to their feet, fell in a huddle at Epstein's feet.

"What in the hell did you do to these suckers, Doobie?" the chunky intelligence man wanted to know. "They act like they were terrorized."

"Oh, I guess it was Sarge Yoric. They couldn't seem to take their eyes off him the whole way back."

Franklin, who with Jones and Epstein had been standing eagerly by, waiting to see what Scruggs and Dubois had caught, was mystified. "Who? We don't have any Yoric on the roster."

"He means the skull, sir," one of the tail gunners said helpfully. "Look inside."

Epstein and Franklin checked inside the track, and the intelligence man laughed outright. "Super, absolutely super. This is the first half of the normal interrogation process—the tenderizer. Now all I have to do is be nice to the poor stupes, and they ought to sing like birds."

By now, the bedraggled Northerners had regained their composure and were standing. Epstein led them into the interior of the bunker along with the base camp interpreter. Franklin, however, had a few words for Dubois.

"I don't care much for your humor, Sarge. But if it suits you, fine. Just pass it around that we've worked damn hard for good relations with the locals, and one look inside a track with one of these souvenirs will blow it all. Understand, Sergeant?"

"Er, yessir. I'll pass the word."

Doobie passed the word, and in a very short time, all the grisly souvenirs had vanished, including Sergeant Yoric.

The arrival of the three special-order POWs coincided with the end of Franklin's base camp days. Hawke, who'd been out in the hills for the better part of a month with Jenks' ACAV section and the dozer tank, was on the way in for a badly needed period of rest, recuperation and repair. The only way, they'd discovered, to keep the tracked fighting machines running, was to cut normal maintenance intervals in half. That meant that each section got eight, rather than four quarterly services per year. The crews lived with wrenches in hand and grease guns nearby.

While Hawke and his weary warriors pulled strong point and reaction force duty, working on the tanks at the same time, Franklin took his thoroughly rested platoon out into the hills and jungles. He'd been looking forward to this day with something that resembled dread. It meant an enforced separation from Tien, just when they'd passed the puppy love stage of their budding romance and were beginning to talk seriously.

When he finally got around to telling her, the night before the platoon was due to move out, she was at first furious with him for not warning her and then instantly contrite and worried about his safety in combat. She'd not shown him this mercurial side of her temperament, and Franklin was still somewhat bemused when he led the line of tanks out the gate past the well bunker.

He sat in the turret, staring fixedly at his map, trying his best to concentrate on the job at hand when Krause, who sat relaxed, yet alert on the loader's hatch, nudged him and pointed.

"It's not too smart not to wave at yer girlfriend, Lootenant. She might not be here when we get back."

Blushing a deep red, Franklin looked up and saw Tien standing by the well bunker, long hair lifting like a banner in the breeze, waving a colored scarf. Suddenly, he felt like an escapee from an old John Wayne movie, and the strains of "Garryowen" tinkled through his mind . . . along with the realization that his infatuation was now out in the open. The troopers had probably known about it all along.

Raising a hand, he waved to Tien, and then was drawn back to business as the platoon moved warily into the hole in the jungle that passed for a road. But that single exchange had lifted a burden off his shoulders. She cared and it was enough.

Chapter Nine

HALF A MONTH HAD GONE BY SINCE EPSTEIN HAD
choppered out in triumph with his three prizes, but
there'd been no communication on the subject. Now,
Hawke and Jones watched with interest as the intelligence officer alighted from the morning chopper—
thunder on his face. The more stoic Weiss, out for a
look-see on Barksdall's behalf, followed. Once they'd
retired to the relative privacy of the M.I. hootch,
Epstein blew up.

"Those stupid cocksuckers up at Two Corps are the
Goddamn problem," Epstein snarled, slamming his
steel pot to the floor. "Their little pea-brains haven't
had an original idea since graduation back in 1902.
That North or South gambit is set in concrete in those
fossilized skulls. Division seems to be coming
around—a little anyway—but they can't overrule
next higher. So here we are, out on a fucking limb."

Trying to calm himself, while Weiss sat and smoldered, Epstein accepted the rum and Coke that Jones put in his hand, continuing. "We, out here in the field, are 'alarmists who don't have the benefit of the overall picture or the benefit of long years in the intelligence field,' to quote the high-Goddamn-command at Two Corps; 'and should restrict our intelligence activities to gathering raw information.'

"I sent up all that beautiful data that we extracted from those three gooks—by the way, that was a light colonel, his adjutant and political officer—and they reinterpreted it to suit their own bat-brained preconceptions." Epstein took a long swig from his drink, and Weiss picked up the narrative.

"I got a good look at the transcript of what Sal dug out of those three prisoners, and it's at least as good as the textbook examples they show you at the Point. "To me it indicates that that bunch was preparing the way for an invasion to follow; but to those fossils, the prisoners were merely primed with misinformation by their superiors. And those uniforms you found were merely NVA surplus shipped down to resupply the VC—not an indication of troop dispositions."

"Well, how do they explain the heavy military supplies and tank ammo we've been finding?" Jones asked.

"Mere red herrings, placed to lead us astray," Weiss said flippantly. "The official doctrine is that when the real thrust comes, the central highlands will explode in diversionary actions which can be safely ignored until the major threat has been reduced."

"What does Barky think about all this?" Hawke asked.

"Officially, he goes along with Corps," Weiss replied. "Unofficially, he told me to tell you to keep up the good work. Sooner or later we're bound to dig up something that'll make even Two Corps sit up and take notice."

"I don't think those idiots would notice a column of T-62s with Russian crews," Sal Epstein was saying, when a breathless runner exploded into the room.

"Jenks has been hit, sir. Most of his infantry are casualties—both tracks disabled and he's wounded—he's under that triple canopy shit on the border where choppers can't go and . . ." The rest of the man's spiel fell on thin air. Hawke and Jones vanished with the first sentence, with Epstein and Weiss following on their heels.

To Hawke's surprise, neither Big Thunder nor Jenks was on the horn when they entered the commo track. A radio operator handed him a mike and announced, "Viper, sir. Cap'n Torrion relaying for Jenks who is so far down under that green crap that they can't even get sunlight in there, much less radio."

Jeremy took the proffered mike and hastily transmitted. "Viper Six, this is Puma. What's coming down, over?"

Torrion's voice came in clear and unagitated—an uncanny counterpoint to the news he bore. "Yore 3-4 and two of his tracks were probing down that old French loggin' road where we saw truck tracks last week, and he got hit by somebody who was waitin' for him. He's taken mine damage in his own track, rockets in his trail element, and thirty percent of his infantry are casualties. Puma 5's been informed, but he has a terrain problem. He can't get there from where he is, over."

As the bad news poured in, Jeremy turned to Riley who'd just arrived and gave him the rotating hand signal that meant "Wind 'em up," only to be told that it had been done.

"Listen outside," Riley said, opening the door of the track. Jeremy heard the rumble of idling diesels as track after track got the word and fired up.

With Hawke busy on the radio, getting sitreps and setting up a reaction force, Riley had a chance to go out and check on progress, intending to make a circuit of the perimeter and pass the word, officially, to the TC and section leaders. Instead, he saw a delegation awaiting him, and a line of waiting combat machines assembling at the gate.

"All up and ready, Sarge," Dubois reported, followed by the E-5 who bossed the HQ tank section. "Dozer and Bravo 6 on line and ready too, sir. Considering the condition of that particular tank, the man, a buck sergeant named Miller, must've pulled off several minor miracles to be confident of taking that hulk in harm's way."

The other two tracks of Jenks' section couldn't be counted because they had no crews, only drivers. They'd lost men to the hospital, R and R and normal rotation; and the remaining crewmembers stood wistfully by their mounts, staring forlornly at the growing line of tanks and ACAVs.

Jeremy's news was all bad. Jenks, with three of Owens' squads riding the tops of his tracks, had been exploring westward on one of the old French logging roads that bore signs of heavy foot and some vehicular traffic. Spotting fresh prints heading west, he thought he might for once be able to catch up with the interlopers and kick a little ass.

Unfortunately, it appeared that the enemy had wanted him to do just that. A mine had caved in and penetrated his track's belly, lifting him and most of the crew out in a cloud of dirt from the sandbag floors. When he came out of unconsciousness, his rear ACAV had been rocketed but not set on fire. Even as he looked, the only mobile vehicle of the section went out—not from fire, but from a stripped transmission.

Cursing blasphemously, he hobbled over to the infantry sergeants, only to find that just one squad leader was left alive. Between the two of them, they set up a perimeter, using the three immobile tracks as the corners of a triangle, intending to keep as many men alive as possible. And to keep the NVA from interfering with any attempt at rescue.

Jenks had gotten on the air to Torrion, because from down in the green canyon, he couldn't reach Puma Base. The captain had immediately launched his company of Strikers, getting in touch with Puma. The fate of the three crippled ACAVs and the remaining grunts now depended on who could get reinforcements into the area first.

Hawke looked expectantly at Weiss, hoping the West Pointer's computerized brain would come up with a brilliant master-stroke. He got one, but not what he expected. "Jeremy, you're facing at least one armor officer that wants a piece of Puma!"

"How do you figure that, Benj?"

"Check very carefully the location of that contact. Consider that this is the first time somebody's found tracks headed west, and remember that Jenks hit an already-laid mine. Somebody wanted to be followed."

Hawke was studying his map with great care as Weiss continued. "Notice that there's only three good heavy equipment accesses to that little bench, the ends of the logging road, and that watercourse which leads through the glade. There's no way heavy armor can come down from above. The cover is too heavy and the slope's too steep. You'd peel tracks like rubber bands if you tried to turn, and nothing we've got could climb back out."

Jeremy's mind was a whirlwind of instantly discarded plans and alternatives—his subconscious knocking down one hair-brained scheme after another—until at last he said, "No one in his right mind would try this, and I'm not going to advise next higher of the gory details. But there is a way."

Picking up a microphone whose radio was turned to Puma's extra frequency, he got in touch with Franklin. "Puma 5, this is Puma. Jimbo, exactly where are you now, over?"

"This is 5, we're damn near above the action, south of the road and cutting west to angle down off this hill to swing back and . . ."

"Negative, negative," Hawke snapped. "Sierra 2 Alpha informs us that there may be a surprise planned east *and* west of the hit. Look at your funny paper. Do you remember what Van Loc told us about that logged-off hill you're on top of?"

"Wait one, Jer," Franklin said, turning to Scruggs who was standing beside him on the tank's hull. "Gator, remember when we had Van Loc out here with us?"

"Yessir, I can find the top of that stream again, and there's nothin' but small stuff growin' along it. The French used it for a log chute back in the forties, Van Loc told me, and there's no sudden drop-offs—just one steep, almost straight shot down. We better send a ground party—say one tanker and a few Nungs down on foot—if there's time. . . ."

"That's roger, Puma," Franklin transmitted. "We

can find the chute PDQ, and we'll recon the access while you're getting on the road."

"Okay, that's part of it," Jeremy said, and then turned to the radio operator. "Switch me back to Viper," he said, picking up the mike.

"Y'all can jest forget about the sucker on the downstream side," Torrion said, when apprised of Hawke's dilemma. "I know where they've got to be, and I can get TacAir in there. As far as the other two are concerned, if you can get 'em engaged, ol' Frankie's boys will be the back side of the nut-cracker."

"Fine, just fine," Hawke said, after Viper had signed off. "That's almost all the damage we can do from here."

Reaching over and tapping the top of Epstein's commo helmet with a knuckle, he asked, "How're you doing, Sal, make contact yet?"

"Negative, I can't raise a single Lurp."

"Rats!" Hawke said. "Well, time's a wasting. Riley, it'll take you the longest to get down there, so you move out first, and I'll follow with two groups—a tank and two crackerboxes each."

"Sir," Riley said. "I think I know where we can find tank commanders for those two loose tracks, and we've got the extra gunners. There's a whole line of cooks and clerks waiting at the gate, as usual, and with Owens' other three platoons on the way by air, there's plenty of replacements available. That is, if you don't mind amateur TCs."

For a few seconds, Hawke was mystified, until he saw where his platoon sergeant was looking. "Oh yeah, prime stock too. A pair of REMFs out to see the world. Officers, even."

"Hey, wait a minute," Epstein said, and then fell silent, realizing that in this company, no matter what the odds, shirking would remove one forever from an incredibly select group. "All I've got is a pistol," he said lamely.

"No problem, sir," the commo sergeant who'd been listening in said, producing an ancient Winchester Model 97 pump shotgun. "The guy who owned this won't be needing it anymore. He got an unplanned rotation—bad case of lead poisoning."

"Thanks a lot, Sarge," Epstein said in an ambiguous tone.

Weiss, calm and efficient, had already walked over to one of the two tracks and was in the gun cupola, checking radios and weapons. Epstein had to grab the scattergun and run for his track.

Climbing up into the newly operable 6-tank, Hawke had to reassure himself that this mechanized refugee from a Bessemer converter was actually combat worthy. "What the hell have you pulled off, Miller? It would take a whole new tank to make this thing even run decently, and the engine sounds like it just came out of the shops."

After a moment of silence, Miller, who was new to Puma, decided he could trust his new boss. "You remember that Charlie company tank that was brand new and hit a two-hundred pound mine up at Dak To?"

"Right, Sarge. They had to put it on a lowboy and haul it back to Battalion. Pity, too. The engine and running gear didn't even have a hundred hours. . . ." His words trailed off as the light finally dawned.

"We parked 'em side by side for two weeks straight, sir. And it's all in here—the whole nine yards—turret hydraulics and all. I've served with Mr. Larsen in Korea and Germany, sir. We understand each other."

That removed one major worry from Hawke's mind. He quickly got in touch with his other TCs as they rolled westward. "Riley, you'll take the near cut-off; the dozer tank and Lieutenant Epstein will go with you. Take your time getting into place because we'll have to go the long way round, and Torrion's people are on foot. The rest of you will follow me. We split up as soon as we've picked up the grunts, 6 out."

By this time, Jeremy thought, the commo people back at Plei Duc, operating on his instructions, would have informed Battalion. And sure enough, Barksdall came in right on schedule, after having informed Brigade that Puma was in a "small action" requiring no outside help.

"Puma, this is Big Thunder. What is your present situation, over?"

"This is Puma. I have three crackerboxes disabled on one of the old French roads, marked on your funny paper as number three. Am proceeding to extract them; Viper, Mongoose and Foxglove 6 are all in the area, if needed. I will be loading Foxglove troops on board in two zero. Puma 6, over."

"Roger, Puma 6, this is Big Thunder. Will rendezvous you then. Big Thunder out."

"You're sure you won't need anything extra, Hawke?" Barksdall asked, while the two stood at some distance from the impromptu LZ, watching the troops load.

"No sir, that man down there has his tail in a royal crack, and any notification to Brigade or Division will only cause more delay in getting warm bodies and hot metal down to him. We've got our plans made, and I don't see what else could be done in the next few hours that would be worth the loss of daylight."

"You're right, of course, son. Dammit, it doesn't feel good having to sneak around like this, just to fight a war."

Jeremy was tempted to tell the older man about the secret frequencies, but he held back the urge.

"There's my signal, sir. The troops are loaded and the squad leaders are briefed."

"Well then, on your way. I'll be overhead and will trade off with Foxglove, acting as Command and Control. And let's hope the radio traffic doesn't attract any sightseers."

"Roger, sir. We probably won't transmit too much out of the valley anyway." Hawke swung into his turret and was gone.

"HOO BOY!" Ballbuster's driver shouted as he nosed the tank down the precipitous slope. "This's gonna be some sleigh ride."

"Shaddup and drive," Gator ordered, nervous in spite of himself. He'd never been all the way down to the bottom; he'd just talked with locals who had.

The plan was for the platoon to follow the intermittent watercourse down to the bench on which Jenks found himself trapped, using the trunks of the small trees as impromptu brakes, almost coasting downhill. If anything went wrong, the only way was still down because no retrieval vehicle could climb up to reach them.

Scruggs looked behind to see Alveretti's Bronco take the plunge, and then the lieutenant's tank plugged the hole in the dense brush, blotting out the sunlight for a few seconds. Now the entire platoon was committed and the rain forest echoed to the shriek of tortured metal and groaning engines accompanied by the maniacal screams of tropical birds and insane howls of primates. Small deer and wild pigs exploded from the dense brush ahead of the thundering tanks.

The farther down the tanks went, the dimmer the sun, but suddenly they were clear of the heavy growth at the forest edge. "Keep the speed down," Scruggs cautioned all drivers. "Once you pick up excess speed at this angle, the brakes won't be able to handle it, and you'll be outa control till you find a tree. You don't want to hit that bench at fifty miles per hour," he warned, "or run over our foot scouts down ahead of us."

Sergeant Harry Jenks was up against it. He'd fallen into a well-laid trap and knew it. Help was on the way, but he suspected that the enemy had reserves close by. He also suspected that it was a deep-laid trap, designed to suck in most of Puma and, if not destroy it, at least deal it a serious blow. He'd relayed these suspicions to Hawke, and the message had come back that steps were being taken. What kind weren't specified.

Jenks, who was a spare, wiry man, and his driver, a short, thin black man who looked out on the world through glasses as thick as Coke bottle bottoms, were the only survivors of a five-man crew. Their ACAV, "Rosie," of which they were extremely proud, was a wreck. Smoke still curled lazily from the hole that'd been blown in the floor by a command-detonated mine.

The ammo handler was compressed out of human

shape into one corner of the interior, and the tail gunners had landed dead some yards from the hull. The guns would still work, though, and after bandaging each other's wounds, Jenks and Willie crawled cautiously back into the Godawful mess that'd been their home, and began clearing them for action.

Simultaneously with the detonation of the mine, an unknown but adequate number of homemade claymores had gone off, sheeting hundreds of pounds of scrap metal against the short column. Only the chance of the directional mines being set a bit low had saved the infantry from annihilation, and they had bought the few surviving armormen time to clear for action.

Right behind Jenks, the following track had suddenly swerved off the dim trail and out into the clearing, avoiding whatever lay in the road in front of it. Now, that track was immobile, as its transmission had failed in the attempt to push over a small tree.

The trailing ACAV also was a smoldering wreck, having been the recipient of three RPG rounds through the body. Fortunately, it hadn't exploded or caught fire, although much of its small arms ammunition had been scattered. Jenks shuddered, thinking of the amount of explosives stored in that machine. It, too, was manned by only two men, but at least they'd been able to get the fifty in action.

Hostile fire came in sporadically, drawn by any chance motion, as if the enemy hadn't enough force in place to carry an assault home.

Jenks, gritting away the pain of multiple burns, cuts and imbedded shrapnel, called out to the single surviving squad leader. "Hey, Mike, me and Willie got two M-60s cleared and ready over here. You got any walkin' wounded to man 'em?"

A burst of AK fire was his answer, and an M-79 gunner plonked a round at the source from a clump of tall weeds. The 40-millimeter grenade went off, accompanied by an inhuman shriek. And the infantryman answered, "Walkin', no. Will a couple of crawlers do?"

"Hell yeah," Willie replied. "We'll set their ass on some ammo crates—send 'em on."

Grimacing with pain from his own cut, bruised, concussed body, he made the shift to haul a couple of ammo cases up to the tail gun positions. And shortly, two pale, grimy, blood-spattered grunts slithered through the rear door. They looked like Red Cross practice dummies after a first aid class had failed their final exams; but with Jenks's and Willie's help, they managed to crank their complaining frames upright and to handle the guns while the two Puma troopers checked Rosie out.

To their amazement, the engine caught immediately. "Blast must've stalled her," Willie guessed as he carefully shifted into the lowest range with both lateral levers pulled back and locked.

They could hear the engine lug down, and Willie slowly released some of the pressure on the bar that controlled the one good track. The cheer that followed the slight lurch forward was short-lived because the sound and motion brought a renewed flurry of incoming fire, green tracers cracking through the jungle-surrounded clearing. Now, however, all three fifties could be manned, and the tail end ACAV, using Jenks's example, had pressed a few damaged grunts into service as gunners.

Slowly, painfully, the balance of fire was being swayed toward the Americans, as more and more men patched by the infantry medic who worked inside the armor of the center ACAV, slid out into the grass and over to one of the other two combat machines. The infantry had bought time for the shattered cavalrymen, and now the guns sheltered the grunts. The remaining squad leader had found a buddy's radio and got into quiet communication with Jenks.

"I got only eight effective for full combat," he reported. "Thirteen wounded, some of whom are in with you guys, and ten dead."

"We're no better off," Jenks replied. "The last track took one into the engine, as well as the body; and number two is gonna need a trannie before it moves again. Rosie here'll probably move, if we can have the time to cannibalize some tread off that wreck back there."

The squad leader thought that one over for a few minutes. "We can slide out into the woods," he suggested, "and work clockwise around while you fire cover ahead of us. There can't be too many of the little shitasses left."

"Yeah, I know. They're just holding us here as bait to bring the rest of Puma in. If we can grease on outa here, it's no trap anymore."

"Goddamn, I hate the thought of this. But it's gotta be done," the infantryman answered, just when Jenks' auxiliary receiver came to life on Puma's private frequency.

"Puma 3-4, this is 5. Hold in place. You and your buddy sit tight and don't do anything rash. Just wait till you hear timber cracking and then open up. You copy?"

Instant relief flooded Jenks, and he had to dig up the energy to switch the transmitter over and answer.

"This is 3-4, them's the sweetest orders I ever got. We'll be here, Lootenant."

Jeremy Hawke was trying desperately to pull off a juggling act for which he had no training and no precedent. For that matter, neither had anyone else on the ground. And with three separate canopy layers between the ground and the Command and Control ships, there could be no help from the sky. Technically, the highest ranking officer should be in charge. In actual fact, Hawke controlled the greatest amount of firepower and the only high-speed mobility. For all practical purposes, he was IT.

Highway 19 ran straight west to the border, with the land falling away to the south of it at this point. Jenks was far below Hawke, and miles south, in an east-west valley that paralleled the highway. During Puma's run toward the west, Jeremy had stopped for half an hour to load infantry on his tanks and tracks.

Where a long, bare hill ran out south of the road, Franklin had swung south, plunging straight down toward that valley floor and the old logging road. Riley, with Weiss riding his tail track, had headed back east, with the dozer tank in the lead, aiming to come up between the NVA and Puma Base.

Meanwhile, Hawke was now rushing at full speed toward the border and had cut down toward the western segment of the road. He would come up between the ambushers and their sanctuary.

Torrion, some of whose troops were already in the area, was heading on foot toward the estimated secondary ambushes, figuring to get between those forces and Jenks.

Mongoose was trying desperately to locate the

enemy tactical HQ, in order to throw a monkey wrench into their ability to coordinate what seemed to be a rather ambitious plan.

Gradually, a noose was gathering, but the southern ambuscade, the one on a point where the streambed leveled out to the valley floor, was still uncovered. "Uncle Frank," however, had sent a cork for that particular bolt hole.

Wu Sung crawled carefully through the thick brush at the head of a side valley. His experiences with Puma had taught him what types of terrain were easygoing for Puma's iron monsters. And his years of battle experience told him that the American captain's guess must be right. Up here where the bushes were thick and the watercourse emerged from the jungle would be where the Communists would expect tanks to try to penetrate to aid their brothers.

Down through the long years since his family had been driven from their ancestral estates in China, he'd nursed a hatred of the Communists, whom he considered to be no more than a more hypocritical breed of warlord. Now, given a chance to hurt them again, he eased up to a position that allowed him to overlook the miniature delta where the flow of water spread out and lost itself in a glade.

He was surprised to hear voices speaking in normal conversational tones. These men must be confident indeed, he thought, to expect nothing but loud, insensitive battle machines to come their way. All right, if that was what they expected, who was Wu Sung to disappoint them? Loud, insensitive machinery it would be. . . .

Even more carefully than he'd arrived, he crept

back out of the glade, crawling like a snake over the rotting leaf mold of the forest floor. At last he emerged into another open space, where his squad waited.

"Tell the American sergeant that he may talk to his kindred in the sky," he ordered a messenger. "It is as the captain suspected, and the pigs are fat for the slaughter." The man rushed off to where a Special Forces sergeant stood, overlooking the valley with a radio and a pair of binoculars.

Wu Sung, for his part, ordered his men to fire the smoke grenades from their Garand rifles when the American gave the word, marking the target. Having given the orders, he slid back into the thick growth, wishing to see the end of this arm of the monster that'd destroyed the culture of China. He'd seen the strikes of the gunships; and the jets, as Torrion called them, couldn't be much more devastating, but they were only faster.

"They must come soon," Wu Sung thought, as the smoke grenades arced over him to land among the startled Northerners. "Or the pigs will . . ." His view was blotted out by a blinding, reddish flash as a concussion wave lifted him clear of the ground. The sound was felt more than heard, and he began bleeding from his ears and nose as he loped away from the scene.

The single 250-pound bomb was rapidly followed by a string of more than a dozen—thankfully going away from Wu, up the defile. He caught only a glimpse of a beautiful, silvery, swept-winged aircraft flashing in the sun. And then a series of extended Brrrrrp's heralded the gun runs, as the F-100s came in, smoking up the target with 20-millimeter warheads. Only then could he hear the crackle of the after-burners fading into the distance as an empty silence fell over the battlefield.

Peering over the edge of the shallow defile that was to have been a killing ground for the Americans, Wu could see only dust and smoke. Then slowly, the pall thinned, drifted and parted. He could see bodies and parts of bodies, gutted carcasses and twisted weapons, smoking uniforms and pools of blood. Something seemed to be trying to scream, then it, too, was silent.

"Good-bye, little warlords," Wu Sung murmured in benediction. "You will not bleed this land—not with Americans here."

Something that Captain Torrion had said stuck in his memory—a quote from one of the American ancestor-figures. "The tree of liberty must be refreshed, from time to time, with the blood of tyrants and patriots. That is its natural manure." And if that is true, Wu thought, a mighty forest must one day grow in this land. . . .

Hawke's infantrymen had dismounted and were probing warily forward on either side of the trail. He was dangerously near the border, working his way back to the site of Jenks's ambush, trying to find the blocking force that instinct told him must be waiting here. He'd taken the most dangerous side, closest to the border, for many reasons; not least of which was his desire to face gun-to-gun an entity he believed had set for itself the goal of exterminating Puma.

He could hear the fitful exchanges between Jenks and the men who'd ensnared him. And in his mind's eye, he could see Riley and the dozer duplicating his approach a kilometer away—on the other side of the fight.

"Puma 3-4, this is 6. Do you hear tank engines and

timber splintering?" Jeremy asked the embattled Jenks.

There was silence, and then a wondering voice, coughing slightly, answered. "Six, this is 3-4, affirmative, but from uphill . . . That's impossible!"

"Not today, it ain't," Jeremy snapped back. Then everything happened at once.

An infantry firefight exploded in the roadside foliage to Jeremy's front, then sputtered to a halt as the grunts, obeying orders, pulled back, allowing Puma to go to work. Hawke turned his gunner, Miller, loose, with orders to shoot high explosive into the curve ahead, then eat up the roadside foliage with cannister.

Once the infantry was clear, he ordered his driver to leave the faint, green-floored roadway and work up the left side of the intended kill zone, while the ACAVs took the other side.

The NVA, deprived of their intended victims, seemed to go insane, swarming aboard the tank as soon as it entered the brush. Jeremy, disdaining the tactic of buttoning up, for a time at least, swung the cannon like a giant club, sweeping a half squad off his back deck while his loader fired into the nearby treetops with a captured AK, keeping would-be grenadiers at bay. By swinging from right to left, he could clip the boarders with the co-ax as well as clubbing them. One individual jumped nimbly over the gun, arming a grenade as he moved. A sudden lift of the gun caught his leg, upsetting him, and then the tube came down, pinning him between the steel deck and his own grenade.

"Button up, boss," the loader shouted as another wave of fanatics clambered up the hull, some getting sucked, screaming, into the tracks in the process. The driver had been running through a patch of thicket that was apparently the command post, and the tactical reserve considered Jeremy to be a nice fat present. Backing hastily out of cover, Hawke called for a back-scratching from Epstein, who had his own problems.

When the tail gunners on Epstein's track swung their weapons to cover the 6 tank, Sal had to contend with a pair of NVA who'd climbed his front while his attention was directed to one side. Now, with his fifty pointed the wrong way, he faced two would-be executioners—one with a grenade.

His frantically groping right hand found the muzzle of the ancient shotgun down by his thigh, and he raised the weapon with one savage stroke, his left hand eagerly clutching the slide as his right hand walked to the trigger. The first NVA grabbed the muzzle with one hand as the spoon flew from his grenade. The twelve gauge blew the soldier's head half off, the grenade falling between his companion's legs. The remaining hostile deftly kicked the little bomb off the side of the hull but two more blasts from the scattergun threw him down on top of it.

By now the infantry had circled back and married up with their armored running mates, and the NVA were being driven steadily back. Hawke, uncharacteristically, remained buttoned up. "We got about a dozen on that pass, Ep," he transmitted. "Keep me covered, I'm gonna try for a few more."

Slowly, the tank rumbled into the thicket, and to Epstein's unbelieving eyes, came out on the other side with three more hostiles on the turret, madly beating on the hatches with riflebutts.

"Wish I had a camera," one of the gunners said wistfully, stroking his trigger.

Then the battle fell into a lull. Jeremy unbuttoned

and began to shuck corpses while his loader heaved empty shell casings out of the turret.

A rolling series of sharp explosions, accompanied by a few whistling claymore pellets announced the springing of one of the Striker's claymore traps. And the steady, rhythmic cracking of the M-2 ball from the Garands punctuated the clean-up. Terse reports from Torrion's noncoms detailed the breaking of both ambushes and the success of the airstrike on the southern group.

The Communist forces had taken a solid shellacking, and were rapidly retreating back to the original ambush site, curling around Jenks as a well-laid trap was hammered to shreds.

Savage battles to the east and west of the clearing were driving weary, angry NVA back to the clearing in which Jenks and his comrades were fighting off continual small parties of Northerners who, unable to carry a full assault, concentrated on individual tracks.

Just now, it was Rosie's turn again, and Willie, tired to the point of numb exhaustion, raised his morphine-doped eyes to the edge of the clearing.

"Fuck, Harry," he said. "This morphine's gettin' to me. I'm not seeing double anymore, I'm seein' triple."

"No you're not, Willie," Jenks reassured him. "There really are three times as many of the little bastards out there."

"Oh thanks, for a minute there I thought I was gettin' so spacey I wouldn't know which one to shoot at."

Punctuating their droll remarks with short, expert bursts of machine gun fire, the two saw more and more hostiles crowding into the clearing, until the tall grass seemed to be alive with them.

"This may be *it*, Willie," Jenks said, catching a

glimpse of yet another assault party forming up. "It's been fun, though."

Willie's answer never left his lips as he was interrupted when the clearing exploded into flame, noise and howling, glowing cannister pellets, interspersed with cracking machine gun fire, exploding high explosive shells and the indescribable wall of sound created by an angry charging tank platoon. Franklin had arrived.

"GET FUCKING DOWN!" Jenks yelled, both aloud and into his radio. The warning was unnecessary because all the weary Americans knew from experience the sound and fury of one of Franklin's frontal assaults.

Gator and Alveretti swung left as soon as they cleared the treeline, while Franklin led Gutierrez and Kim around to the right, linking up with Riley's contingent—as Hawke and Epstein entered triumphantly from the west.

Weiss, riding the last track of Riley's section, sat in utter awe of these men and their accomplishments. As events would have it, he was the only one on a radio while the separated elements of Puma held a short, loud, profane reunion.

"Puma 6, this is Big Thunder 6. What the hell is going on down there, Hawke, over?"

"Big 6, this is Sierra 2, Alpha. Riding a Puma track; the situation is resolved, and we are consolidating, over."

After a short period of silence, Barksdall queried. "And just how did you get involved in that fracas, Alpha?"

Weiss, at a loss for a suitably evasive answer, said, "Big 6, this is 2 Alpha. Puma needed a pair of Tango

Charlie's and the representative from Golf 2, and I got shanghaied, over."

A strangled sound, something resembling a groan and a laugh, came with Barksdall's next transmission, as he ordered Weiss to give him a full report upon his return to Oasis.

Chapter Ten

THE M.I. SHOP AT PLEI DUC HAD, BY TACIT AGREEMENT, become Puma's intelligence/operations shop. While Jones was officially the M.I. resident, in practice, either Weiss or Epstein could be found there much of the time. Jones coordinated widely varying sources, and Epstein came in periodically and swapped information with the border troops.

Epstein's Division-wide contacts allowed him to shed a bright light on what appeared to be unconnected happenings in the border AO. At the same time, intel harvested from his unofficial border sources often "jelled" puzzles up at Division. Weiss, for his part, kept Barksdall informed of local goings-on.

A week and a half after the ambush which had severely damaged several of Puma's ACAVs, Weiss and Epstein had arrived at Puma Base for an information swap. Finding Hawke out circulating on Puma business, they spotted Franklin sitting in a lawn chair under the thatched awning of the M.I. shop, one jaw lumped out of shape.

"What happened to you, Jimbo?" Epstein cracked. "Get in a fight with Tien?" After his romance with the lovely Vietnamese girl had come out in the open, Jimbo had become the subject of the usual kidding from his buddies and took it in good grace.

"Naw," he mumbled uncomfortably. "Three teeth gone—abscess at the same time. I got choppered out to Pleiku Air Force Base, and just got back from a triple extraction . . . . Goin' back out tonight, too. Never saw a woman get so happy and so sad so quick."

"Man, that's the pits," Epstein said sympathetically. "I had one of those in high school. How come you're goin' right back out? I thought you'd be glad for some goof-off time after that Chinese cluster-fuck down in the jungle a couple weeks ago."

"Things're warmin' up a bit," Jones interrupted. "Torrion called in yesterday, all bent out of shape about missing a couple of NVA messengers. And we converted a two-tank sweep—that's Scruggs and Alveretti—into a taxi run to deliver their Nungs to Benteen, who's going to try to short-stop the couriers. He oughta have something for us by late today, or early tomorrow."

"That's why I've got to get back so quick," Franklin said. "We're suspecting that the ambush on Jenks was a deliberate attempt to cripple Puma. Those NVA had an uncommon number of RPGs with them."

"I begin to think so, too," Epstein said. "By the way, how's battle damage repair coming?"

"Super," Franklin said, grinning lopsidedly. "You

know that those two crazies, Jenks and Willard, conned us into hauling that rambling wreck of theirs back in?"

Epstein shook his head remembering how close he'd come to obliteration himself.

"Well," Jimbo said, "one ACAV was totaled, and they cut a section of side armor out of it to patch Rosie's belly. And then Jenks and Riley came up with the idea of putting double bellies on all the tracks with a layer of ironwood in between. That'll save us about a ton of weight in the form of sandbags, and cut trannie loss to nothing."

"Damn good thing something is working right," Epstein replied. "The pattern hasn't changed up at Division or Two Corps. They all think the big one will come either north or south. But I'm betting it'll come right through here—all we need is proof. Goddammit, why doesn't something break?"

Miles to the west of Puma Base, Eli Benteen and Wu Sung were preparing to intercept the NVA couriers, hoping to find the last piece in Epstein's puzzle.

Eli was crouched by the side of a border trail, his eyes locked with those of a Bengal tiger. The predator stood, nose questing, stopped in midstride by a familiar scent.

"Don't try it, pussycat," Benteen's hooded gray eyes seemed to say as his hand caressed the CAR-15. "Screw up my day, and you're vulture food!" Resentfully, the huge feline blinked—and was gone. . . .

The great cat had learned, early in its life, that the two-legged combatants were the real masters of the jungle. It would not go far, however; these forest altercations had become a fairly reliable source of meat for the aging tiger. . . .

Wu Sung, whose twenty men were temporarily working with the Amerindian ranger, slid into place beside Benteen. "They come," he whispered. "Fifteen soldiers and two with pistols and dispatch cases. Are we hidden well enough?"

For an answer, Eli pointed at the fresh pug marks in the moist earth of the jungle trail. "Only two minutes ago," he said, enjoying the surprise on Wu Sung's normally stoic face.

Benteen, his four Lurps and Wu Sung's section of two squads were on a critical hunt. Torrion's CIDGs had spotted what appeared to be an NVA courier team, escorted too heavily for them to tackle, and had passed the word to their HQ. The Special Forces captain had no patrols in the area, and any attempt to insert Americans by helicopter could easily scare off their quarry.

A fast consultation with Hawke had resulted in the diversion of one of Puma's mechanized sweeps to a point where the Nungs could pull off a forced night march. Benteen, also reached by radio, had been diverted from his rounds; and by an incredible feat of land navigation, had intercepted Sung and his men—at night.

Working swiftly, the two experienced jungle warriors had set up one of the most deadly and risky ambushes in existence. For this operation, their normal L-shaped claymore/machine gun trap would be too destructive. They wanted the couriers alive, and the escort dead. So it would have to be a man-for-man ambush.

The NVA party had been seen working its way across a stream and was reported to be holding excellent troop intervals, indicating experienced men who would maintain that dispersion in heavy going.

Benteen picked a relatively straight segment of trail, not the sort of location where a jungle-wise commander would be expecting an ambuscade, and set up his forces. With knowledge of the size and spacing of the oncoming unit, a trap could be set to match it.

One man would be walking point. He could be allowed to pass unharmed and policed up later. Behind him would come seven armed men, then two with dispatches, then seven more. All that was required to take them would be sixteen men who could count.

When the main body of the NVA entered the trap, Sung's number one man counted off "one." When the sixteenth man passed him, he would shoot to kill. At the other end of the kill zone, the last man waited; he would let only the point through, and kill the next man. Waiting in the center were Benteen, the Lurps and Wu Sung. When the couriers were in front of them, they would leap, armed only with short-cut lengths of mahogany.

The springing of the hastily planned ambush was announced only by a short rattle of gunfire, one startled yell, and a violent scuffle in the center of the NVA patrol. Benteen and Sung arose, grinning from ear to ear.

"Numma-fuckin'-one G.I.," the Nung said. "Now get point man."

"Maybe not," Eli said, looking down the trail after the last NVA, who'd vanished, covering the pug marks with his own rubber-sandaled prints. "Listen!"

A coughing feline roar, far down the trail, was punctuated by an agonized scream. Then silence fell over the jungle again . . .

* * *

Benteen, bone-weary after a night march, ambush and fast aerial extraction, had dropped two leather dispatch cases and two prisoners off with Jones. And all five Mongoose team members had gone to ground in the cool sanctuary of their bunker.

While the Lurps stacked Z's, however, the atmosphere in the M.I. shack became extremely electric. Epstein, once he heard that Mongoose had made a hit, had decided to stay over, putting his interpreter to work on the two batches of NVA documents. The Viet national who'd been assigned to Epstein was an ARVN lieutenant, and his eyes were bulging as he read the pages before him.

"One pouch contains operational battle plans, sir, and the other contains lists of local contacts, estimates of village sympathies, that sort of thing. I can only do one at a time. Which do you want first?"

Epstein, whose thirst for info had been triggered by what little had been translated, turned to Jones and Franklin, who were the only Puma officers in base. "We need both batches translated simultaneously. Can you get me Van Loc?"

"No way," Franklin replied. "He's out in the hills doing some politicking, trying to convince some other village honchos to stick with our side. They all know there's another invasion coming, but not who'll win."

Epstein, who had, for all practical purposes, dual mental processes, had been reading over his interpreter's shoulder as he talked, and now he picked up a completed page, showing it to the other two.

"Red herrings, my ass," he crowed. "The 65th NVA is just across the border, and they have a battalion of PT-76s with them. Whatever's coming through here is gonna be a bit more than a diversion. You gotta find me another translator ASAP."

Tien Van Loc was never very far from Jimbo Franklin's mind, and now the fact that she, like many educated Vietnamese, was trilingual, crossed his mind. "I think I can get us an interpreter," he told Epstein, reaching for a field phone. "Wait one."

The phone was wired into the commo track and was answered immediately. "Smitty, send a runner for Miss Van Loc, and tell her it's urgent," Franklin ordered. "And is Lieutenant Hawke there?"

"No sir, he's in town. Said he was going to check with Doan about that last row of trip flares, and then he was going to get a haircut. Do you want me to have the runner look him up, too?"

"No, I'll find him when I go in, but keep an eye out for Lieutenant Weiss; he's around someplace."

As soon as Franklin replaced the phone, Epstein had another high point for him. "They're going to hit here, Jimbo. Just like I figured. Here's a reference to exploitation units available if a successful breakthrough is achieved."

Flipping pages, Epstein picked out another. "Regimental Task Force to move east on Highway 19, will use existing supply roads that have been upgraded to handle armor and will intersect 19 at . . . Dammit, the coordinates are in code, and we haven't found the cipher book yet." He was reaching for another page when Ti flowed through the door, temporarily stopping all conversation.

Favoring the other men with a smile, she went directly to Franklin, who blushed. "Hi Jimbo, how is toothache today?"

"Fine, fine," he mumbled, shifting the cotton wad. "Benteen, the one you call the 'Yankee Ghost,' just brought back an incredibly important NVA message catch, and we need an extra interpreter. Will you take this pile and start translating it for us?" He pointed to a table where the contents of the second dispatch case had been spread out. Tien sat down, nodding her head, suddenly lost in the documents.

"They appear to be lists of villages, miss," Epstein said, pointing out some columns on the top sheet. "This one is a village name, the next over is the chief contact in the area, and the third column is the expected sympathy and reaction to liberation. The last one is the immediate tactical disposition . . ." Ti gave him a blank look at the unfamiliar word, and he explained. "That is what those so-called liberators will do to any given hamlet."

Understanding, she nodded her head again, sending a shimmer of light down through her glossy hair, sending a shimmer through Franklin at the same time. He decided to get out while he still had some self-control. He'd always acted the perfect gentleman with the woman, especially in front of the G.I.s, but the more time they spent together, the stronger their mutual attraction grew.

If he didn't watch it, he'd make a damn fool of himself. "I can't do anything more here," he said. "I'm going to pick up the platoon's laundry with a jeep. Call me if anything breaks; I'll keep a helmet radio handy." No one answered as he left; even Tien was buried in the mass of information.

Jeremy, unsuccessful in his search for Le Doan, had stopped in at Van Loc's restaurant, intending to refuel on one of Mama Van Loc's American-Vietnamese concoctions. A meal of Buffaloburgers, fried rice and stir-fried veggies made quite a good combination.

Jeremy asked how the family was, and Mama Van Loc informed him that Tien had been called by

Franklin to help with interpreting. That bit of info got him to speculating just what had been in those dispatches, but Tien's mother distracted his attention with a long series of questions about Franklin.

Unlike most Viets, the elder Van Locs took no exception to the attention Jimbo was paying to their so-beautiful daughter. In fact, they seemed to be openly pleased with the developing relationship, much to Jeremy's amusement. His exec had been converted from self-proclaimed bachelor to ardent suitor in one electrifying moment.

Finishing his meal, Hawke escaped from the questions by professing his need to find Doan, and slinging his poncho over one shoulder, went out into a misty, gloomy day. Monsoon must be starting up early, he thought, as he walked the almost deserted village street.

The horse-drawn generator had been installed in a vacant shop, and a contented purring issued from its stack as Jeremy passed, waving to the Viet mechanics and the two American sergeants who were tending to the requirements of the temperamental machine. Another bond between native and Yankee, he thought. There always seems to be a jeep parked outside the miniature electric company.

Rounding a corner, still deep in thought, he came into the narrow street where Mama-san Lin's laundry sat opposite the barbershop cum whorehouse owned by the venerable Vo Thuot. Jeremy had time only to notice that a mud-spattered jeep and trailer sat in front of the laundry, before a squall of rain came hissing down the alley. Ducking absentmindedly into the first shelter available, he broke one of the cardinal rules of the Vietnam War: "Don't go anywhere alone."

"Welcome, welcome, Lieutenant Hawke," Vo's tinny voice whined. "No business all day, you first customer, please to take seat."

With a grandiose gesture, Vo whisked a canvas cover off the old French barber chair that was his prized possession. The gold-trimmed, leather-cushioned chair had fascinated Hawke since the first time he'd seen it. A relic of the former imperial tenants of the country, it bespoke an earlier, more genteel time —of flower-lined verandas and the sweetness of thousands of bougainvillea lining stuccoed walls.

With a sigh, Hawke plopped into the rich softness of the cushioned chair. The base camp routine, the late hour and digestive contentment all combined with the hypnotic drumming of the rain on the tin roof. Hawke's guard was down, and he fell into a near doze as Thuot yammered on, praising the glories of U.S. technology and products.

The haircut and shave completed, Vo inquired if he might clean the lieutenant's ears and nostrils, to which Jeremy mumbled a sleepy assentive from somewhere out in never-never land. Smiling secretly, Vo rummaged among his utensils, seeking one special instrument.

Epstein, Jones and Weiss were poring over the shoulders of the two Vietnamese who were laboriously translating the now critically important documents. Most of their attention went to the ARVN lieutenant who was assigned to Epstein, because he was handling the operational orders. Tien was simply copying, tediously, long lists of names, places and analysis.

They now had the rough composition of the opposing forces, but couldn't predict just exactly how many would be committed, or where, because of Russian war doctrine which was controlling the preparations. Whichever thrust made the most progress would get the most reinforcement. Their job was to find the trigger for invasion and then try to convince higher powers to give them some backing.

"Here, maybe, it is," the Viet officer said, holding a document aloft. "This says that NVA will strike two days after mass assassinations, when confusion is at its highest, before the enemy (ARVN and U.S. forces) have time to install deputies."

"Oh fine," Epstein said. "Now all we have to do is wait for a few hundred people to get knocked off. They didn't happen to include a list of prospective corpses, did they?"

Epstein had thought he was being very funny, but the ARVN officer soberly ruffled through the mass of paper before him and selected a two-page list of names. "I have not look at heading before now," he explained. "It was only another list like Tien work on."

Excited now, Jones grabbed the list, anxiously checking for some of the known friendly locals that he and Captain Dawson had been working with. Running his practiced eye down the death list, he suddenly stopped, almost paralyzed with shock. "Jeremy Hawke is on this list," he said quietly, "along with all our civil action people—and Van Loc."

The room had gone deathly still, and Weiss stepped over to Tien's side. "Who are the cadre for Plei Duc, Miss Van Loc?" She hadn't gone that far down the list yet, and her eyes flew down the page, stopping at the little town's entry.

"The old barber, Vo Thuot," she said, and then her hands jumped to her mouth, stifling a shriek.

Jones wasted no time. He stepped over, punched Puma frequency into his radio and sent out a general alarm. "Any and all Puma stations. Find Puma 6, he is under assassination orders. Find and apprehend Vo Thuot, he is VC."

"I'll give 'em a few seconds and repeat this," he said, turning around, but he was talking to an empty room and the sound of running engines could be heard, receding into the distance. Resolutely, he turned back to the mike. "Any and all Puma. . . ."

Jimbo Franklin had been spending a pleasant half-hour kidding with Mama-san Lin, the middle-aged proprietress of one of the town's laundries, when he saw Hawke disappear into Vo's establishment. Something not quite Kosher about the situation tickled his consciousness, but another of Lin's attempts at fractured English claimed his attention. He continued the banter, until she asked, "Why you no turn off helmet?"

"What helmet?" he asked blankly. And she pointed to the G.I. steel pot on which his elbow was resting. It was equipped like Hawke's, with one of the miniature radios. Both tankers, however, had been so deafened by 90 millimeter guns and RPG hits, that they couldn't hear them unless they were actually wearing the rigs. When his attention was focused on it, though, he could hear a tiny, insect-like voice issuing from it. Now the tone was frantic. Curiously, he set the helmet on his head, and Jones's voice blasted into his ears.

Jeremy, almost totally supine in the reclining barber chair, had just sleepily given permission to Vo for the extra service, when the side of Vo's head instantly erupted in a grisly shower of blood, bone fragments and gray matter as the crash of a .45 filled the small hootch with deafening sound.

"HOLY SHIT!" Hawke screamed, flinging himself from the chair in a diving roll, drawing his own .45 from a shoulder holster.

"Gettin' kinda careless, ain't ya, Jer?" Jimbo snickered, leaning insolently against the doorframe, holding a still-smoking Colt. "Ya get dead real quick when you forget where you're at, pard. Lucky for you I saw you come in here, and even luckier that Mama-san Lin could hear this radio—or you'd be history. Look at what that little shit was gonna clean your ears with!"

Trying to avoid the mess, all that remained of the barber's head, Jeremy looked at Vo's right hand, and what might have been, turned his heart to ice. Protruding from the old man's clawed fingers was a six-inch needle-pointed ice pick. As he sat back down in the chair, the ice pick in his own hand, four jeeps skidded to a halt in the narrow alleyway and a dozen people rushed in, all talking at once.

Chapter Eleven

VAN LOC'S ANNOUNCEMENT HAD BEEN LIKE A KICK IN THE belly to Franklin, as he, Hawke and Jones were gathered with the village elders in Loc's restaurant after the assassination attempt. The old man had informed them that his daughter, Tien, would be departing within the week for college—in Paris, where she would be safe from whatever the future held.

Franklin's heart had skipped a beat, his love-shrouded mind reeling at the thought of not having her around to talk to. Neither Jimbo nor Ti could do anything but stare sadly at one another.

Franklin was in a cloud for the remainder of that day, and into the night. He'd never been taken by anyone to the degree that Ti had overpowered him. That little slice of his daily life that he looked forward to was being snatched away from him. Sure, it would be much safer for her to be out of the country; he knew that. But the selfish part of a lover's psyche could not be denied. She'd become his daily jolt of sweetness. His reminder that there was indeed something worth preserving in this hellhole they'd been thrust into. He felt cheated, denied and empty.

He'd let himself go, his mind flying, soaring over the grit and blood of war around them whenever he and Ti were able to get away by themselves, outside the village. He would lay back against a rock or tree, listening to the light melody of her innocent voice, floating on the softness of her childlike desires and her descriptions of the natural beauty of her country. To him, Tien Lin was peace, beauty, love and happiness, all bound into one incredibly simple, giving human being. James Franklin had been unconsciously planning his life around her; he didn't sleep at all well that night.

Somehow he sensed that Ti would be at the well bunker earlier than usual the next morning, and he was waiting just as the sun's rays first cracked over the low-lying cloud bank to the east.

She slipped into the dark coldness of the bunker without a sound, her head held low, her hands clasped tightly together in front of her. In the pale light of dawn, Jimbo could see the large tears tracking the softness of her cheeks.

She did not take her usual place on the hard concrete bench next to him. Instead, she came directly to him, sliding silently astride his knees, surrounding him with the warmth of her arms and perfumed veil of her long hair.

He'd touched her only once before, a brief kiss on the cheek. Now, the magnetic touch of their bodies seemed to ignite another life within her. Suddenly, she was torn with wretching sobs, flooding his face with tears. Her crying tore at his heart, ate at his very being, making him forget what he'd worked so hard at planning to say to her.

Regaining some composure, Ti took his face in her hands, kissing him softly on the mouth. "I love you, my American Jimbo. I love you more than my life. I know that my father means well for me, to keep me from harm. You know that I must do as he wants. I do not want this for you, for me. I want for you to be with me forever. My heart hurts with a pain so terrible that I cannot describe. I do not want to leave, my Jimbo. Please help me be strong."

Again her composure disappeared in a flood of new tears and sobbing.

"Tien Lin, you will always be with me, always in my heart. No matter what happens here, or later, I will forever love you," he whispered, looking deeply into her liquid brown eyes.

The astounding information that they'd discovered the day before had not only jarred Van Loc, it had triggered Hawke as well. Jones, Hawke and Van Loc had gone into Oasis that afternoon. Hawke would be having an operational briefing with Barksdall, while Jones and Van Loc would continue on to Pleiku with Dawson on "unspecified civil business," probably involving a certain missionary with leftist leanings. All three would be gone until sometime tomorrow.

Franklin had been left in charge and had been busy all day supervising the preparation of Puma's ACAVs for whatever might be coming their way. After a few beers with Riley, he made his way to the bunker and flopped into his cot, grateful for the new "base camp" mattress. With Jones gone overnight, he was all alone.

Shortly after midnight he heard a light scraping in the sand on the wood step leading into the bunker. Grabbing his carbine, he moved to the foot of the cot, next to the wall enclosing the bunker entrance, shielding him from the doorway.

A low, barely perceptible whisper broke the quiet of the bunker's tomblike interior. "L'tenant Jimbo, there is someone who must see you now, please," came the choppy, unmistakable voice of Doan.

"Doan, what the hell is it? Who wants me now?" Franklin croaked to the shadow in the opening.

Without a sound, another figure broke from the deep shadows of the entrance and Doan disappeared in the darkness. Before he could speak, Franklin was smothered in the flower petal softness of Tien's kisses. Franklin tripped backward and they both sprawled onto the mattress in a groping, caressing heap. Fortunately, the bunk was a G.I. issue, steel model.

Ti had shed her clothing and her supple warmth was locked to his body. "I love you for all my life, Jimbo. Somehow, somewhere, we will be together again. I come here to give you my childhood. I want no other man, ever. Make love to me, Jimbo, all this night. Hold me. I want to feel your life in me. I want to feel that when I am so far away from you," she whispered hoarsely, kissing his face, his eyes, his lips—her tiny hand shyly tracing the hardness between his legs.

They cried, sobbed and laughed their love to one another in the close blackness of the bunker, oblivious to the reminders of war—the eerie golden shadows cast by the night watch's flares that popped overhead every so often. They knew only themselves, the screaming ecstasy of her first shattering climax, the giving of her very soul.

At last they gave themselves up to delicious exhaustion, locked in the embrace of their final lovemaking. And only when Doan slipped silently into the bunker and shook them did they awaken.

The night had barely begun to fade into the gray of first light when he held her for the last time, seated on the cold bench of the well bunker where they'd first spoken.

"Your absence will leave a big hole in my life, Ti."

"I will not forget you, my love, my tall American. I know of the temptations and distractions you fear for me in Paris. But I will always be faithful to your love. When you leave my country, please remember Tien Lin. America is such a big wondrous place with many beautiful, yellow-haired women."

"Ti, no one could ever take your place. When I leave here, I'll be in Paris two days after touching down in San Francisco. I will make you my wife, lovely Tien Lin."

"I will not see you again before I go to Pleiku, Jimbo. I do not think that I could bear the hurt of leaving you again. My father will go with me to Pleiku. He says that your colonel has arranged for a helicopter to take us there. You know, I have never flown before."

"I must go now, Jimbo Franklin. Remember me in your dreams," she whispered, kissing his fingers and placing his hand over the warmth at her loins.

He could only shake his head dumbly, tears streaking the stubble on his cheek. "Go with God, Jimbo. My heart is with your heart. I will always be yours."

Breaking their embrace, she began to sob and turning quickly, fled into the red glow of the new dawn.

He sat unmoving for a long time in this cool place, their place. He was not afraid to cry.

* * *

When Hawke stepped off the helipad at Oasis, he found Epstein and Weiss waiting for him. "Time's a wastin', Jer; the wheels are starting to turn," Epstein said. "Barky wants us in his personal office five minutes ago at the latest. What took you so long?"

"Hey, lighten up. That's only a Huey, not an F-100, and even my present exalted rank doesn't rate a private chopper."

"You may wish you had your own gunship after this operation," Weiss said. "The intel breakdown is looking even worse than yesterday's skimming."

"Well, here we are," Epstein said as they approached the sandbagged trailer. "It's your Battalion, you knock on the dragon's lair."

"Come in, gentlemen, sit down," said a surprisingly cordial Barksdall.

"I don't have to tell you how grave the situation is. You were instrumental in obtaining the data. Division, at first, was a bit sticky about your preempting the digestion process, until Epstein reminded them that Hawke wouldn't have survived had you not done so.

"Division is now processing those documents, and the couriers that Benteen provided have been most cooperative . . . they seem to have been somewhat ill-treated on their journey back to HQ."

Jeremy grinned wickedly at that comment. Having one's supposedly professional escort annihilated and then being clubbed unconscious by a war-whooping Amerindian would have to be a bit unsettling.

"Their data must've revealed quite a lot, sir, otherwise we wouldn't have been called in," Hawke said. "And Franklin tells me that his line platoon has been alerted direct, instead of through the Mike Force relay."

"That is correct, Hawke, due to the present, shall we say, unbalanced disposition of our forces. Puma is now the only armor in the area, and I don't have to spell the consequences out for you. Due to that fact, Division has given me a free hand, and I intend to play it to the utmost. Epstein, you have the advantage of the latest info from the wizards at HQ. Suppose you give us a quick digest of just what we're facing."

"Yessir, I do," Epstein said, opening a manila folder. "First off, we now know for certain that at *least* one NVA main force regiment is just across the border—with an indeterminate number of both T-54 and PT-76 Russian tanks. They are now fully supplied and marshaling to move. The courier carried a personal alert message to the VC, B3 Front Officer, stating that an invasion force would be crossing the border tomorrow night and that he was to render whatever assistance he could. The size of the force was not specified, but it will certainly contain armor.

"Second, they are to make a night march into the Republic of Vietnam (RVN), and assault a large number of objectives, some of which we think are simply too hard for what we *think* they have available. They would seem to have something besides armor up their collective sleeves . . .

"Third, acting on Benteen's data, another Lurp team, code-named Ferret, has found and traced a large, high-speed trail." Now Epstein stood and picked up a pointer, stepping to the colonel's private situation map. "Right about here, north of 19W, where it crosses over into Cambodia."

Barksdall stood, interrupting Epstein. "Thank you, Lieutenant, that's got us up-to-date. If the NVAs' intelligence is at least half accurate, they know, sure as hell, that we don't have squat in the way of armor to counter any mechanized thrust into our area. With the 10th Cav out east on the roads, and our own line companies up north, all I have to plug the dike with is Puma."

"Sir, how can we do any good with an ACAV force?" Hawke asked. "All I have in the immediate area are two M-48s, Bravo 6 and the dozer tank. Franklin's platoon is so far back in the hills that it's doubtful if he could even get there by tomorrow night. Plus, he'll need a refueling for any extended operations."

"Bear with me, son," Barksdall said, moving the pointer to a freshly inked-in route. "The Lurps found, further east, along that high-speed trail, a potential kill zone, past this twisted section here. But before the NVA could cut into 19W, the road traverses a steep-sided slope. The south side drops off into a 150-foot vertical cliff. The north side is blocked, for a length of over two hundred meters, by a vertical rock outcropping about one meter high. Once any unit is in that stretch, they cannot maneuver to their flanks."

The pointer moved again, northward up the slope. "If you get into position here, along this ridge, you will command the kill zone. If you hit them at night from atop this ridge, you could inflict maximum casualties. Because of the terrain angle, neither the T-54 or PT-76 can elevate its gun high enough to reach you. They would have to break out of the death strip and get past the rock wall to turn your flanks."

"That comment about turning our flanks is what bothers me, sir."

Barksdall smiled, turning to Epstein. "Your turn, Epstein. I believe you've arranged for some extremely competent light infantry who know the area."

Epstein again put on his conspiratorial grin. "Our good buddy, the Green Beanie type from Georgia, will be riding his Mike Force people with you, Jer. While you're getting into position, he'll lay a good number of anti-tank mines in areas that any tank would have to traverse to get out of the ambush. Plus, his little people have about thirty RPGs that they seem to have acquired from some mysterious source."

That relieved Hawke's mind considerably and he quickly thought over the possibilities. "We'll have TacAir and Arty laid on, naturally; and that leaves only setting up the restocking for Puma heavy. . . ."

"That's already laid on, son," the colonel said. "Weiss here is handling that, and has already laid on the Chinooks. He'll personally escort Franklin and his new maps out to the platoon, and find out if there's anything else they need.

"Now," the colonel said, rising and heading for the door, "Lieutenant Epstein's boss wants him back ASAP. Weiss has his job to do. Hawke, you'll come with me down to the tank park, I've got a new type of combat vehicle for Puma."

"Shouldn't I be getting back to base, sir?" Hawke asked as he and Barksdall walked across the dusty, bunker-dotted Oasis. "There's plenty for me to do before 1700 which is move-out time."

"Well that's what you have a platoon sergeant for, Hawke," the colonel said. "Weiss will pick up Franklin in an hour, and he's dropping SGM Hagerty off at the same time. If he and Riley can't run Puma's checklists off, we're all in trouble.

"Now, young Mr. Hawke, you're going to relieve me of a white elephant that I believe will be of more use to you than me."

"What's that, sir?"

Shaking his head at the vagaries of DOD, Barksdall replied, "The 88th, like every other armored unit in the theater, has been issued a 20-millimeter anti-aircraft vehicle for evaluation. Since AA equipment often adapts to armor use, I want you to *evaluate* this beast for me. Have fun!"

They'd entered the gloomy depths of a framed maintenance tent, and Barksdall pointed to a peculiarly rigged APC. Walking closer, Jeremy looked intently at the machine, noting that its crew, who were standing nervously by, had painted the name "Hagar" on the gunshield, which housed an ominous-looking cluster of 20-millimeter gun barrels. The Gatling gun, modernized and driven by a high-torque electric motor, had reentered the field of combat.

The weapon, snuggled in Hagar's cupola, was capable of delivering up to 100 half-pound warheads per *second* of operation. For years, these guns, known as Vulcans, had been part of aircraft armament and had been used in thousands of strafing runs.

As Jeremy eagerly swung into the gun mount, Barksdall said, "We have no use for close-in air defense in this war, so take it, and you're welcome. Just watch your ammo consumption."

"THANK YOU, sir," Hawke said, and was unable to resist a boyish-sounding, "Oh boy, wait'll Jimbo sees this sucker!"

"Good God, Jimbo! How the hell do you run tanks in that green carpet down there?" Weiss asked.

"Very carefully," Franklin answered, shouting over the roar of the Chinook's turbines.

The two officers were riding the lead ship of the two that were to restock Puma's tank platoon from the air, making a fast cross-country run possible. Each chopper carried ammo and rations internally, and a 500-gallon "Blivit" of diesel fuel was slung underneath. In addition, Franklin was custodian of the usual bag of mail from the World, and several sacks of Mama-san Lin's carefully mended and ironed laundry.

The co-pilot turned to where the two were sitting on jumpseats and addressed Franklin. "Sir, there's a voice like a cement mixer on the air; says he's Puma 1-4. And how big an LZ do we want?"

Taking the mike, Franklin got in touch with Scruggs. "Yo, Gator, we're bringing in two hooks with fuel and ammo, get to it!"

"That's a roger, Lieutenant," Gator said, turning to the group of tank commanders who were gathered on Ballbuster's back deck. "All right you apes, get to it. Form on me, two meter interval, let's clean off the top of this hill."

As soon as the TCs were aboard, the five tanks formed a line which, pivoting like the spoke of a giant wheel, made three full circles around the top of the hill, leveling even trees up to a foot in diameter. Once this was accomplished, they separated into two groups, one at each end of the combat LZ. Maneuvering cautiously, the giant copters set a blivit on one tank deck in each group. And as soon as the crews had unshackled the ungainly bladders, the birds settled delicately to earth in the center of the new LZ.

While the crews went about the business of resupplying the needs of their war machines, the TCs again gathered on Ballbuster's deck, where Franklin and Weiss brought them up-to-date.

"Enemy tanks, by God!" Scruggs exclaimed, a predatory gleam in his eyes. "I ain't laid sights on a Communist tank since Korea, and these M-48s are sure as hell a lot more tank than a Sherman ever was. You think we can get this mob on up there in time to horn in on the fracas, sir?"

"Depends on the condition of those streams and our buddy, Chuck, Gator," Franklin said as he continued to enter new information on maps and hand them out to the tank commanders.

"Best of luck, Franklin, and give 'em hell!" Weiss hollered over his shoulder as he loped over to the last of the hooks.

Giving his friend a reassuring wave, Franklin slid off the platoon sergeant's tank and walked over to his own Big Bastard. "Crank 'er up, Dean. Let's go find the war!"

Chapter Twelve

FROM HAWKE'S VANTAGE POINT, THE POSITION ATOP THE ridge, north of the trail, commanded a perfect view of the route below. Ambushed along this stretch, any force below would have no place to go, save over the steep embankment to the south—a near vertical drop of over two hundred feet. Torrion's sappers had nearly completed laying the large anti-tank mines. They'd also sprinkled some claymore mines along the kill zone on the south edge of the trail.

Two 55-gallon drums of napalm had been hauled along on Hawke's APCs and planted at either end of the beaten zone. Blocks of TNT under them made a fugasse that would both propel and ignite the jellied gasoline. The flaming hell would be blasted over each end of the NVA column when the ambush was triggered. Above anything else, the average soldier hates fire. The fear of being burned alive can turn the best trained, toughest soldiers into a raving, uncontrolled mob.

Darkness came quickly as the Puma crews settled into their vehicles, ready at their guns, awaiting the enemy column from the west. Captain Torrion had set out two deep LPs (listening posts), the first over 500 meters to the west, beyond the series of turns leading into the ambush site.

The second was set up at 250 meters, again to the west, but further up the ridge to the north. One-third of the CIDG Strikers manned defensive positions in a half-perimeter just north of the Puma Force, covering its back. The remainder were interspersed with the PCs, below the military crest of the ridgeline.

The first sign of the NVA was a report received from the far LP. Several NVA, carrying perfume lamps, had passed their location heading east. They could also hear the faint sounds of vehicles, also apparently heading east. . . .

Hawke's skin crawled at that bit of news. C'mon, Jimbo, get here with your big guns, he prayed silently.

Puma, at this point, had only two tanks, set in ambuscade, loaded with their precious few heat rounds. Those two tanks were dug in at the west end of Hawke's line with orders to await enemy armor, and not reveal themselves until ordered. They were Jeremy's insurance policy.

"Puma, this is Viper," came the whispered call from Green Beret Captain Torrion. "Lima Poppa 2 reports that the first group of gooks is now passing them. Lima Poppa 1 now has a solid column of NVA passing below them. The sound of the vehicles is louder, but still well behind the foot troops."

"Roger, Viper," Hawke said. "Keep yer eyes open

to the north. Don't fire until I hit the claymores and the foo-gas. I want 'em shittin' all over themselves in panic."

"We're ready, Puma. Viper out."

"Six, I've got 'em in front of my position now," the voice of Sergeant Riley croaked in Hawke's ears.

"Roger, 2-4, stand by."

Now Hawke could make out the faint blue points of light made by the perfume lamps below him. Behind them, he saw more lamps and an unending shadow of men marching on either side of the road. By the time they reached the edge of the kill zone, there would be a couple hundred men strung out below along the trail, totally oblivious of the curtain of steel awaiting them.

"Blue lights just passed," reported the track at the eastern end of the line. This group of less than a dozen would be taken care of by Torrion's little people when the balloon went up.

"Stand by, Puma."

"FIRE."

The charges beneath the 55-gallon drums of napalm were set off first. Set into the ground at 45 degrees, their flaming, jellied contents were blown across an area fifty meters wide, and nearly as deep. Anything within that blast cone received a coating of the clinging, fiery hell.

At least a quarter of the kill zone, at either end, was lit up by flaming torches; once men, now mindless lumps of pain, stumbling blindly around their burial ground.

Hawke lifted the small board containing a switch and ten sets of wire terminals. Throwing the switch, electrical impulses raced down ten sets of wire to ten M-18A1, claymore mines, evenly distributed along the entire length of the killing zone. In one merging series of white flashes, 7500 white-hot, steel ball bearings tore through the confused, milling file of terrified NVA, killing dozens of troops not kissed by the agonizing caress of the napalm.

Every gun on the ridge opened fire as the claymores blew. Ruby tracers plunged into the crowd of men below. A few green and white tracers left the trailbed in a futile response as communist gunners opened up. The northern edge of the trail was bordered by a three-foot bank, offering some protection—but not enough. The rain of whining, spattering, bouncing rounds found all corners of the zone.

Now, more ruby tracers joined the chaos, streaking in from the east and west, cutting down those attempting to find safety there. Torrion's flank security had moved closer to the fray and was adding an additional demoralization factor to the shrieking horror of the moment. Puma's corpse factory was in full production.

Suddenly there was no noise. Only the scattered popping of a few rounds cooking off in some flames below. A thick cloud of cordite smoke clung to the earth below the tracks, almost masking the scene of death. Cries and moans could be heard from the wounded. A few shapes could be seen staggering around the smoldering graveyard. But the remainder of the NVA battalion had fled the field.

Another sound also faded to the west . . . the re-treating crackle of exhausts and metallic clanking of tracks. The instant overwhelming volume of fire from the ridge and the blasts of the claymores and fugasse must have decisively moved the intruders to another, less costly course of action—but definitely not in

Puma's direction. "Thank the saints for that," Hawke said, removing his CVC helmet. He emptied a canteen of water over his sweat-soaked head.

The NVA had blindly walked into a massive ambush, confident that they were safe in their Cambodian sanctuary and infiltration routes. They reeled in a blind rush and fled back to their supposedly safe haven.

Maybe someday Puma would be unfettered by stupid rules of non-engagement and political cowardice, allowing them to go after the enemy's sanctuaries, to interdict their lines of supply, and to inflict maximum casualties on the NVA in their own backyard. Wasn't that the way wars were supposed to be fought? Take the war to the enemy . . . defeat him in every way! Find him, fix him, kill him. Some war! Body counts and body bags. . . . Where the hell was Jimbo?

Alveretti heaved up out of the inky water into the red-tinted beam of Franklin's flashlight and the subdued glow of Bearcat's nightlights, pouring muddy water and curses. "Sir, we'll never get the tanks across this damn crick while it's dark. There's too many damn boulders and big holes to be safe."

"I mighta guessed as much," Franklin growled as he watched Bronco's TC shuck off his dripping clothes and safety rope. "We're going to have to keep working west, upstream, till we find a crossing."

"Shit!" came an obviously worried voice from behind him. "Then we won't be gettin' there in time to help Lootenant Hawke and the Strikers—they're on their own for a while."

"You got that right, Krause," Franklin answered. "And by the looks of things, the man could use a little help right about now." Turning eastward, he pointed at the sky. "Just look at that shit-storm, will you, those tracers make it look like the northern lights."

Indeed, the eastern ridgelines were lit up like the Aurora Borealis, as green, white and orange tracers shot into the sky like dying fireflies, and the orange glow of tank guns fought through the triple canopy of jungle. What they'd guesstimated as a battalion-sized force of NVA must have stumbled straight into Jeremy's mechanized ambush.

Without any real "hard" intelligence data, Franklin wondered if any of the T-54 or PT-76 tanks, spotted in Cambodia a week ago, had accompanied the force into Vietnam. Hawke's M-48s would have little trouble with any ComBloc armor, but the ACAVs would be sitting ducks, even with LAWs (Light Anti-Tank Weapons). . . . Enough second guessing. This platoon had to get across this damned river before first light or risk observation by enemy patrols.

Toggling his mike switch, Franklin ordered his men to crank up and move out along the riverbank. They continued on their westerly course for nearly an hour, searching for a crossing, but steadily drawing away from the fireworks to the east. The battle had grown in intensity, with the orange glare of artillery and the intense white of air-dropped flares adding to the multi-hued brilliance of that piece of sky. The fiery red tongue of Puff the Magic Dragon licked across the ridgeline, lapping up lives by the dozen.

Finally, Kim's voice cut through the crackle in Franklin's headset. "Five, this is 1-5. We just struck it lucky. Mister Chuck just fuck up big-time. Come see, quick!"

Halting the column, Jimbo grabbed his carbine

from its ready spot on the cupola, and vaulted from the front slope into the tracks of the lead tank. Pungi stakes were an everpresent danger, especially along possible routes of travel—so he took no chances. As he stalked past Bearcat, Kim's diminutive figure emerged from the shadowed bulk of the tank, gesturing to the edge of the stream.

"Lookie here, Lieutenant. Charlie's got a regular highway goin' through here, and watch this. . . ." Much to Franklin's amazement, the little sergeant appeared to be walking on water as he crossed the stream.

The NVA had built a bridge over the watercourse below the surface. In the dim cat-eye lights of the tank, Franklin could see that the secondary layer of tree branches overhead had been lashed together, making the installation undetectable from the air. Checking the sides of the bridge, he could see a well-traveled corrugated surface of bamboo and packed earth.

Franklin had switched his headgear to the steel helmet with the miniature radio, and he reached up and keyed the transmitter. "All Big Boys follow Bearcat across the blue line, then stop and set up temporary security; 1-4, you're in charge for a while."

After hearing Scruggs's gravel-voiced affirmative, he turned to Kim, who also served as the platoon's demo expert.

"After you've got your tank across, move on up the road about a hundred meters. Have your gunner keep his IR light on the trail—just in case. Then hot-foot it back here with a couple of satchel charges. We're gonna rig a big surprise for our little buddies."

Not too long after Ballbuster had rolled over the subsurface bridge, Kim came charging back down the column. "I brought along some trip wire for the fuses, Lieutenant," he puffed. "And you might like this little jewel, too."

Dropping the canvas bags, he handed the astonished Franklin a large, conical engineer-shaped charge —thirty pounds of aimable explosive.

"Where in the hell did you dig that thing up, Kim? I haven't seen one of those since Armor Officers' Basic."

"Let's just say that a certain engineer sergeant owed me a small favor. I'd suggest that we put it at one end of the bridge, in some of that soft gravel-sand, and aim it straight up."

It took less than an hour to set the automatic ambush. First, they dug a hole for the shaped charge, arming it with a variety of cross-linked fuses. If a vehicle didn't set off the charge with a pressure device, its front wheels would catch a submerged trip wire. As an extra bonus for any inquisitive VC sappers, several booby-trapped claymores and isolated blocks of C-4 were set in the bushes bordering the stream. Franklin had just finished setting the last explosive snare, when Krause came running down the road.

"Lieutenant Hawke's on the horn, sir. He needs you ASAP!"

Stepping up to the nearest tank, Franklin picked up the external handset, switching it over to radio transmit. "This is Puma 5. Hey, Jer, haven't you kicked their asses yet? Over."

"Never saw so many of the little bastards close up," Hawke reported excitedly. "We caught them all packed together in a nice long column, right on that improved trail we suspected. Must've been a couple hundred got into the "L" before we opened up. We heard engines coming up behind this bunch, but they high-tailed it when the shooting started. Torrion's little people are out there now, policing up after our mess.

"Where the hell are you guys, Jimbo? We thought you might have cut into some of these people's flankers, over."

"This is 5. No such luck. We got hung up by one of those unmarked streams and had to find a crossing. Ole Charlie's put up one of those underwater bridges like the Russians used in WWII. We're across, but we've modified the architecture a bit—if you get my drift, over."

"Good thought, Jimbo. Just mark it on the map for our side. How soon do you think your element will be able to get up the trail we're on? Over."

"We're on our way now, Puma, but it will not be before daybreak, over."

"Roger, 5. I don't think that the people who survived and bugged out are going too far back right now. You know what valley we're in. Do you think you can cut onto their road and get ahead of them? Over."

"Puma, this is 5, wait one."

After an intense map scrutiny with his TCs, Franklin again got hold of Hawke. "Six, this is 5. As far as I can tell, we're on the same road unless it takes an unpredicted turn over one of these green mountains, which I doubt."

"That's what I hoped," Hawke replied. "Take a look at your map. Do you see a stream paralleling the border from the south, bending across the trail?"

"Rog, Jer. I don't have the red line on my map, but the terrain features match up, over."

"Okay. Now you see where the stream bends; the

trail has to cross there because of the escarpment and high banks to the north, and the same problem to the east. It's an old geological fault. Can you get there?"

Franklin had been tracing the line of the NVA road under the red battle light inside his turret, and he suddenly figured what Hawke was up to.

"Gotcha, Puma. Looks like some pretty heavy timber to the west of that cut. What does Viper say? Will it hide our tanks? Over."

After a brief consultation with Torrion, Hawke came back with an affirmative; and Franklin came up with a final suggestion.

"Okay, leader, we'll mosey on up there and get set. I'd suggest that you move out just before light, and kinda keep pressure on the buggers—just to keep their minds on losing and moving."

"That's a rog, Jimbo. We'll lean on them from this end and keep the little bastards honest."

"Roger. We'll be in touch as soon as we're in position, 5 out."

Franklin put the column in motion, with Kim in the lead, scanning the road ahead with his searchlight on infra-red. Because of the near total darkness created by the interwoven branches above and the muffling effect of the foliage, the tanks moved in cloaking silence. Even the noise of their engines would not be heard by anyone up ahead until the last moment.

Gator, putting Ballbuster in the tailend slot, swung his IR light to the rear, covering their backs while the rest of the TCs swept the sides of the jungle trail with the IR binoculars.

The five tanks rolled smoothly along the well-constructed trail, encountering no obstacles except for a few stream crossings. At one of these the lead tank commander waded cautiously through the ford, and

Franklin began to wonder about the accuracy of his map. They'd investigated several fuel caches, finding them unguarded, almost as if. . . . No, he put the thought out of his mind. They couldn't have gone that far west, even if this was a branch of the Ho Chi Minh Trail.

Three hours after the conversation with Hawke, the procession slowed and Kim came back on the air. "Five, this is 1-5, the land is starting to drop off up here, and I feel water in the air."

"Puma heavy, this is 5. Shut 'em down," Franklin ordered, straining to hear any sound of water before the tropical night chorus resumed. "Can you see water, Kim?"

"Negative, but I can hear it. I got a man out now, checking. By the looks of my IR picture, the ground opens up for a hundred meters or so, along the blue line. The picture across the stream is solid, straight up, and the road curves left along the base of the escarpment."

"Roger, Bearcat, we copy," Franklin acknowledged. "Tango Charlies, meet me behind the lead tank, 5 out."

Before long, Franklin and his four tank commanders were squatting in a circle behind Kim's tank, and the lieutenant was laying out his intended trap.

"Here we are on the map," he said, pointing at a crossing. "And right out there is the water." Lighting up a portion of ground with his red-lensed flashlight, he smoothed a section of dirt, drawing a crude picture with a fingertip.

"This line is the stream, there; and here we are on the road." He drew another line, with five dots on it.

"Now Kim and Alveretti will cut left, or downstream, and keep inside the treeline. Scruggs and

Gutierrez cut right; and all four tanks set up at least twenty meters inside the brush. I'll roll forward and slide just off the road, even with you. Once you're in place, shut 'em down and check out your areas. When you've got some daylight to work with, set out at least three claymores each."

The circle of noncoms had been quietly nodding their heads as he talked, and there were no questions. As he stood up, they all silently melted into the darkness. And one by one, the 52-ton murder machines growled into life, crunching off into the heavy foliage—TCs walking ahead, feeling the way.

Soon, Franklin was in place too, scanning the crossing with their only starlight scope. Along with the night sounds of insects, he could hear the gurgle of the river and the far-off howling of a lovesick orangutan.

The "all set" report had been sent to Hawke, who'd now broken out of ambush position and was rolling after the NVA. No danger sound could yet be heard, but the predawn quiet was broken by the hushed voice of Hawke, using the private Puma frequency.

"Five, this is Puma. Be advised that a LRRP unit, just extracted, spotted the NVA headed back your way in the company of three PT-76s, and four truckloads of assorted dinks and gear. The tanks are leading; and get this, with their guns to the rear, we must really be getting on their nerves. As best as I can tell, they're two klicks from you. Good shooting, mate! Over."

"This is 5, I copy, out," Franklin replied, the pre-battle knot tightening in his stomach.

"Puma heavy, you all copy that, over?"

One by one, the TCs checked in, the roll call ending with salty old Scruggs's "Hot Dawg, it's clobberin' time!"

The humor, though, failed to evict the butterflies,

now grown to the size of buzzards, from Franklin's digestive tract. Only the noise and confusion of wild combat could do that—and then only for a while.

Gradually, the indigo of the moonless night gave way to the misty gray of early dawn. The nighttime chorus of frogs and insects gave way to the morning serenade of awakening birds and primates. The area surrounding the river crossing slowly revealed itself to the concealed warriors.

The river was approximately thirty meters wide, and at this point, quite shallow. Half oval clearings met the banks on both sides, and no attempt had been made to hide the passage of both wheeled and tracked vehicles. Again, an uneasiness assailed Franklin. The NVA were never this careless, unless . . . Maybe he'd somehow gotten into Cambodia.

A faint sound of engines began to be audible, and Franklin's attention focused to the east side of the river where the road came curving out of steep cliffs. Both up- and downstream the river was walled in, preventing any escape or maneuver. By blind luck, they'd set up a perfect killing ground.

Rapidly the sound of engines swelled to a threatening roar, and panicked jungle birds erupted from the green tunnel across the river. The clinging mist had nearly dissipated when the bow of the lead tank pushed its way around the bend. Its gun had been swung to the front, angled off to one side.

The second tank still had its turret faced to the rear. As the driver of the lead machine ground down through the gears and entered the water, the third one was revealed as a BTR-50. Not a tank, but an armored personnel carrier, crammed with small brown men in green fatigues and pith helmets.

All of the visible enemy personnel seemed more

concerned with what lay to their rear than what might be ahead. Franklin was conscious of the subtle movement of the turret as Krause hand-cranked the massive gun to the target, avoiding the giveaway mechanical howl of the turret motor. Just as the lead tank began its exit on this side of the stream, two trucks loaded to the rails lurched into the clearing, closely followed by two more. Then several columns of infantry, quick-marching in ragged formation, came into view, and Franklin could actually feel the predatory anticipation of his troops.

"Okay, Krause," he said quietly, "let 'em have it!"

The concussive BLAM-WHAM of a tank gun firing and hitting at close range blew away Jimbo's butterflies and triggered the other four nineties. Krause's first HEP round blasted a gaping hole in the PT-76's gun mantlet, sending the gun back into the rear of the turret. His second shot only rearranged the junk created by the first.

On either side of Big Bastard, Bronco and Bandido fired in unison. The BTR was hit nearly broadside from the right, and the second PT-76 at the base of the turret. The second hit on the BTR split open its fuel cell and the Russian-made PC blew itself apart in a shower of flaming fuel, shards of melted aluminum, and bits of human bodies. Another hit on the remaining PT blew its turret off the hull, throwing it forward where it stuck, gun down in the stream, like a giant sign.

High explosive rounds from the other two tanks exploded among the troops who were clinging to the trailing trucks, sending mangled, screaming bodies in all directions. Ruptured fuel tanks ignited, spewing fiery diesel in all directions over the remnants of the NVA lead unit. The chatter of machine guns and the sharp "cracks" of exploding claymores were added to the cacophony, sounding counterpoint to the tanks' booming cannons.

Far back in the distance, the heavy yammer of Browning .50s indicated that some of the NVA's trailing units had turned to their rear, only to be given the choice between the ACAVs and the cannister-belching tanks. Hell's hornets were now howling across the river ford, shredding any exposed hostile.

"Puma 5, this is Puma. What's your status? Sounds like hell just opened the mass entry gate, over."

"This is 5," Franklin responded, "I do believe we made a very big dent in somebody's master plan. Two light tanks and one BTR amphibian are now a flaming garbage dump. And I don't know how many dead and wounded are lying around. This place is a goddamn turkey shoot, Jer. Hell, they looked like they were taking a Sunday afternoon stroll before we hashed them up, over."

"Roger, Jimbo, we should be at your location in about zero five. So keep your shooting low and at home, over."

"Wilco, Puma, break, break; Puma five elements, did you monitor Puma's last? Over."

"That's affirm," came the answer from Scruggs, the rattling noise of his co-ax in the background. . . . "Wait one. A whole new crew just busted. . . ." A triple brain-jarring roar of departing cannister punctuated his conversation, and he came back on the air. "Sorry, 5, they were getting a bit too close, but that's solved now."

The scattered clanking of AKs was evidence that at least some of the NVA force had gathered their wits and were going to make a fight of it. Downstream, the almost continuous song of Kim's co-ax and the thudding of his .50 said that he was doing business as usual.

Franklin had just finished a quick roll and sitrep call, when the sharp PLOOH of Sims's M-79 brought his attention to his own tank's situation. He saw a 40mm round detonate among a group of NVA clustered around a 75mm recoilless rifle at the side of one of the trucks. Whipping the cannon with the override as Sims dropped back into the hatch, he turned the turret crew loose on the weapon. Cannister followed by HE mangled the 75mm and crew, overturning the truck in the process. The truck was slowly being driven back across the ford by explosions.

The loud popping of a stream of tracers six inches from Jimbo's head directed his attention to the heavy brush in front of him, just as he heard the double "clang" of a driver going to ground and slamming his hatch. Following the line of fire, he caught a glimpse of the ugly snout of an RPG-7, just as it fired. Before he could react, the warhead hit the front slope of the tank at a sharp angle, blasting pieces of the right headlight and molten chunks of armor all around.

Krause was already sending cannister back when Jimbo realized that the blast of heat he'd felt on his neck and upper arm was, in fact, shrapnel from the rocket. Most of his right sleeve was in tatters and blood was beginning to seep. He had good mobility, but numbness had begun to set in. He also had a hot stinging in his neck. He made a quick, alarmed roll call. Krause was too busy shooting to answer and Sims was loading like a glistening sweating automaton.

"Dean," Jimbo yelled over the gun-thunder, "you dead or just counting battery caps?"

"Shit, Lootenant, that sucker was aimed right at me. . . ." Dean was saying, when a string of light explosions, like a chain of Chinese firecrackers ripped over the clearing, ripping into the bushes that concealed the offending group of NVA. Again and again, like a fiery whip, that string lashed the battle zone, boring like an explosive drill into cover and concealment. When it shut down at last, there was no answering fire . . . nor any motion at all.

"What the fuck was THAT?" Sims shouted, staring at the shredded foliage ahead.

"That, my man," Franklin replied, "was one of Mr. Hawke's surprises. Puma 6 is now a vulcan track—brand spanking new. He should be coming around the bend in a few seconds."

Franklin's prediction was right. In less than a minute, Jeremy's "maneuver element" began streaming around the bend, circling into a half-perimeter in the opposite treeline.

Staring at the total devastation around him in stunned silence, Hawke picked his way through the twisted, charred metal and torn, smoldering bodies to Franklin's tank.

"My God, what a slaughter!" he exclaimed. "You really meant it when you said 'turkey shoot.'"

Clambering up on the turret beside Franklin, Hawke went on. "There's gotta be at least two hundred corpses out there."

"Yeah, we busted a few, Jer. But I can't get over how they just came sauntering into us. You can see that it was a total surprise."

"Jimbo, I think that you might want to take a look at something we discovered after our shoot-out back up the road."

"First, hadn't we better call the Old Man and let him know about this? The whole Division hasn't had this many kills in over two months."

"Listen up, man," Hawke said. "Remember the red line your map doesn't have?" The little tickle he'd harbored in the back of his mind since they found the bamboo road had become one large itch.

"You're telling me that we are where I think we are? Oh shit. Now how do we tell the Old Man we're in Cambodia without letting the cat out of the bag?"

"Well first, Jimbo, let's take a look at what we have here, before we go calling anybody."

Their walk through the cauldron was like a stroll through the nether regions of Hades. Many bodies, charbroiled from fuel fires, were still smoking. Others were simply not recognizable as parts of humans. The river, like that little stream outside of Enari, was littered with human flotsam.

The high explosive plastic rounds from the tank guns had twisted the light Russian reconnaissance tanks like beer cans in the hands of drunken troopers. The PT hit by Krause had had its 76mm gun wrenched from its mounts and slammed through the rear of the hull. Passing the de-turreted hulk of the second tank, they came to the BTR which, by the looks of its extensive radio gear, had been a command vehicle.

Most of the crew had been immolated by the exploding fuel cells, but many of the passengers had been thrown clear. Franklin turned one over with his foot, letting out a low whistle. "I think we really hurt them bad, Jer. Come look."

Stretched before them, a grinning death mask on his face, was a full colonel of the Peoples Army of Vietnam. Scattered around him were a number of canvas bags and dispatch pouches—all full of maps, orders of battle, unit manning charts, signal codes.

. . . All the important documents of a Regimental, not Battalion HQ.

Jeremy knelt by one of the bags, looking for any maps which would apply to their area, only to be interrupted by Jimbo, who'd rolled another corpse onto its back.

"Jer, I think we got another honcho here. This one's got a pistol, dispatch case and red collar tabs. Might be the political officer."

"No wonder these guys were in such a hurry to get back into Cambodia," Hawke said, leafing through the contents of the leather pouch. "I think we messed up part of a damn big operation."

"We still have to make some kind of a report of this to the CO, Jer," Franklin reminded his friend.

"The location of the border in this region is really vague," Hawke said. "The SF boys themselves don't really know the precise location. The canopy's so thick that accurate mapping would depend on ground surveys, which the bad guys tend to interfere with.

"I would recommend that we call this party in, and place it on or near the 'red line.' That way, if we *are* in Cambodia, the map you're operating with shows that river as inside Vietnam. We can just merely lose my map."

"Okay, leader," Jimbo said, grinning. "Let's do it!"

Coming back to Franklin's still-smoking iron steed, they mounted over the rear sprocket, avoiding the overly warm bow.

"Krause, hand me a mike and punch in the Battalion Admin freq."

"Why the admin push, Lieutenant?" Krause inquired as he switched frequencies and connected a hand mike.

"You know where we think we are, Krause. We don't want the whole world listening to the conversation. Get my drift?"

"Oops, yessir," came the reply from inside the turret as the mike was extended.

Hawke picked it up and nervously squeezed the transmit lever. "Big Thunder 6, this is Puma, over."

"Puma, this is Big Thunder 6, send your info."

"Wow, Barky must've been sitting right on the radio," Hawke said to Franklin before reporting in.

"Six, this is Puma. At approximately 0615 this morning, Puma 5 elements ambushed a November Victor unit retreating from last night's contact with Puma 6 elements. Contact was made along the blue line, heading west. Coordinates Yankee Zulu 4650-8903. Because of the heavy cover and the indefinite locations of the red and blue lines on the funny papers, these coordinates are suspect.

"Puma 5 elements engaged a reinforced battalion of NVA, supported by two PT-76 tanks, one BTR series command vehicle, and four heavy transport trucks. Puma 5 elements destroyed all of the NVA vehicles; we have a confirmed body count of two hundred sixty-six NVA KIA.

"Two of the NVA are tentatively I.D.'d as a regimental CO and his political officer. We need a Golf Two to confirm. There are no U.S. KIA, only one WIA; local medic says no problem, over."

A long, dead pause followed Hawke's startling report. Even the troops on the scene were awed by the sheer numbers. Finally, though, 6 answered.

"Puma, this is 6. Confirm 2-6-6 KIA? Seven vehicles? Including two tanks? . . . Uh, over," came the astounded response from the Battalion Commander.

Grinning from ear to ear, Hawke confirmed. "This

is Puma, that's affirmative. We're standing in a pile of mangled bodies and scragged vehicles, over."

"This is 6, roger. Does your WIA require dustoff? Over."

"Negative. Medic here has well in hand; request resupply of Poppa-Oscar-Lima, Ninety mikemike, 7-6 deuce and Charlies, over."

"Roger, Puma. I will be at your location in about three zero. We'll arrange for a G-2 from next higher on the way out. Big Thunder 4 will lay on a hook for POL and other needs. Is Viper 6 with you?"

"That's affirmative," responded Torrion. "I confirm Puma's report with one correction. Add one zero KIA as a result by Mike Force elements now closing on this location. Your boys didn't leave much for us to chase, Big Thunder, over."

"This is 6. Roger Viper, break; Puma, do you have an adequate LZ?"

"Roger 6, we have a six to ten ship Lima Zulu, secured by Puma and some of Viper's little people."

"See you in three zero. Six out."

Chapter Thirteen

BARKSDALL'S COMMAND AND CONTROL CHOPPER SOON APpeared over the clearing, and Jeremy lobbed out a yellow smoke grenade as the escorting Cobra gunships began a criss-cross pattern.

"Identify yellow smoke," the pilot responded to the visual signal.

"Affirmative, Gambler, come on down," Franklin answered. And the chopper settled to earth, kicking up a small cyclone of dust that blended with the acrid smoke, obscuring vision for a few seconds.

Leaping to the ground as the bird settled in, Barksdall and Carlisle were frozen in place by the total devastation around them.

It was as if the hammer of a wargod had smashed unbelievers and their weapons back into the primordial elements of the jungle floor. The broken bodies of the NVA command group lay where they fell, covering an area easily two hundred yards in diameter. Though the heat and flames of burning fuel and ammunition had subsided considerably, the smoke from multiple funeral pyres joined into a single pillar, reaching high into the azure morning sky. Winged predators were circling and furtive scufflings in the brush announced the arrival of their four-footed competition.

"Gentlemen, I have witnessed some fairly nasty battle sites in my day, but this has got to beat all," Barksdall stated as he returned the salutes of the two Puma leaders. "And you say that only one of your people was wounded. . . . That's you, Franklin, obviously. How the hell . . . ?"

"They came out of that hole in the jungle across the river there," Franklin said, "and we were set up in a 'U' of tanks on this side. The rest is what you see. They never knew we were here till we opened up."

Barksdall had been sweeping the area with his binoculars. "Where are the two officers you spoke of?" he asked.

"Just beyond the burned-out BTR, sir," Hawke answered. He led the way as the group followed. As they crossed the clearing, yet another Command and Control ship fluttered down, throwing up its wall of dust.

"That'll be Division G-2," Carlisle said. "When I gave him an outline of this fray, he nearly crapped his pants."

"You're the first to go gun-to-gun with enemy armor," Barksdall said, "since the 69th had that go at it with PT-76s up at Ban Het."

Like the CO of the 88th before him, the short, angular LTC who was Division intelligence, stood agape at the sight in front of him before he and his assistant, Salomon Epstein, trotted across the clearing to the group of tankers.

"Gentlemen, this is *some* kind of ass-kicking you've laid on old Charlie," the colonel said, "and this was definitely *not* just another probe. Where are your two prizes?"

"We were just heading that way, Colonel," said Franklin, gesturing toward the hulk of the BTR. "Follow me." Falling in beside Hawke, Epstein, for once at a loss for words, walked awestruck through his friends' handiwork.

Flies had already begun to gather on the two NVA officers, who'd been laid out neatly beside their dispatch pouches and canvas bags. The G-2 officers brushed the flies aside, quickly searching the dead officers' pockets. Now Epstein drew a buck skinning knife and cut the collar and unit patches from their uniforms, while the colonel attacked the document bags.

After rifling through the assembled documents, the intelligence specialist stood, obviously more than a little bemused.

"This is something very interesting, gentlemen," he said to the armor officers. "We don't have any kind of make on this unit designator. You have indeed uncovered something big. Judging by the appearance of things, our little friends were setting up a real shit-storm for somebody. Also, judging by the composition of this command unit, this is not the only bunch of armored vehicles in the main force."

While the man continued to talk, Hawke's attention was taken by Torrion who, after checking on his arriving Strikers, had abruptly darted back into the clearing, motioning insistently for Hawke to join him.

"What's up, Frank?" Jeremy asked, puzzled over the excited manner of the usually bomb-proof Special Forces captain.

"Come see what ole Uncle Frankie and his little people found," Torrion urged, taking Jeremy by the sleeve and almost dragging him into a thick clump of bamboo and wait-a-minute weeds.

Entering the clearing in the center of the stand of bamboo, Hawke whistled in shock at the appearance of the prisoner. Heavy black European combat boots protruded from beneath standard green NVA combat fatigues and a battered pith helmet lay next to him. He wore the usual web gear, but there was no insignia on his uniform. A long, clean gash oozed blood through close-cropped, thick blond hair, down the high forehead and into the terrified yet arrogant eyes of a Slavic face.

Barksdall and the G-2 colonel were deep in conversation when Hawke strode up to them, while Franklin was helping Epstein sort and stack the NVA paperwork.

"Er . . . Sirs, do we have anyone in the command who understands Russian?"

The question stopped all conversation, and Epstein filled the silence with, "Yeah, Jer, my family left Russia as refugees in '17, and I'm still fluent. Don't tell me you've found Russian paper?"

All eyes were on Hawke, and he was tempted to draw out the suspense for a moment. "No," he answered, "but Torrion's Strikers have apparently got a live one right over through those bushes!" Hawke was almost trampled by two light colonels in the rush into the bamboo.

The blond East European remained where they'd found him, surrounded by Torrion's Strikers. His head wound had been treated and swathed in a G.I. battle dressing. The man, though injured, retained an overt air of pride and arrogance. Epstein knew that getting even one word from this individual would be an effort without the use of the more drastic tongue-loosening methods used by less controlled "Spook" troops.

Kneeling beside the now handcuffed man, Epstein removed a Salem from the C-rat pack in his pocket, lit it, and placed it between the lips of the prisoner. Surprised, but accepting, the man puffed gratefully. Epstein sat and watched him for better than ten minutes, a disturbing basilisk stare roving over the man as if here was a thing to be examined, rather than a live human.

Unmindful of the circle of humanity, Sal continued watching the Slav, meeting the now somewhat confused glare of the captive. The man seemed to be doubting his vaunted Slavic superiority and wondering if this small American Semite had some supernatural power with which he could enter the minds of helpless captives.

Suddenly Epstein smiled disarmingly and rattled off a few sentences in Russian. The Slav's eyes bulged and he started to answer. He'd uttered no more than a half-dozen words when his tongue stopped as if bitten off, on the word Spetsnaz.

Rising, Sal clapped the man familiarly on the shoulder, and turned to his boss. "I told him that if he was very cooperative we wouldn't turn him over to the widows of people whom he's *liberated*. He started to tell me that a Spetsnaz can't be broken, and then clammed up."

"Well I do believe the Puzzle Palace boys will have a field day with this package," the G-2 colonel said, slapping a congratulatory hand on Epstein's shoulder. "What say we wrap him up and get him back to the head shed?"

Leaving Torrion and the Strikers to bring the captive out, the party headed back toward Barksdall's ship, only to be intercepted by a sergeant from the intelligence party.

"Sir, Bronco 6 is zero five out, and wants us to hold tight until he gets here."

As if on cue, two additional Cobra gunships appeared, joining the four already on station, and the general's private chopper hammered its way into the center of the impromptu LZ. As the turbine of the Command and Control ship shut down, the imposing figure of the general stalked over and the armor officers went silent, waiting.

"Gentlemen, I don't know if I should raise hell with you or pin medals on you," the general said, addressing Hawke and Franklin. "You know we have somewhat of a problem with your map coordinates."

The two lieutenants were beginning to sweat when Barksdall interrupted. "We have an even more pressing matter to deal with, General. It adds a new dimension to the picture, and puts any border violation in a different light. Look over there."

Following the line of Barksdall's arm, the general saw two of the Strikers leading the Spetsnaz troop out on the end of a rope.

"Well I'll be damned," whispered the tall general. "We've heard rumors of these guys working with the NVA along the border, but I never dreamed we'd have the good fortune of getting our hands on one of them."

"General Pierce, Lieutenant Epstein here has already determined that the man is Soviet Spetsnaz," the G-2 colonel interjected.

"Well, how did he do that?" the general asked, turning to Epstein.

"Sir, he came right out and admitted it," Epstein replied. "Before he had control of himself."

For once the general was jarred out of formality. "The Spooks back at Disneyland will shit when they find out what you boys have come up with. We'd best sit down for a few minutes and get our act together. Let's try to find out exactly where we are first. That will be our biggest problem if the politicians down at USARV or MACV—or the damned, self-righteous press—get hold of this, Russian or not.

"Gentlemen, shall we adjourn to one of the lieutenant's tracks and get to work?"

When the small group of officers had settled in the rear of Jeremy's 20mm track, the general went straight to the heart of the matter.

"Gentlemen, we are treading on *very* thin ice. While it is true that you two lieutenants and this incredible task force of yours have probably saved the life of a nation today, you also know just how much hay the anti-war people and their media sycophants could make of this. The North Vietnamese are privileged to invade South Vietnam at whim, while we must respect their damn sanctuaries in other conquered nations."

Barksdall was shaking his head gravely. He'd been there before. Hawke and Franklin, however, were looking at each other in disbelief. Was their accomplishment, then, to go unreported and their men unrewarded because of the clamoring and rabble-rousing of a horde of unwashed freaks in the streets of the United States?

Seeming to read their minds, the general continued. "You and your men, Hawke, will, when we leave here, have a suitable awards ceremony back at Oasis. But it will be a partial smokescreen—Puma will have to disappear for a while. We're pulling enough Cav back here, along with one of Barksdall's wandering companies, to be able to hold the fort. At the same time, an Air Cav brigade-sized independent combat team down on the coast has put in a request for heavy armor. It appears they've found out the hard way that full air mobility ain't all we thought it would be."

Hawke and Franklin were starting to perk. This sounded interesting.

"You're aware, of course, that the army runs in-country R&R facilities?" the general asked. Both lieutenants nodded their heads, not quite believing their ears.

"We'll move Puma, in toto, down through the refit facility at Qui Nhon, and let those boys of yours have a week on the beach while their machines are in the shops. For the time being, you can consider yourselves OPCON to Commanding General 1st Field Force Vietnam, as an Armored Special Force. Does that suit you?"

"YES SIR!!" the two answered in unison.